Kevin Brockmeier

Kevin Brockmeier lives in Arkansas, USA. The first chapter of *The Brief History of the Dead* appeared in the *New Yorker*, and the novel has been published throughout the world. Kevin Brockmeier is also the author of *The Truth About Celia*, a collection of short stories entitled *Things That Fall from the Sky*, and two children's novels entitled *City of Names* and *Grooves: A Kind of Mystery*.

Praise for *The Brief History of the Dead*

'Brockmeier is a lyrical yet subtle writer . . . A powerful read'
Time Out

'His confident voice, observational brilliance and playful humour dazzle to the end'
The Times

'Such is his sensitivity and skill that Brockmeier contrives a mystery that is . . . subtle, absorbing and ultimately satisfying'
Guardian

'The themes are united with wonderful delicacy . . . *The Brief History of the Dead* must be accounted a prodigy of imagination, insight and overwhelming tenderness'
Independent

'Gripping – and moving – stuff'
Sunday Times

'Ingenious . . . Highly impressive'
Financial Times

The Brief
History of the
Dead

The Brief History of the Dead

KEVIN BROCKMEIER

JOHN MURRAY

© Kevin Brockmeier 2006

First published in Great Britain in 2006 by John Murray (Publishers)
A division of Hodder Headline

Paperback edition 2007

The right of Kevin Brockmeier to be identified as the Author of the Work has been
asserted by him in accordance with the Copyright, Designs and Patents Act 1988.

2

A CIP catalogue record for this title is available from the British Library

ISBN 978-0 7195-6830-5

Printed and bound in Great Britain by Clays Ltd, St Ives plc

Hodder Headline policy is to use papers that are natural, renewable and recyclable
products and made from wood grown in sustainable forests. The logging and
manufacturing processes are expected to conform to the environmental regulations
of the country of origin.

John Murray (Publishers)
338 Euston Road
London NW1 3BH

For my Dad

Many African societies divide humans into three categories: those still alive on the earth, the sasha, and the zamani. The recently departed whose time on earth overlapped with people still here are the sasha, the living-dead. They are not wholly dead, for they still live in the memories of the living, who can call them to mind, create their likeness in art, and bring them to life in anecdote. When the last person to know an ancestor dies, that ancestor leaves the sasha for the zamani, the dead. As generalized ancestors, the zamani are not forgotten but revered. Many . . . can be recalled by name. But they are not living-dead. There is a difference.

—JAMES LOEWEN, *LIES MY TEACHER TOLD ME*

Contents

The Brief
History of the
Dead

One

THE CITY

When the blind man arrived in the city, he claimed that he had traveled across a desert of living sand. First he had died, he said, and then—*snap!*—the desert. He told the story to everyone who would listen, bobbing his head to follow the sound of their footsteps. Showers of red grit fell from his beard. He said that the desert was bare and lonesome and that it had hissed at him like a snake. He had walked for days and days, until the dunes broke apart beneath his feet, surging up around him to lash at his face. Then everything went still and began to beat like a heart. The sound was as clear as any he had ever heard. It was only at that moment, he said, with a million arrow points of sand striking his skin, that he truly realized he was dead.

Jim Singer, who managed the sandwich shop in the monument district, said that he had felt a prickling sensation in his fingers and then stopped breathing. "It was my heart," he insisted, thumping firmly on his chest. "Took me in my own bed." He had closed his eyes, and when he opened them again, he was on a train, the kind that trolleys small children around in circles at amusement parks. The rails were leading him through a thick forest of gold-brown trees, but the trees were actually giraffes, and their long necks were reaching like branches into the sky. A wind rose up and peeled the spots from their backs. The spots floated down around him, swirling and dipping in the wake of the train. It took him a long time to understand that the

3

throbbing noise he heard was not the rattling of the wheels along the tracks.

The girl who liked to stand beneath the poplar tree in the park said that she had died into an ocean the color of dried cherries. For a while the water had carried her weight, she said, and she had lain on her back turning in meaningless circles, singing the choruses of the pop songs she remembered. But then there was a drum of thunder, and the clouds split open, and the ball bearings began to pelt down around her—tens of thousands of them. She had swallowed as many as she could, she said, stroking the cracked trunk of the poplar tree. She didn't know why. She filled like a canvas sack and sank slowly through the layers of the ocean. Shoals of fish brushed past her, their blue and yellow scales the single brightest thing in the water. And all around her she heard that sound, the one that everybody heard, the regular pulsing of a giant heart.

The stories people told about the crossing were as varied and elaborate as their ten billion lives, so much more particular than those other stories, the ones they told about their deaths. After all, there were only so many ways a person could die: either your heart took you, or your head took you, or it was one of the new diseases. But no one followed the same path over the crossing. Lev Paley said that he had watched his atoms break apart like marbles, roll across the universe, then gather themselves together again out of nothing at all. Hanbing Li said that he woke inside the body of an aphid and lived an entire life in the flesh of a single peach. Graciella Cavazos would say only that she began to snow—four words—and smile bashfully whenever anyone pressed her for details.

No two reports were ever the same. And yet always there was the drumlike thumping noise.

Some people insisted that it never went away, that if you concentrated and did not turn your ear from the sound, you could hear it faintly behind everything in the city—the brakes and the horns, the bells on the doors of restaurants, the clicking and slapping of different kinds of shoes on the pavement. Groups of people came together in parks or on rooftops just to listen for it, sitting quietly with their backs turned to one another. *Ba-dum. Ba-dum. Ba-dum.* It was like trying to keep a bird in sight as it lifted, blurred, and faded to a dot in the sky.

Luka Sims had found an old mimeograph machine his very first week in the city and decided to use it to produce a news-paper. He stood outside the River Road Coffee Shop every morn-ing, handing out the circulars he had printed. One particular issue of the *L. Sims News & Speculation Sheet*—or the *Sims Sheet*, as people called it—addressed the matter of this sound. Fewer than twenty percent of the people Luka interviewed claimed that they could still hear it after the crossing, but almost everyone agreed that it resembled nothing so much as—could be nothing other than—the pounding of a heart. The question, then, was, Where did it come from? It could not be their own hearts, for their hearts no longer beat. The old man Mahmoud Qassim believed that it was not the actual sound of his heart, but the remembered sound, which, because he had both heard and failed to notice it for so long, still resounded in his ears. The woman who sold bracelets by the river thought that it was the heartbeat at the center of the world, that bright, boiling place she had fallen through on her way to the city. "As for this reporter," the article concluded, "I hold with the majority. I have always sus-pected that the thumping sound we hear is the pulse of those who are still alive. The living carry us inside them like pearls. We survive only so long as they remember us." It was an imperfect metaphor—Luka knew that—since the pearl lasts much longer than the oyster. But rule one in the newspaper business was that you had to meet your deadlines. He had long since given up the quest for perfection.

There were more people in the city every day, and yet the city never failed to accommodate them. You might be walking down a street you had known for years, and all of a sudden you would come upon another building, another whole block. Carson McCaughrean, who drove one of the sleek black taxis that roamed the streets, had to redraw his maps once a week. Twenty, thirty, fifty times a day, he would pick up a fare who had only recently arrived in the city and have to deliver him somewhere he— Carson—had never heard of. They came from Africa, Asia, Europe, and the Americas. They came from churning metropolises and from small islands in the middle of the ocean. That was what the living did: they died. There was an ancient street musician who began playing in the red brick district as soon as he reached the city, making slow, sad breaths with his accordion. There was a jeweler, a young man, who set up shop at the corner of Maple and Christopher Streets and sold diamonds that he mounted on silver pendants. Jessica Auffert had operated her own jewelry shop on the same corner for more than thirty years, but she did not seem to resent the man, and in fact brought him a mug of fresh black coffee every morning, exchanging gossip as she drank with him in his front room. What surprised her was how young he was—how young so many of the dead were these days. Great numbers of them were no more than children, who clattered around on skateboards or went racing past her window on their way to the playground. One, a boy with a strawberry discoloration on his cheek, liked to pretend that the rocking horses he tossed himself around on were real horses, the horses he had brushed and fed on his farm before they were killed in the bombing. Another liked to swoop down the slide over and over again, hammering his feet into the gravel as he thought about his parents and his two older brothers, who were still alive. He had watched them lift free of the same illness that had slowly sucked him under. He did not like to talk about it.

This was during a war, though it was difficult for any of them to remember which one.

~

Occasionally one of the dead, someone who had just completed the crossing, would mistake the city for heaven. It was a misunderstanding that never persisted for long. What kind of heaven had the blasting sound of garbage trucks in the morning, and chewing gum on the pavement, and the smell of fish rotting by the river? What kind of hell, for that matter, had bakeries and dogwood trees and perfect blue days that made the hairs on the back of your neck rise on end? No, the city was not heaven, and it was not hell, and it certainly was not the world. It stood to reason, then, that it had to be something else. More and more people came to adopt the theory that it was an extension of life itself—a sort of outer room—and that they would remain there only so long as they endured in living memory. When the last person who had actually known them died, they would pass over into whatever came next. It was true that most of the city's occupants went away after sixty or seventy years, and while this did not prove the theory, it certainly served to nourish it. There were stories of men and women who had been in the city much longer, for centuries and more, but there were always such stories, in every time and place, and who knew whether to believe them?

Every neighborhood had its gathering spot, a place where people could come together to trade news of the other world. There was the colonnade in the monument district, and the One and Only Tavern in the warehouse district, and right next to the greenhouse, in the center of the conservatory district, was Andrei Kalatozov's Russian Tea Room. Kalatozov poured the tea he brewed from a brass samovar into small porcelain cups that he served on polished wooden platters. His wife and daughter had died a few weeks before he did, in an accident involving a land mine they had rooted up out of the family garden. He was watching through the kitchen window when it happened. His wife's spade struck a jagged hunk of metal, so cankered with rust from its century underground that he did not realize what it was until it exploded. Two weeks later,

7

when he put the razor to his throat, it was with the hope that he would be reunited with his family in heaven. And, sure enough, there they were—his wife and daughter—smiling and taking coats at the door of the tea room. Kalatozov watched them as he sliced a lemon into wedges and arranged the wedges on a saucer. He was the happiest man in the room—the happiest man in any room. The city may not have been heaven, but it was heaven enough for him. Morning to evening, he listened to his customers as they shared the latest news about the war. The Americans and the Middle East had resumed hostilities, as had China and Spain and Australia and the Netherlands. Brazil was developing another mutagenic virus, one that would resist the latest antitoxins. Or maybe it was Italy. Or maybe Indonesia. There were so many rumors that it was hard to know for sure.

Now and then someone who had died only a day or two before would happen into one of the centers of communication—the tavern or the tea room, the river market or the colonnade—and the legions of the dead would mass around him, shouldering and jostling him for information. It was always the same: "Where did you live?" "Do you know anything about Central America?" "Is it true what they're saying about the ice caps?" "I'm trying to find out about my cousin. He lived in Arizona. His name was Lewis Zeigler, spelled L-e-w-i-s. . . ." "What's happening with the situation along the African coast—do you know, do you know?" "Anything you can tell us, please, anything at all."

Kiran Patel had sold beads to tourists in the Bombay hotel district for most of a century. She said that there were fewer and fewer travelers to her part of the world, but that this hardly mattered, since there was less and less of her part of the world for them to see. The ivory beads she had peddled as a young woman had become scarce, then rare, then finally unobtainable. The only remaining elephants were caged away in the zoos of other countries. In the years just before she died, the "genuine ivory beads" she sold were actually a cream-colored plastic made in batches of ten thousand in Korean factories. This, too, hardly mattered. The tourists who stopped at her kiosk could never detect the difference.

Jeffrey Fallon, sixteen and from Park Falls, Wisconsin, said that the fighting hadn't spread in from the coasts yet, but that the germs had, and he was living proof. "Or not living, maybe, but still proof," he corrected himself. The bad guys used to be Pakistan, and then they were Argentina and Turkey, and after that he had lost track. "What do you want me to tell you?" he asked, shrugging his shoulders. "Mostly I just miss my girlfriend." Her name was Tracey Tipton, and she did this thing with his earlobes and the notched edge of her front teeth that made his entire body go taut and buzz like a guitar string. He had never given his earlobes a second thought until the day she took them between her lips, but now that he was dead he thought of nothing else. Who would have figured?

The man who spent hours riding up and down the escalators in the Ginza Street Shopping Mall would not give his name. When people asked him what he remembered about the time before he died, he would only nod vigorously, clap his hands together, and say, "Boom!," making a gesture like falling confetti with his fingertips.

~

The great steel-and-polymer buildings at the heart of the city, with their shining glass windows reflecting every gap between every cloud in the sky, gave way after a few hundred blocks to buildings of stone and brick and wood. The change was so gradual, though, and the streets so full of motion, that you could walk for hours before you realized that the architecture had transformed itself around you. The sidewalks were lined with movie theaters, gymnasiums, hardware stores, karaoke bars, basketball courts, and falafel stands. There were libraries and tobacconists. There were lingerie shops and dry cleaners. There were hun-

9

dreds of churches in the city—hundreds, in fact, in every district: pagodas, mosques, chapels, and synagogues. They stood sandwiched between vegetable markets and video rental stores, sending their crosses, domes, and minarets high into the air. Some of the dead, it was true, threw aside their old religions, disgusted that the afterlife, this so-called *great beyond*, was not what their lifetimes of worship had promised them. But for every person who lost his faith, there was someone else who held fast to it, and someone else again who adopted it. The simple truth was that nobody knew what would happen to them after their time in the city came to an end, and just because you had died without meeting your God was no reason to assume that you wouldn't one day.

This was the philosophy of José Tamayo, who offered himself once a week as a custodian to the Church of the Sacred Heart. Every Sunday, he waited by the west door until the final service was over and the crowd had dissolved back into the city, and then he swept the tile floor, polished the pews and the altar, and vacuumed the cushions by the Communion rail. When he was finished, he climbed carefully down the seventeen steps in front of the building, where the blind man stood talking about his journey through the desert, and made his way across the street to his apartment. He had damaged his knee once during a soccer match, and ever since then he felt a tiny exploding star of pain above the joint whenever he extended his leg. The injury had not gone away, even after the crossing, and he did not like to walk too far on the leg. This was why he had chosen to work for the Church of the Sacred Heart: it was the closest one he could find. He had, in fact, been raised a Methodist, in the only non-Catholic congregation in Juan Tula. He frequently thought of the time he stole a six-pack of soda from the church storage closet with the boys in his Sunday school class. They had heard the teacher coming and shut the door, and a thin ray of light had come slanting through the jamb, illuminating the handle of a cart filled with folding chairs—forty or fifty of them, stacked together in a long, tight interdigitation. What José remembered was staring at this cart and listening to his teacher's footsteps as the bubbles of soda played over the surface of his tongue, sparking and collapsing against the roof of his mouth.

The dead were often surprised by such memories. They might go weeks and months without thinking of the houses and neighborhoods they had grown up in, their triumphs of shame and glory, the jobs, routines, and hobbies that had slowly eaten away their lives, yet the smallest, most inconsequential episode would leap into their thoughts a hundred times a day, like a fish smacking its tail on the surface of a lake. The old woman who begged for quarters in the subway remembered eating a meal of crab cakes and horseradish on a dock by Chesapeake Bay. The man who lit the gas lamps in the theater district remembered taking a can of beans from the middle of a supermarket display pyramid and feeling a flicker of pride and then a flicker of amusement at his pride when the other cans did not fall. Andreas Andreopoulos, who had written code for computer games the whole forty years of his adult life, remembered leaping to pluck a leaf from a tree, and opening a fashion magazine to smell the perfume inserts, and writing his name in the condensation on a glass of beer. They preoccupied him—these formless, almost clandestine memories. They seemed so much heavier than they should have been, as if they were where the true burden of his life's meaning lay. He sometimes thought of piecing them together into an autobiography, all the toy-sized memories that had replaced the details of his work and family, and leaving everything else out. He would write it by hand on sheets of unlined notebook paper. He would never touch a computer again.

There were places in the city where the crowds were so swollen you could not move without pressing into some arm or hip or gut. As the numbers of the dead increased, these areas became more and more common. It was not that the city had no

11

room for its inhabitants but that when they chose to herd together, they did so in certain places, and the larger the population grew the more congested these places became. The people who were comfortable in their privacy learned to avoid them. If they wanted to visit the open square in the monument district, or the fountains in the neon district, they would have to wait until the population diminished, which always seemed to happen in times of war or plague or famine.

The park beside the river was the busiest of the city's busy places, with its row of white pavilions and its long strip of living grass. Kite vendors and soft drink stands filled the sidewalks, and saddles of rock carved the water into dozens of smoothly rounded coves. There came a day when a man with a thick gray beard and a tent of bushy hair stumbled out of one of the pavilions and began to bump into the shoulders of the people around him. He was plainly disoriented, and it was obvious to everyone who saw him that he had just passed through the crossing. He said that he was a virologist by profession. He had spent the last five days climbing the branches of an enormous maple tree, and his clothing was tacked to his skin with sap. He seemed to think that everybody who was in the park had also been in the tree with him. When someone asked him how he had died, he drew in his breath and paused for a moment before he answered. "That's right, I died. I have to keep reminding myself. They finally did it, the sons of bitches. They found a way to pull the whole thing down." He twisted a plug of sap from his beard. "Hey, did any of you notice some sort of thumping noise inside the tree?"

It was not long after this that the city began to empty out.

~

The single-room office of the *L. Sims News & Speculation Sheet* was in one of the city's oldest buildings, constructed of chocolate-colored brick and masses of silver granite. Streamers of pale yellow moss trailed from the upper floors, hanging as low as the ledge above the front door. Each morning as Luka Sims stood cranking away at his mimeograph machine, sunlight filtered through the moss outside his window and the room was saturated with a warm, buttery light. Sometimes he could hardly look out at the city without imagining that he was gazing through a dying forest.

By seven o'clock, he would have printed a few thousand copies of his circular and taken them to the River Road Coffee Shop, where he would hand them out to the pedestrians. He liked to believe that each person who took one read it and passed it on to someone else, who read it and passed it on to someone else, who read it and passed it on to someone else, but he knew that this was not the case, since he always saw at least a few copies in the trash on his way home, the paper gradually uncrinkling in the sun. Still, it was not unusual for him to look inside the coffee shop and see twenty or thirty heads bent over copies of the latest *Sims Sheet*. He had been writing fewer stories about the city recently and more about the world of the living, stories he assembled from interviews with the recent dead, most of whom were victims of what they called "the epidemic." These people tended to blink a lot—he noticed that. They squinted and rubbed at their eyes. He wondered if it had anything to do with the virus that had killed them.

Luka saw the same faces behind the coffee shop window every day. HUNDREDS EXPOSED TO VIRUS IN TOKYO. NEW EPICENTERS DISCOVERED IN JOHANNESBURG, COPENHAGEN, PERTH. Ellison Brown, who prepared the baked desserts in the kitchen, always waited for Luka to leave before he glanced at the headlines. His wife had been a poet of the type who liked to loom nearby with a fretful look on her face while he read whatever she had written that day, and there was nothing that bothered him more than the feeling that he was being watched. INCUBATION PERIOD LESS THAN FIVE HOURS. EXPOSURE AT NOON, MORTALITY AT MIDNIGHT. Char-

13

lotte Sylvain would sip at her coffee as she scanned the paper for any mention of Paris. She still considered the city her hometown, though she had not been there in fifty years. Once, she saw the word "Seine" printed in the first paragraph of an article and her fingers tightened involuntarily around the page, but it was only a misprint of the word "sienna," and she would never see her home again. VIRUS BECOMES AIRBORNE, WATERBORNE. TWO BILLION DEAD IN ASIA AND EASTERN EUROPE. Mie Matsuda Ryu was an enthusiast of word games. She liked to read the *Sims Sheet* twice every morning, once for content and once for any hidden patterns she could find—palindromes, anagrams, the letters of her own name scrambled inside other words. She never failed to spot them. "TWENTY-FOUR-HOUR BUG" CROSSES ATLANTIC. FATALITY RATE NEARING ONE HUNDRED PERCENT.

The people who went knocking on the doors of the city began to notice something unusual. The evangelists and traveling salesmen, the petitioners and census takers, they all said the same thing: the numbers of the dead were shrinking. There were empty rooms in empty buildings that had been churning with bodies just a few weeks before. The streets were not so crowded anymore. It was not that people were no longer dying. In fact, there were more people dying than ever. They arrived by the thousands and the hundreds of thousands, every minute of every hour, whole houses and schools and neighborhoods of them. But for every person who made it through the crossing, two or three seemed to disappear. Russell Henley, who sold brooms that he lashed together from cedar branches and hanks of plastic fiber, said that the city was like a pan with a hole in it: "No matter how much water you let in, it keeps pouring right through." He ran a stall in the monument district, where he assembled his brooms, marketing them to the passing crowds, which barely numbered in the low hundreds these days. If the only life they had was bestowed upon them by the memories of the living, as Russell was inclined to believe, what would happen when the rest of the living were gathered into the city? What would happen, he wondered, when that other room, the larger world, had been emptied out?

Unquestionably, the city was changing. People who had perished in the epidemic came and went very quickly, sometimes in a matter of hours, like a mid-spring snow that blankets the ground at night and melts away as soon as the sun comes up. A man arrived in the pine district one morning, found an empty storefront, painted a sign in the window with colored soap (SHER-MAN'S CLOCK REPAIR. FAST AND EASY. OPENING SOON), then locked the door and shuffled away and never returned. Another man told the woman he had slept the night with that he was going to the kitchen for a glass of water, and when she called to him a few minutes later, he did not answer. She searched the apartment for him. The window beside her dressing table was open, as though he had climbed out onto the balcony, but he was nowhere to be found. The entire population of a small Pacific island appeared in the city on a bright windy afternoon, congregated on the top level of a parking garage, and were gone by the end of the day.

But it was the people who had been in the city the longest who most felt the changes. While none of them knew—or had ever known—how much time they had in the city, or when that time would come to an end, there had usually been a rhythm to their tenure, certain things a person could expect: after finishing the crossing, you found a home and a job and a company of friends, ran out your six or seven decades, and while you could not raise a family, for no one aged, you could always assemble one around you.

Mariama Ekwensi, for one, had made her home on the ground floor of a small house in the white clay district for almost thirty years. She was a tall, rangy woman who had never lost the bearing of the adolescent girl she had once been, so dazed and bewildered by her own growth. The batik cotton dresses she wore were the color of the sun in a child's drawing. Her neighbors could always spot her coming from several blocks away. Mariama was a caretaker at one of the city's many orphanages. She thought of herself as a good teacher but a poor disciplinarian, and it was true that she often had to leave her children under the watch of another adult in order to chase after one who had taken off running. She read to the smaller children—books about long voyages, or about animals who changed shape—and she took the older ones to parks and museums and helped them with their homework. Many of them were badly behaved, with vocabularies that truly made her blush, but she found such problems beyond her talents. Even when she pretended to be angry with the children, they were clever enough to see that she still liked them. This was her predicament. There was one boy in particular, Philip Walker, who would light out toward the shopping district every chance he got. He seemed to think it was funny to hear her running along behind him, huffing and pounding away, and she never caught up with him until he had collapsed onto a stoop or a bench somewhere, gasping with laughter. One day, she followed him around a corner and chased him into an alley and did not come out the other end. Philip returned to the orphanage half an hour later. He could not say where she had gone.

Ville Tolvanen shot pool every night at the bar on the corner of Eighth and Vine. The friends he had at the bar were the same friends he had known when he was alive. There was something they used to say to each other when they went out drinking in Oulu, a sort of song they used to sing: *I'll meet you when I die / At that bar on the corner of Eighth and Vine.* One by one, then, as they passed away, they found their way to the corner of Eighth and Vine, walked gingerly, skeptically, through the doors of the bar, and caught sight of one another by the pool tables, until gradually they were all reassembled. Ville was the last of the group to die, and finding his friends there at the bar felt almost as sweet to him as it had when he was young. He clutched their arms and they clapped him on the back. He insisted on buying them drinks. "Never again . . . ," he told them, and though he could not finish the sentence, they all knew what he meant. He was grinning to keep his eyes from watering over, and someone tossed a peanut shell at him, and he tossed one back, and soon the floor was so covered with the things that it crunched no matter where they put their feet. For months after he died, Ville never missed a single night at the tables—and so when he failed to appear one night his friends went out looking for him. They headed straight for the room he had taken over the hardware store down the street, where they banged on the door and then dislodged the lock with the sharp edge of a few playing cards. Ville's shoes were inside, and his wristwatch, and his jacket, but he was not.

Ethan Hass, the virologist, drank not in the bars at all but from a small metal flask that he carried on his belt like a Boy Scout canteen. He had been watching the developments in his field for thirty years before he died, reading the journals and listening to the gossip at the conventions, and it sometimes seemed to him that every government, every interest group, every faction in the world was casting around for the same thing, a perfect virus, one that followed every imaginable vector, that would spread through the population like the expanding ring of a raindrop in a puddle. It was clear to him now that somebody had finally succeeded in manufacturing it. But how on earth had it been introduced? He couldn't figure it out. The reports from the recently dead were too few, and they were never precise enough. One day he locked himself in the bathroom of the High Street Art Museum and began to cry insistently, sobbing out something about the air and the water and the food supply. A security guard was summoned. "Calm down, guy. There's plenty of air and water for you out here. How about you just open the door for us?" The guard used his slowest, most soothing voice, but Ethan only shouted, "Everybody! Everything!" and turned on the faucets of the sinks, one by one. He would not say anything else, and when the guard forced the door open a few minutes later, he was gone.

It was as though a gate had been opened, or a wall thrown down, and the city was finally releasing its dead. They set out from its borders in their multitudes, and soon the parks, the bars, the shopping centers were all but empty.

One day, not long after the last of his neighborhood's restaurants had closed its doors, the blind man was standing on the steps of the church, waiting for someone who would listen to his story. No one had passed him all day long, and he was beginning to wonder if the end had come once and for all. Perhaps it had happened while he was sleeping, or during the half minute early that morning when he had thought he smelled burning honey. He heard a few car horns honking from different quarters of the city, and then, some twenty minutes later, the squealing of a subway train as its brakes gripped the tracks, and then nothing but the wind aspirating between the buildings, lingering, and finally falling still. He listened hard for a voice or a footstep, but he could not make out a single human sound.

He cupped his hands around his mouth. "Hello?" he shouted. "Hello?" But no one answered.

He experienced an unusual misgiving. He brought his hand to his chest. He was afraid that the heartbeat he heard was his own.

Two

THE SHELTER

The wind had been blowing for twenty-three days, first from the east and then from the south, making a prolonged death moan inside the vents. Occasionally a gust of ice would push its way through the hut's system of turns and baffles, and hundreds of clear gray crystals would come fanning out over the room, peppering down onto the desk and the floor. Laura would stop whatever she was doing and watch them melt. She was disheartened by how long it took. The heating panels were obviously breaking down, if not crippled beyond repair. Next the lights would go, and after that, if she was still alive, it would be the food stores. What a total damned disaster.

The trouble had started nearly a month ago, when the antenna had snapped off the communications array. She and Puckett and Joyce had reconstructed the event as best they could. The antenna was a slender aluminum stilt sheltered inside a large satellite dish, and a thick casing of snow and ice had collected around it. The wind had driven the temperature above freezing for a day or two—the same freak wind that was slowly melting the ice shelf out from under them—and the mass of snow and ice had slipped from the bowl of the array in one giant chunk, taking the antenna along with it.

That was it. That was all that had happened. The whole thing was unbelievably stupid.

Why hadn't the dish been constructed out of thermogenic

metal? Or, failing that, why hadn't someone positioned it so that it would remain empty? Or, at the very least, why hadn't the three of them been provided with the equipment they might need to repair it? Sometimes it seemed to Laura that the entire expedition had been slapped together by monkeys. But no. It had been planned and financed entirely by the Coca-Cola Corporation, as either a publicity exercise or a research expedition, depending on where you read about it: an internal document or a news release.

The idea was to send a team of people to the Antarctic to explore methods of converting polar ice for use in the manufacture of soft drinks. The ice cap was already melting, after all, pouring into the ocean by the tankerload, and the corporation might as well take advantage of it while they still could. That was their reasoning. The advertising department had even devised a new slogan: "Coca-Cola—made from the freshest water on the planet," which, if it caught on, they planned to modify in a year or two to "Coca-Cola—now *that's* fresh!"

The expedition was supposed to last for six months. The planning board had appointed Michael Puckett the polar specialist, Robert Joyce the soft drink specialist, and her, Laura, the wildlife specialist. There was some debate as to whether they should call her a "wildlife" specialist or an "animal life" specialist—was Antarctica wild in the same way that, say, the Amazon of the last century was wild?—but the argument was quelled when someone suggested that the board consider the word "wild" in its original sense, as a neglected or uncultivated region. So it was that the photograph of Laura that appeared in all the newspapers, the embarrassing one that depicted her stuffing underwear into a military-style canvas bag, bore a caption that read, "Laura Byrd, wildlife specialist, prepares for the long winter." Her first lover had been a journalism professor, and she was well aware of the subtle ways that newspaper editors contrived to mock the stories they found absurd. Even now, with the cold gradually folding itself around the hut like a pair of hands, she could feel the color rising to her cheeks as she thought about it.

Photographs. Wildlife. Monkeys.

Wasn't there an old television commercial that showed a family of monkeys sharing a bottle of Coca-Cola at Christmas? She was pretty sure she remembered seeing something like that when she was a little girl.

In any case, it was not long after the antenna splintered free of the satellite dish—two days, to be exact—that the radio gave a few last sputters of white noise and chopped-up syllables and then went silent. Why couldn't she stop rehearsing the details? The web and telephone connections fell dead along with the transceiver, so that the three of them—she, Puckett, and Joyce—had no way of contacting the corporation for help. Puckett insisted that they search the shelter for any spare parts they could use to patch the radio or the transceiver back together. There were only two rooms to go through, a living area and a sleeping area; nevertheless, the operation took them half the day. They uncovered several hundred bags of pemmican and jerky, a jar of ten thousand vitamin C tablets, a bundle of electric blankets tied together with elastic cords, two kerosene lanterns, six cans of freeze-dried coffee, a Primus stove, an extra pair of collapsible tents, and even a rudimentary tool chest, but nothing that would help them fix the radio or the broken antenna.

The equipment register was plain. Laura knew they wouldn't find anything else.

The fact was that if even one of their communications systems had been working, they could have requested the material they needed to repair any of the others. But with each and every one of them broken, they were flat out of safeguards.

The people at Coca-Cola knew everything there was to know about advertising and market research and product positioning, but not quite enough, as it turned out, about polar exploration.

The three of them waited almost a week for the corporation to reestablish contact with them. Puckett kept digging out his ice cores, and Joyce kept testing the water to see if it met the company's purity specifications, and Laura kept searching the area for even the slightest sign of wildlife. She couldn't help but think that the work they were doing was a waste of time, that the corporation already knew everything they cared to know about the continent from their dozens upon dozens of feasibility studies. After all, if the expedition had been a serious scientific endeavor and not just a way of drumming up interest in Coca-Cola's newest product line, wouldn't the powers that be have sent more than three people along? Wouldn't they have conducted a more rigorous training program? No, the expedition was a publicity stunt—nothing more than that—and they all knew it. Still, the three of them kept working. It was the best way they could think of to kill the time as they waited for help to arrive. These weren't the days of Shackleton and Scott, after all, when you could disappear into the polar waste for years at a time before anyone noticed you were missing. Expedition protocol required that they submit a statement of progress to the corporation every twenty-four hours, by three in the afternoon Pacific Standard Time, and until the radio went dead they had never missed a day. Of course, three in the morning and three in the afternoon could be indistinguishable so far south, where the sun might float in the sky for months at a time, and it was possible that they had mistaken the one for the other from time to time. But there was every difference in the world between missing a deadline by a few hours and missing it by four, five, six, seven days. The corporation must have realized something was wrong by now.

Soon enough, someone would cut through the wind and the snow to rescue them. Laura could picture it even with her eyes open. A sledge would come slicing across the ice, a team of riders would climb out, and the supplies they needed would be dropped at their front door. Or a helicopter would chop down from overhead, unload a new transceiver, and screw itself back into the air, leaning forward in the wind like a dragonfly.

In the meantime, she could just sit playing cards with Puckett and Joyce. They stared at the reinforced arches along the inside of the hut. Every so often, one of them would press a palm against the door to feel the cold seeping through the metal. They had plenty of time. The three of them began to hear voices calling out to them, dogs barking, the digging noise of engines—sounds that were couched inside the wind like plants flexed inside a seed. Eventually, though, they realized they were just imagining things. No one was coming for them. They had been forgotten.

Laura was the last of them to reach this understanding. When she did, she became so dizzy that she saw spots of light in her eyes—thousands of them, exploding like distant stars. She thought she was going to faint. She muttered something about being out of luck, to which Puckett insisted that you could never really claim to be *out* of luck, since you never knew when things would get worse—or better, for that matter. Luck was not a limited resource, and there was no sense in trying to measure it. To which Joyce responded that the world was full of stories about people who ran out of luck: look at Prometheus, chained to his rock, with that eagle wresting out his liver for the rest of time. *There* was a person whose luck had been exhausted. To which Puckett suggested that maybe luck wasn't the sort of thing people could be said to possess at all: maybe there were currents of luck, good and bad, that ran through the world, and sometimes we found ourselves in one current, sometimes in the other, but the water itself was never truly a part of us, we were just trying to stay afloat in it. To which Joyce said, "If you've never felt luck inside you—really inside you, Puckett—then you have no credibility on this matter."

Laura had been exasperated by the conversation at the time. It was the sort of spiritless debate that the men would toss back and forth for hours on end just to keep themselves entertained. She had threatened more than once to walk to her death in the snow if they didn't stop. Now, though, she would have given anything to hear their voices again. Or any voice, for that matter.

Puckett and Joyce had been gone for nearly three weeks. When it became obvious that the corporation was not going to send any assistance, they had set out with a loaded sledge toward the western rim of the Ross Sea, where a station studying the migratory habits of emperor penguins was supposed to be located. Their plan was to contact Coca-Cola, explain what had happened, and then, if they could, borrow a radio and a spare transceiver before heading back to the shelter. The sledge ran on the latest fuel cells, designed to operate for sixty days on a single charge. Even if the ice had gone soft or the ridges were lined out against them, it shouldn't have taken them longer than a week to reach the station. They ought to have returned a few days later. Laura was beginning to resign herself to the idea that they weren't coming back. She was alone in the hut, and she was frightened.

Outside, the wind made a ringing noise between the cables. The tone shifted and pulsed in slow bands of sound that faded to silence at the upper end of her hearing register. It reminded her of the bells that used to ring at the summer camp she went to as a girl. There were two of them, at opposite ends of the camp, and she had discovered a place by the docks no bigger than her own body where the sounds would cancel each other out. She would stand there listening to the crickets and the lapping of the water inside a bulging pocket of silence. She walked back and forth in the confined space of the hut trying to locate such a pocket. In the corner above the computer station, maybe, or in the chink of space underneath the bed. Then she gave up and sat in her chair by the door and poured herself a glass of wine. It was a '27 Merlot, their only bottle. It tasted wonderful.

Polar bears. In the Coca-Cola commercial. It was polar bears, not monkeys.

~

Four days later, she found a digital music player inside Joyce's footlocker. She was washing her face on the other side of the room when the lock sprang open with the abruptness of a gunshot, and she couldn't resist looking inside. Joyce had taken his journal, his toiletries, and most of his clothing with him, but he had left behind a stack of carefully folded long johns and a pocket-sized Bertelsmann player with a selection of several hundred tracks on it. Laura set the dial to shuffle, and for the next three weeks, until the day she ventured out of the hut into a hard, clear evening of windless snow, the shelter resounded with the music of Beethoven and Link Springs, Handel and Schoenberg and Charlie Parker.

She settled into a routine of reading, exercising, and cooking, marked by long periods of sitting quietly in a chair with the music wrapping itself around her like a cloak. For one hour after lunch every day, she tried to add a page or two to her journal analyzing the effect that the corporation's cola production methods would have on the continent's indigenous plant and wildlife— her only official duty of the expedition. The task was made more arduous, and more absurd, by the almost total absence of indigenous plant and wildlife in the area. All the seals and penguins were concentrated along the rim of the ice shelf, where holes and fissures gave them easy access to the ocean. And the only vegetable life on the continent was in the ocean itself, where various forms of algae and seaweed lived. Occasionally she fiddled with the radio, hoping to summon up a signal she could navigate back to the corporation. Once, for less than a minute, she heard a dolphinlike series of clicks, squeaks, and whistles, but then the receiver went dead again, and she couldn't make out another sound. She played solitaire every so often, but she always stopped when she realized she had been shuffling the cards for too long without laying out a hand. Sometimes she paced back and forth between the bed and the door, counting off her steps. *Four, five, six, seven.* She tried to sleep for eight hours a night, but because of the slow deterioration of the heating panels, she often woke after just three or four, the muscles in her calves bunching painfully together in the cold. She made a point of checking the thermometer every morning. The temperature inside the hut was dropping by about two degrees a night. Soon it would be below the freezing mark, and she would have to punch through a lid of ice just to get to the water in the drinking basin. Already, she could see her breath making tiny little vanishing blemishes in the air. How cold would it have to become before she began to develop frostbite?

One night, shortly after she had eaten dinner, when she could have sworn there wasn't a thought in her head, she became terribly sad. She felt it as a sort of aching in her joints, as though her body were suddenly collapsing in on itself. What was this? she wondered. The feeling seemed to rise up from out of nowhere. First she was just standing by the broken transceiver, listening to a Shostakovich recording and absentmindedly conducting the orchestra with her finger, and then she was sitting on the edge of her bed, shaking and weeping uncontrollably. She cried until her stomach made a fist inside her, and then she doubled over and placed her head between her legs, gasping until she was able to pick up the rhythm of her breathing again. Every night after that, at exactly the same time, it happened again—the wild sobbing and then the clutching feeling in her gut that made her forget everything that had ever happened to her.

She was starved for conversation and laughter, for the simple tangency of other bodies. She tried to remember the times she had spoken to other people—people who had taken her knee and leaned in to whisper in her ear, people who had shouted her down in classrooms and committee meetings—and when she couldn't remember them, she imagined them, which was the next best thing. She missed Puckett and Joyce, their ridiculous arguments, even the sound of their breathing. She suspected more and more that they had gotten lost somewhere between the hut and the Ross Sea station, or that they had made it to the station but decided not to risk the return trip. She missed her mother and father, too, and her friends, and her neighbors from the apartment building where she used to live. Sometimes she thought about them so much her head became filled with their voices.

"Come on, sweetie, time for bed," she heard her father saying, and then it was fifteen years later, and her college roommate was telling her, "I'm staying with Kyle for the weekend, so you've got the room all to yourself." Next it was ten years after that, and she listened to her boss as he rapped on the door of her office and said, "I'm going to give you one word, and you tell me what you think: *Antarctica*." And a year before that, her boyfriend had told her, "That's the lipstick. You should wear that color from now on. God, it makes me want to bite your lips off." And then, just a week before she left for the Pole with Puckett and Joyce: "What, you can't spare a lousy dollar? Miss New-Black-Shoes-with-Her-Fancy-Matching-Belt. Miss Too-Busy-to-Give-a-Damn-About-Anyone-but-Herself." This was the man who begged for change outside the Coca-Cola building.

She would listen to their voices until the wind drowned them out, and then she would emerge from the fine open air of her memories into the low gray arches of the hut and the endless hours of sitting and pacing.

She looked for ways to draw out her routine, teasing it apart into its various threads and following each one to the end, no matter how wispy and frail it became. She wasn't going to allow herself to go crazy, she decided. She exercised for a full hour in the morning, rather than just fifteen minutes, jogging in place in her coat and gloves. She read books that forced her to pay attention to every word. The meals she cooked became more and more laborious: pot roasts, stews, and casseroles that used up her store of vegetables and needed to simmer for half the afternoon. She pounced at every interruption, suspending whatever she was doing in order to tug out a crease in her blanket or sweep a trace of snow up from the floor. But nothing seemed to help. The truth was that no matter how many times she lifted herself out of her chair, trying to simulate a feeling of urgency, she was never truly going anywhere. She was stuck right where she was, and she knew it.

She was making a minor repair to the stove one morning when she nearly chopped off her left hand. It happened like this: She heard a bolt rattling above the burner, and when she couldn't get the leverage she needed to tighten it, she climbed on top of the stove, trying for a different angle. She could see straight down the crevice in back. A metal tailing of some kind had come loose from the wall. It was trembling and jerking, brushing against the stove as the wind shook the cabin. That was where the noise was coming from; it wasn't the bolt at all. She knew the noise would drive her crazy if she let it continue, and so she tried to twist the tailing back into place with her fingers. When that didn't work, she tried to saw it off with her pocket knife. And when *that* didn't work, she decided to hack it loose with a hatchet she found in the tool chest. She steadied herself against the stove with her left hand, brought the hatchet up with her right, and just before she reversed her swing, she lost her grip.

Her hand was so numb from the cold that she didn't even realize it was empty until the ax came tilting past her head and crashed into the top of the stove. It made a bell-like rolling noise and then clattered to the floor.

When she looked down, she saw a silvery gash in the stove, curling down into itself like a coring of frozen soil. The gash was right at the tip of her fingers—she might have been pointing to it.

That was the moment when she realized how truly alone she was. If the hatchet had fallen just an inch or two to the left, she would have bled to death before anyone found her—weeks or, she was prepared to imagine, even years later. She would have to be more careful from now on.

She began to remember certain incidents from her life—meetings, conversations, and various other episodes—with a clarity that amazed her. Once, when she was in college, she had spent an entire day at the Chicago zoo watching a baby giraffe, the last the world would see, swirling and jiggling a length of iron chain with its long black tongue. On the day she began her first job, working behind the counter of a dry cleaner's, a customer had given her a pair of pants with a ring-shaped stain on the crotch and asked, "Can you get Formula 44-D out of polyester-rayon?" Then there was the time her mother took her to the birthday party of a school friend and afterward scolded her for singing the phrase "When are we going home?" over and over again, to the tune of the "Happy Birthday" song. Laura had been only four years old at the time.

She wondered if she was undergoing the same rush of memories that the dying are said to experience—only much, much more slowly.

Laura Byrd, wildlife specialist, prepares for the long winter.

And then there was the crying again, which always came as a complete surprise. She couldn't understand why she wasn't able to anticipate it. Maybe it was like the pain that women underwent in childbirth, those million agonies of cramping and stretching that washed the mind clean as they took place. Or maybe it had something to do with the upwelling of memories that seemed to place her so firmly in her past life, a life that had overtaken and caught hold of her just as her present was becoming more and more indistinct and her future was fading to the merest suggestion. Maybe the crying was part of her other life, her real life, the one that was unfolding before her eyes, and maybe she was nothing more than a visitor there.

One day, not long before the thermometer stopped working, she realized that the hum she was so accustomed to hearing from the shelter had gone silent. This was the sound the hut made as it converted the vibrations of its atoms into heat. It emanated from deep inside the walls, a tone so uniform and regular that she barely recognized it as a sound at all. She wouldn't even have noticed it was missing if it hadn't been for a brief lapse in the wind that brought a nearly perfect stillness to the air. She took off her glove and touched her fingers to one of the heating panels. She could feel the cold biting through her skin. When she lifted the frame from around the panel and slid the locking plate loose, she saw that the coil inside had faded to a pale, lusterless gray. She looked behind the other panels and found exactly the same thing: dozens of dimmed-out heating coils, like dead worms washed onto the sidewalk after a rain. She had known all along that it would happen, and it had. The heating panels had finally quit working.

There were two tents left in the storage closet (Puckett and Joyce had taken the others), and she set one of them up in the center of the living room so that she could sleep inside it. It was surprisingly well insulated—with its own limited heating system, one of the new so-called "soft coils"—and before long she was spending most of her day in there. The light that filtered through the fabric gave the air a milky pink coloring, and the dome inhaled and exhaled slightly as the air pressure shifted in the hut. She had the absurd impression—a dream, really—that she was living inside a jellyfish. Early in the morning, before she was wholly awake, she would lie in her sleeping bag listening to the watery lurching of the wind and imagine that she was pumping slowly across the floor of the ocean as millions of yellow diatoms sailed around her. Dreaming was easier than screaming, and screaming was easier than worrying, and worrying was easier than crying, which was what she knew she would be reduced to if she didn't keep a hard eye on herself.

She left the tent each morning to make breakfast and to exercise, and every so often to use the bathroom, and then again in the evening to cook dinner. The shelter retained only a small amount of the heat it had stored over the past six months, and the stove warmed it up a little bit more, but she still had to put on her coat and gloves every time she climbed outside the tent. She didn't yet know what she would do when the electricity finally gave out completely. It had flickered off a few days before, coming back on in a series of arrested spurts. She had counted every second between the bursts of light and darkness, feeling sick in the pit of her stomach. But for now, at least, it was still flowing.

Flowing. Blowing. Snowing.

She often found herself spinning out word associations as she lay drowsing in the tent. It was a game she had begun playing as long ago as elementary school, as she tried to run a knife through the empty minutes between recess and the end of the school day.

Snowing. Snowball. Ball game. Ball bearing. Bering Strait. Straight man. Man about town.

Man about town. Laura had been working for the Coca-Cola Corporation for less than a month when they instituted what they called their "man about town" campaign. This was during the last big water-safety scare, when all the talk shows and newspapers were full of reports that the terrorists were planning to poison the nation's drinking water. The corporation hired some ten thousand good-looking men and women to dine in the restaurants of New York, Los Angeles, and a handful of other large cities and say to anyone they spotted ordering a glass of water, "Wouldn't you feel safer drinking a Coke?" By the third week of the operation, domestic sales had increased by forty percent, and by the fifth week they had increased another twenty. The campaign was Joyce's idea, and its success had landed him the promotion that would eventually send him to Antarctica—and,

Laura speculated, to the bottom of a crevasse somewhere. Puckett had been chosen because of his knowledge of the polar landscape (though in truth he was no more than a hobbyist) and Laura because, of the dozen or so environmental impact specialists in her department, she was the only one who had seniority enough to be eligible for the trip but too little seniority to decline. This was how such things were usually decided.

Four days after the electricity began to falter, it snapped off with a conspicuousness that she knew was final. A scent of cordite spread through the shelter—though it couldn't possibly have been cordite—and the Bertelsmann player stopped dead in the middle of an Etta James song. If she had understood anything at all about how the generator worked, she might have been able to repair it, but she knew next to nothing about electromechanics, only the few scraps of theory she remembered from her freshman year of college. She turned on the flashlight she had placed in the pocket of the tent. The air around her still had the same slightly pink quality to it, but now that the light was reflected back in on itself, rather than filtered through from outside, it was twice as sharp as it had been before. Everything inside the tent seemed to shine with a finely edged clarity. There was a box of granola bars in the recess by the tent's entrance. She unwrapped and ate one. She was astonished by the distinctness of the individual grains, which were cemented together with such cohesion that they resembled tiny puzzle pieces. This was the kind of food she would be eating from now on, she knew: hunks of pemmican, dehydrated biscuits, beef jerky, and granola bars—food that was meant to last through an apocalypse. She could always hook up the Primus stove or try to construct a fire, of course, but even then she expected the provisions to run out in less than a month. The expedition was supposed to have ended weeks ago, and their reserve of supplies had always been meager.

So this was her situation: no heat, no electricity, and soon there would be no food.

She knew what she had to do—knew, in fact, so immediately that she realized she must have been pondering the question for weeks.

Her only chance was to outfit the second sledge, abandon the shelter, and set off after Puckett and Joyce. If she made it to the western rim of the Ross Sea, she would find food, shelter, and companionship; if not, she would be no worse off than she already was. She didn't want to leave. The thought of venturing out across the ice, into all that cold and emptiness, terrified her. But there was no other choice.

She spent the next half-day gathering the supplies she needed: boxes of condensed and dehydrated food, a jar of multivitamins, a few cans of coffee, a dozen rolls of toilet paper, one change of clothing, her tent and sleeping bag and thermal lining, her first-aid kit, a bottle of sunblock, a coil of Alpine rope, several waterproof boxes of matches, the Primus stove and a few cans of heating oil, a bundle of candles, the spare tent, a small magnetic compass (the sledge was equipped with a GPS monitor, but she didn't want to take any chances), her flashlight and a box of extra batteries, the tool box, a cooking pot, a second cooking pot for melting ice into water, a few pieces of plywood, an ice ax, a pick, a sledging shovel, her pocket knife, and, finally, a harness and a pair of skis and ski poles, in case the sledge broke down and she had to haul the supplies across the ice herself. She used up more than an hour looking for an extra fuel cell for the sledge, but she wasn't able to find one. Which meant that either the corporation hadn't thought to provide them with one or that Puckett and Joyce had taken it with them. In either case, she would have to make do without it.

She was concentrating so hard on culling and sorting the equipment that she didn't even notice that the wind had stopped blowing until she swung the door of the hut open to a paling sky and a motionless field of snow. She stepped outside, tucking her hands in her armpits. The air was absolutely still. No matter where she looked she couldn't see a single cloud, though from somewhere a sparse, floury snow was falling.

It was one of the sunset days—that was how she had come to think of them—when the sky fills for hours at a time with trailers of pink and gold. A bare freckling of stars was just beginning to show through the atmosphere, and she began to count them. The longer she stared, though, the more she was able to see, and soon she gave up.

She squatted down to examine the condition of the ice. Thousands of parallel ridges—sastrugi, they were called—stretched from the door of the hut all the way to the horizon, combed into the snow by the southern wind. But the ice was not too soft, nor was it too hard and dry, and she thought that it would make for good traveling.

She began to chip away at the mass of ice covering the sledge, setting the sharp end of the pick against it and hammering down with her palm. It was like breaking the stone from around a sculpture, and as the shards rained down around her feet by the thousands, she contemplated the distance that lay ahead of her, and the industry, and the luck, it would take to cross it.

Three

THE ENCOUNTER

It was hot in the office, a terrible, parching heat that lifted the smell of ink from the mimeograph machine and filled the air with it. For a long time Luka sat at his desk fanning the fumes away from his face. Then he opened the window and pulled the vines out of the way, waiting for the breeze to come blowing through. The quiet outside was nearly transcendent. There were no cars idling at the stoplight, no children running past with balloons. There was nobody down there at all. The air tasted like granite and river grass. He took a few deep breaths and returned to his stencil.

He was working on the latest edition of the *Sims Sheet*. The headline read ALONE IN THE CITY, and the subheading, in a slightly smaller type, EDITOR WONDERS, IS THERE ANYBODY OUT THERE? That was as far as he had gotten.

He had spent the better part of the morning stationed outside the River Road Coffee Shop with a full stack of the early edition in his hands. From seven to eleven-thirty he had stood there, completely alone, reading the headline to himself: THE GREAT LEAVE-TAKING CONTINUES. Four and a half hours of waiting by the plate-glass window where dozens of bodies used to sit shifting about on rickety wooden stools, inching their coffees to the left as the sun came slowly into view. Four and a half hours of counting the birds on the ledges and the bits of trash blowing by on the street. Four and a half hours, and he saw not a single human soul, not even the people he considered his regulars, like the woman who wore the white beret, or the thin man in the wrinkled business suit, or the dessert chef who always poked his head outside just as Luka was packing up to leave.

In all his years in the city, this was the first time such a thing had happened. Who or what had taken everybody he didn't know. But that wasn't the question that was bothering him. The question that was bothering him was, Why hadn't it taken him as well? He allowed himself a few extra minutes to wait out any stragglers before he finally gave up and walked home. On his way, he dumped the entire run of newspapers in a garbage basket, then thought better of it and fished them back out, then thought better of it again and threw them away, but he kept a single copy, a memento, which he pinned to the wall behind his desk. It would serve as a memorial for something—the day his hope died out, maybe.

Why was he still working on the newspaper at all? He wasn't sure. Habit, he supposed—something to keep his hands busy, something to keep his mind occupied. He could already sense where the whole thing was heading, though: down, down, down, into the deepest, most embarrassing form of solipsism.

He wasn't looking forward to it. He had always been the paper's only writer, and now he was its only reader, too. Soon, if he wasn't careful, he would be issuing reports on his own bowel movements.

The *L. Sims News & Speculation Sheet: All the Sims That's Fit to Print*.

Or, better yet: *All the Sims That's Sims to Sims*.

A tiny licking breeze came into the office and stirred the air. He heard the vines that had fallen back over the window rustling against the brick. He bent over his desk to tinker with his lead: "At approximately 11:30 this morning, the editor of this newspaper concluded that he was the last human being in the city. And perhaps, aside from the birds, the last creature of any kind." Or should he use a comma before the "and"? Or a dash? Or a parenthesis? When he was in his early thirties, five or six years before he died, he had taught an Introduction to Journalism course at Columbia University and been astonished to discover how many of his students—some of the best students in the city, mind you—were incapable of writing a good opening sentence. Not only did they bury their leads, they burned them, dismembered them, and *then* buried them. This had been one of his favorite classroom jokes, though it had never gotten so much as a single laugh. No wonder. He stuck the course out for three semesters—three semesters, two hundred students, and one love affair, to be exact—before he decided to resume writing full-time. He hated to say that reporting was in his blood, but it did seem to offer him something that nothing else did: the exhilaration of a million small facts. When he was working on a story, he felt as though he were a paleontologist uncovering a set of bones, chipping away at the world until he had enucleated some small, hard object he could catalogue and carry away in his hands: a skull, say, or a breastbone. That was the real reason he kept on writing the newspaper: he didn't know how else to behave.

He was a fool, of course, and he knew it. He had traded the pleasures of conversation and friendship, pleasures available to anybody who so much as stepped out his front door, for a million hours of sitting alone in his office piecing together the next day's copy. He had taken it for granted that the community of the dead, and earlier the community of the living, would always be there, waiting just outside, and so he had neglected it, choosing to watch and listen from the periphery rather than actually participate in it. He ought to have set his notebook down, gone to one of the bars, and sought out a few drinking buddies. He ought to have fallen in love with somebody, or at least tried.

There were so many things he ought to have done, but he hadn't, and now it was too late.

He decided to add the comma to the "and," and then he moved on to the next sentence, and before long he had lost himself in the story he was telling.

He must have been working for half an hour before something finally snatched his attention. He lifted his head.

For just a moment he was sure that he had heard a tapping noise. He set his paper aside and listened.

There it was again, the same tapping noise, like a tree limb brushing against a street sign. The sound seemed to be coming from down on the street. When he went to the window and looked outside, he saw the flag end of a coat disappearing around the corner. *Holy, holy, holy*. He kept repeating the word, first in his head and then out loud. It was a broken-off exclamation of surprise, something he was hardly even aware of thinking until he heard his own voice.

He bounded out of the office and took the stairs at a gallop. The street directly in front of the building was deserted, but he knew which way the coat had gone. He followed after it. He felt the kind of rolling surge of high energy he had sometimes felt as a teenager, when he would have to stop whatever he was doing to rush into the field behind his house and hurl a softball or a tennis ball as hard as he could, then push off from the grass to chase it down. He smacked a parking meter with his hand as he rounded the corner of the sidewalk. At the end of the block, he saw the coat vanishing behind the shining silver window of a building, the polished black heel of a shoe flashing in its wake. He redoubled his speed.

"Wait!" he shouted. "Hold up!"

He was halfway down the street before the figure in the coat reappeared, taking two steps away from the corner of the building. He stood there with all the calm of a street sign, the wind parting slowly around him. Something about the way he held his arm extended toward the brick wall, like a diver keeping his line in reach, told Luka that the man was blind, though he was not wearing dark glasses or carrying a cane. The tapping noise Luka had heard from his office must have been the sound of his shoes striking the sidewalk.

Luka slowed to a jog as he closed the gap. "Hey." He was still breathing hard from his run down the stairs. "Hey, I'm—" He gasped. "I'm Luka—" Another gasp. "Luka Sims."

The blind man cocked his head to one side. "Are you real?" He placed a peculiar stress on the word "real."

It felt so satisfying to be talking to somebody that Luka found himself letting out a noise: a quick gust of genuine laughter. "Are *you*?" he said.

Something tightened inside the blind man's face. "It's been a long time since I could say so with any certainty."

"Here," Luka said. "Take my hand," and cautiously the blind man reached for it. The hand he gave Luka was dry and callused, particularly at the fingertips, and it twitched when Luka squeezed it. "There," Luka said. "I'm as real as that. That's about all I can guarantee."

The blind man nodded as if to say *Close enough*, then withdrew his hand.

"I didn't think there was anybody else left around here," Luka admitted, though it seemed ridiculous now, like a nightmare that had lost all its power as soon as the sun rose.

After a moment, the blind man asked, "What's happened? Can you tell me?"

"All I can give you is a theory." He switched into reporting mode. "It looks like the world—the other world, I should say—is shutting down. From what I can gather, there was some sort of virus over there, and it knocked out most of the population. Maybe all of the population, I don't know. And when they go, so do we. That seems to be the way it works. Mind you, all of this is just a theory. It doesn't explain what the two of us are still doing here."

"I came here across a desert," the blind man said.

And that evening, as he sat lightly on the cushions of Luka's sofa, like a paper kite poised to catch the wind, he was still recounting the story. He had finished off the last of the red wine and fettuccine Luka had prepared, and he was tearing tiny pieces of his napkin off and collecting them in his palm. "I thought it was only the whistling of the wind at first. It took me a while to hear the pulse." The blind man repeated the exact same detail for what must have been the sixth or seventh time, and Luka made another little affirmatory noise. He was unwilling to let the blind man go, unwilling to leave him alone for even the few seconds it would take to rinse the dishes or put the leftovers away, for fear that he would disappear. "All that sand, and it wouldn't stop moving," the blind man said, and when he brought his hands together, the confetti pieces of his napkin drifted to the floor.

They stayed up talking until long after the sun had set. Then Luka offered the blind man a place on his couch to sleep, and because it was late and the blind man was still tipsy from the wine, he accepted.

Luka lay awake half the night listening to him breathe.

The next morning he was still there, sitting on the sofa, running his hands over a wing-shaped piece of driftwood that Luka had fished out of the river. He had folded the blanket Luka had given him into a perfect square, positioning it in the center of his pillow. When he heard Luka come into the room, he said, "I think there must be more of us."

"More of us?"

"More of us left in the city."

"Why do you say that?"

The blind man was quiet for a long time. "Instinct."

And though Luka couldn't say why, he was inclined to agree. Since he had noticed the tapping noise outside his window, he had been quick to investigate any unusual sound: a nut falling from an oak tree, his refrigerator hatching another clutch of ice cubes. He would let the sounds sail around in his short-term memory until he was satisfied that he could identify them. Then he would get up and head to the window or the kitchen just to make sure. It was as though every sound that was not the wind or the birds or the river was by definition human. He imagined people all over the city, hundreds of them, trying everything they could think of to pierce through the walls of their solitude, but uncertain there was anybody out there. Hundreds of faces behind hundreds of windows. Hundreds of coats gliding around hundreds of corners. He was determined that he wouldn't stop looking until he had picked out every last one of them.

He and the blind man spent the day searching for anyone they could find. Luka tried to offer him his elbow as they started out, but the blind man refused it. "A man who's walked as far as I have doesn't need anybody's help," he said. Instead, he navigated by trailing his hand along the wall of whichever building they were passing, listening to the echo of his hard-soled shoes as they hit the sidewalk.

The two of them began at Luka's apartment building, venturing outward in a series of linked rings. "We should stay in one place," the blind man argued. "Other people are going to be out searching, too." And he had a point—someone could easily happen by the apartment building while they were away—but Luka was too restless to stay put. He preferred to take his chances in the city.

They walked down street after street, the blind man shouting out, "Hello?" and Luka shouting out, "Anybody?" every ten or twenty steps.

"Hello? Anybody? Hello? Anybody?"

They passed bus benches and empty storefronts and hundreds of abandoned cars, some of them stalled out in the middle of the road. There were paperback novels lying open on the sidewalk, and carry-away bags from Chinese restaurants, and even the occasional briefcase or backpack. Once they found a skateboard rolling back and forth in a drainage culvert, struggling against the wind. But they did not see any people. It occurred to Luka that this was the first morning in years he had failed to complete an edition of the *Sims Sheet*. And though it was true that the only reader he had discovered so far was a blind man, and so probably not a reader at all, he felt for a moment like a kid who had forgotten to do his homework. It was something he knew about himself, something he had long known: there was always a teacher standing somewhere over his shoulder.

As the day wore on, he and the blind man spiraled farther and farther away from their starting point, reaching the river on one side and the skirts of the conservatory district on the other, until the soft white-blue of the sky began to bruise over and they headed back to Luka's apartment building. It was understood between them that the blind man would stay another night. Or another two nights. Or another three. That he would stay as long as it took for them to discover or be discovered by someone.

Luka had no idea where the man usually made his home. He didn't seem to be the type of person who would have a pet or a lot of possessions to take care of. Luka wouldn't have been surprised if he slept in a different place every night, on whichever couch or bed or carpet he happened to find himself.

He woke up early the next morning to the smell of something cooking. He went into the kitchen.

The blind man had found a jar of batter in the refrigerator and was pressing waffles into shape between the hinged metal pans of a waffle iron. Luka could see the batter sizzling and darkening as it spilled over the circumference of the pan.

"You know you talk in your sleep," the blind man said.

As far as he could tell, Luka had not made so much as a sound as he entered. "I do? What do I say?"

"'They're still down there.' 'The best thing I've ever done.' That sort of thing."

Luka thought about it for a minute. "I have absolutely no idea what that means," he said.

He ate a plateful of the waffles, which were surprisingly well cooked—a perfect crisp brown at the edges, but fluffy at the center—and then the two of them set off into the city. They explored the same terrain they had covered the day before, but in straight lines this time rather than linked circles, to make sure they hadn't missed anybody. They had to take shelter under the awning of a liquor store during one of the city's sudden thunderstorms, but the rain lasted only a few minutes, and then they were off again.

It wasn't until late that afternoon that they found another survivor.

~

Her name was Minny Rings, and they spotted her trying on gloves behind the window of a discount clothing store. She gave a start and clutched her chest when Luka tapped on the window. Then she rushed outside exclaiming, "Thank God! Thank God!" She looked as though she wanted to wrap her arms around the two of them. Instead, though, she just put her fingers to the cuffs of their jackets for a moment. She had been dead less than a week, she said, when the only other people in her building, an old Russian woman and her son, who was even older, slipped out the bottom of the funnel. She hadn't seen anybody since. She had spent the last few days walking around her neighborhood, watching the birds fly from rooftop to rooftop, and rattling doorknobs to find out whether they were unlocked. She had made her way into dozens of empty shops and apartments, looking through piles of clothing, stacks of antique maps, and display cases full of jewelry. She had turned up a library of old books inside someone's painted wooden trunk, and she had filled most of the last couple of nights reading one of them.

"What book?" Luka asked.

"The Master and Margarita."

"Mikhail Bulgakov. I love that book."

"Me, too," she said. Luka watched as she brought her thumb and her forefinger to the corners of her lips. It looked as though she were trying to tug her smile down into a frown. A nervous tic, he supposed.

The blind man, who was leaning against the wall, took off one of his shoes and beat at the heel until a pebble rolled out. Then he squeezed his foot back inside. "The air is getting colder," he said suddenly, and sure enough, the sun was falling. The tops of the trees still caught its full light, but the trunks and the scaffolding of the lower limbs were sliced off by the hard shadows of the buildings, so that when Luka's vision blurred, he saw only the very highest branches. They looked like ornaments floating in the sky.

Minny touched Luka's arm. She asked, "Are you okay?"

"Why?"

"You looked like you were about to faint there."

"Did I? I'm just tired from walking, I guess. Tired and hungry. We haven't eaten anything since this morning."

"Mm-hmm. Look, what do you think about the two of you coming back to my place with me?" she said. "I don't want to be too—what? Forward. Pushy. But I'd rather not let you out of my sight right now. I'm just around the corner," she said hopefully, and she pointed her finger.

So Luka and the blind man followed her back to her apartment, which was a small one-bedroom on the ground floor of a converted school building, sparsely furnished with a few folding chairs and a coffee table. She brewed a pot of coffee, and later, after they had eaten, as the dishes soaked in the sink, she brought their talk gradually around to the crossing and

44

the other world. She wanted to know how the two of them had died.

"A car accident," Luka said. "I always knew I would die in a car accident, and that's exactly what happened. I was on the highway, and I hit the front wedge of one of those concrete dividing walls, and the car broke apart into a million pieces. It was like my body stopped and the rest of me just kept on going. Like a dream almost. It wasn't even raining. I just lost control of the wheel."

"And what about you?" Minny asked the blind man.

"Old age," he said after a short pause, which, like all his pauses, might have been either thoughtful or oblivious—Luka couldn't tell. "Old age and neglect."

The night had deepened outside, so that the lamps in the apartment, which had seemed so weak just an hour or so before, glowed like miniature, shining suns.

"And what happened to you?" Luka asked Minny.

"The same thing that happened to everyone else," she said. "The Blinks."

She seemed reluctant to say anything more, and Luka didn't press her.

He already knew most of the broad details, anyway. The rapidly progressing illness that began with an itching behind the eyes. The flight of the population from the coasts and the cities. The looting and the vandalism. The desperation and the brutality. He must have conducted a hundred interviews in the last few weeks of the newspaper, and the story had always been the same.

The conversation fell away, and the three of them sat quietly listening to the faucet drip into the sink. Every so often, the water would strike the edge of a metal pan with a whispery, cymbal-like brushing sound before it shifted and began falling into the soapy water again.

After a while, Minny excused herself to go to the bedroom. She wanted to finish reading her book. "I'm only about twenty pages from the end. It won't take me long. You don't mind, do you?"

"Go right ahead."

"Fantastic." She came back half an hour later, already dressed in her pajamas, and slipped the book onto a small wooden shelf that was recessed into the living room wall. She stood there for a long while with her hands resting on her hips. "I'm trying to remember what it was I was supposed to do," she said to herself. Then, after a few seconds, "Oh, well. I guess it will come to me eventually."

They stayed up another hour or so discussing their plans for the next day. Though Minny knew almost nothing about the city as it existed beyond the few blocks of her neighborhood, she wanted to join Luka and the blind man in their hunt for other survivors. It was decided that when morning came, if the three of them were still there and no one had disappeared, they would head deeper into the conservatory district together. It was Luka's feeling that where there were three people there were bound to be four, and where there were four there were bound to be five. "I'm not so sure about six and seven, though," he said. He tried to work up a little chuckle, a half-laugh for his half-joke, but he was too tired and it came out as a yawn.

The blind man had already fallen asleep in his chair. Luka swallowed a second yawn, and Minny took his arm.

"Look, I only have the one bed, but you're welcome to one side of it."

"Are you sure?"

"Mm-hmm. I'll sleep better that way."

"All right. Good," Luka said. He ended up brushing his teeth with his index finger, then washing his face with a shell-shaped piece of soap he found sitting on the rim of the bathroom sink. By the time he was finished, Minny had already turned off the bedroom light, but he could still see well enough to find his way to the other side of the bed. He stood above her for a moment. He was trying to adjust himself to the idea of sleeping next to another body. The world had swung around like a carousel, it seemed, and given him another chance.

"I think I need to finish my story," Minny said.

"The Bulgakov? I thought you did finish it."

"No, the other story. My story."

He pulled the blanket down and slid beneath the covers. "Shoot."

"Well, I was away from home when the virus hit. That's the important thing." She spoke slowly and deliberately, as though the story were a complicated maze of rooms she was trying to pick her way through for the first time. "I was at a sales convention in Tucson, Arizona. Office supplies. I used to sell office supplies to hospitals and state agencies. There were probably five hundred of us in the hotel, from all over the country. When the news came through, we all rushed for our rental cars. I just kept thinking that I wanted to see my dad again. Isn't that strange? It didn't make any sense. I hadn't spoken to my dad since I was a kid, and he was dead anyway, but he was all I could think about. Not my mom, not my boyfriend. My dad. But the hotel had set up a quarantine around the edge of the parking lot, and they wouldn't let any of us leave. I guess they thought somebody might have carried the virus in from out of state. I don't know. I managed to get one of the last few Cokes out of the vending machine in the lobby, then I went back up to my room. Most of the TV networks were already down, but a couple were showing footage of the virus from Great Britain. It was horrible. Bodies lying dead on the grass or propped up against trees. You're lucky you didn't have to see it." She shuddered. "Honestly. There was this one shot, from London, of these hundreds of shoes lying scattered around on a flat stretch of highway. Nothing but shoes. People must have thrown them off when they were running from something, I guess. Who knows what? I couldn't help turning the TV back on every so often to see if there was anything new, but there never was. By the end of the day the networks were nothing but static, except for one of the gossip channels that was airing some show about Hollywood weddings. A repeat, of course. No more Hollywood weddings. I think it was the next morning that I started to feel sick. I remember going into the bathroom for a glass of water, but not much else after that."

Here she stopped for a moment, and the remembering tone fell out of her voice. "I guess that's the whole story. I'm sorry. I just had to tell somebody."

"Can I ask you one question?" Luka said.

"Ask."

"How long was it before you died?"

"I don't really know," Minny answered. "My guess would be that I didn't make it through to the night."

She was resting on her side, hunched and facing away from him. All this time her feet had been swaying in slow half circles beneath the blankets, one grazing on top of the other, like waves covering each other over on the beach. He felt as though he could listen to the rustling sound they made forever. Just before he fell asleep, he heard her mutter, "The dishes," and the next thing he knew it was morning.

Once more, the blind man was already awake. He was helping Minny in the kitchen, filling the coffeemaker as she plugged the toaster oven into the wall. The three of them ate a light breakfast of English muffins with strawberry jelly, and then they started off into the city.

The streets seemed even emptier than before. Most of the trash—hamburger wrappers, ticket stubs, styrofoam cups—had been blown down to the river or collared inside the necks of various alleyways. The few pieces that remained were either too heavy or not aerodynamic enough to be lifted by the wind. A windup alarm clock. A rubber doorstop. A compact disc. They looked like part of some vast, citywide art installation: *Things We Left Along the Way*.

A banner was flapping between two flagpoles on the side of a building, tightening and relaxing like a sail luffing in a gentle breeze, but on the pavement everything was perfectly still. Luka kept his eyes open for any sign of human activity. He matched his step to Minny's. The blind man stayed a few paces ahead of them, running his hand along the walls and the windows, never stumbling as he stepped over the curb into the intersections of the empty streets.

Luka planned to lead them back to his office before the day was out. He was afraid he had neglected to close his window. Whether or not they found anybody, he didn't want to leave his equipment exposed to the rain. The mimeograph machine, in particular, barely worked on even the best of days: the crank often got stuck, or the drum fell loose, or the paper came through clotted with ink. He hated to imagine how it would operate with a few gallons of rainwater irrigating the machinery.

They stopped for a few minutes at a small, enclosed park on the corner of Seventeenth and Margaret Streets, where they lined up on one of the wrought-iron benches to rest their legs. Minny took her shoes off and began rubbing the soles of her feet, massaging them with her thumbs and then with her knuckles. "This is what a lifetime of driving from the door to the mailbox will get you," she complained. "Little-girl feet."

A pair of basketballs had drifted to a stop against the chain-link fence. Every so often a gust of wind would pass between them, and they would roll apart and come back together again with an oddly resonant thumping noise. Minny slipped her shoes back on, Luka tapped the blind man's shoulder, and the three of them headed back out toward the conservatory.

It was still early in the day when the blind man brought them up short, extending his left arm. "Did you hear that?" he asked.

Luka hadn't noticed anything. Neither had Minny.

"It sounded like a gunshot," the blind man said. "A few miles away."

He cocked his head and pointed. "There! There it was again!"

All at once, and without another word, he struck off at a fast walk. Luka and Minny had no choice but to follow after him. He appeared to know exactly where he was going. He made a right onto Third Avenue, sheering around a car that was tilted up onto the sidewalk, then took a left by the Ginza Street Shopping Mall. He never turned down a blind alley or into a courtyard, never even paused. Luka couldn't figure out how he did it. Maybe it had something to do with the shape of the wind, the way various sounds came together or frayed apart in his ears. Or maybe it was his sense of equilibrium, which must have been as finely calibrated as a compass. Luka made a note to ask him whenever they got where they were going.

The blind man took them past a library and a gymnasium— four blocks, eight blocks, ten—leading them swiftly toward the river and the monument district. By the time the next gunshot was fired, the sound was much clearer. "Damned if I can't hear it," Luka said.

"It's a signal." The blind man scraped past a wooden barrel and let out a huff. "Someone's trying to get our attention."

"Why didn't *we* think of that?" Luka asked.

"We did," the blind man said. "But I didn't imagine either of you were likely to have a gun."

It was two more blocks before they broke out from behind the mass of buildings. They rounded the concrete wall of a parking garage, took a few steps up a wheelchair ramp, and saw stretched out before them the broad, grassy clearing at the center of the monument district. A spokelike pattern of walkways radiated from the monument, which was a polished marble obelisk supported on a narrow pedestal. A man with a pistol was standing beside it firing into the air.

And milling all around him, their voices raised in conversation, must have been two hundred people. A half dozen others were trickling in from the other side of the field, converging at the sound of the gunshot.

Minny gasped and took a step back, knocking heavily into Luka. "I'm sorry," she began. "It's just . . . it's just that," and she swallowed and slowly shook her head. "It's just that I never thought I would see so many people again."

"It's a big city," Luka said, by which he meant to say, *Neither did I.* And without thinking, he took her hand and pressed it to his chest. Then they followed the blind man out of the shadows and into the body of the crowd.

Four

THE MILES

The first two days of the journey went by without trouble. From her seat in the sledge, Laura followed a steady course to the northwest, using the GPS system and the onboard navigational equipment to plot her course to the station. She had never driven a sledge before, but the controls were surprisingly easy to operate. The weather was clear and there was a glasslike transparency to the air, so that she rarely had to stop for more than a few minutes at a time. The runners beneath the sledge, heated to diminish the abrasion of the ice, were capable of carrying her over all but the largest gaps and fissures, and the only time she had to vary her path was when a shoulder of rock or ice lanced its way up through the ground and forced her to circle around to the other side. She drove through the long daybreak of the Antarctic fall, resting only when the sun was high enough to rise up off the ice in a disorienting glare. Then she continued driving until the day was over and the evening was snuffed from the sky.

At sunset, when she stopped to rest, she had to unpack her equipment. The tent was easy to assemble. It was ornamented with a pull cord that caused it to pop from its bag and stretch out like a life raft until it fully expanded. She would walk around the edges knocking stakes into the ground, and then, when the wires were secure, she would carry her sleeping bag and cooking gear inside and bed down for the night. That was it; the whole procedure took less than fifteen minutes. In the morning, when she was ready to leave, all she had to do was tug on the pull cord again to make the tent collapse in on itself, withering into a perfect little cylinder that made a hissing noise as it shrank. A tag above the entrance read, WARNING: ALWAYS LEAVE DOOR OPEN WHEN DEFLATING TENT, and every time she saw it, she imagined the thing exploding like a balloon as it tightened around its bubble of trapped air, drifting to the ice in a thousand tatters of pink cloth. It was the kind of tent that was purchased by wealthy corporate executives who intended to hike the Rockies or the Appalachians someday but never quite managed to leave the city. Eventually, their children would set it up in the middle of the living room, between the sofa and the fireplace, and pretend they were pioneers.

And who's to say they weren't?

Ever since she was a little girl, Laura had felt like a pioneer, passing over into the wilderness of the rest of her life. She remembered lying beneath her bed on her twelfth birthday, staring up into the orchardlike rows of the box springs and thinking how strange it was that she had no idea where she would be a year later, on the day she turned thirteen, and that she had had no idea where she would be today the year before, on the day she turned eleven. Certainly she could never have guessed that she would find herself lying underneath her bed staring at the box springs and wondering about the way time was put together. Why was it that everything that had happened to her in the past seemed so clear, but as soon as she turned toward the future, it all went dim and faded to nothing? Was that what it meant to be alive—moving from a brightly lit corridor into a darkened room at every step? Sometimes she felt that way.

The tent kept her warm at night, or as warm as she could reasonably expect to be. She found the hum of its soft coil oddly comforting, like the sound of car wheels hissing over wet asphalt—a sound she always associated with the million rainy fall nights she had spent listening to the traffic flow past her bedroom window. But it was obvious that the heating system had not been designed for polar use. The heat from the coil radiated though the bottom of the tent, which caused the ice to melt, flow toward the edges, and refreeze, creating a sort of ovenlike seal. When she woke in the morning, there was always a shallow puddle beneath the floor that rippled back and forth as she shifted her weight. It made her feel as if she were sleeping in a waterbed.

She tried to knock the ice from the fabric before she pried the stakes out of the ground, but she was never able to get rid of it all, and when she activated the pull cord and the tent deflated, fragments of it would invariably crack and go spitting through the air, gliding across the ridges for twenty yards or more. She was usually able to load the sledge and set off again before the sun got too high. She estimated that she had covered sixty miles on her first day of travel and eighty miles on her second—better time than Puckett and Joyce had made, she imagined. The wind and the snow had long since covered their tracks, but for her the weather had been nothing but stillness and sunshine. It felt good to be moving. The crying fits that had come over her in the shelter seemed to have fallen away. She felt stronger than she had in weeks.

Soon she would wind her way down the ice stream and through the coastal pass. She would cross from the land mass onto the Ross Ice Shelf. And not long after that—a matter of days, probably—she would make it to the station. What a relief it would be to have other human beings to talk to again.

But on her third day of sledging, the temperature dropped and the sky clouded over, and the wind began whipping up pennants of ice and snow. Before she knew it, she was in the middle of a blizzard. She could still move forward, but the wind was coming from the northwest now, directly in front of her, which made the traveling slow and difficult. Pellets of hardened snow tapped against the window of the sledge, so much of it that it sounded like leaves crackling in a fire. Her headlights bored a narrow tunnel through the blizzard, but the snow confused her vision, making everything go white. She kept altering her focus as she tried to see more deeply into the storm, and the snow would catch her gaze and carry it back to the windshield in a series of shifting planes. Before so much as an hour had passed, her eyes had begun to ache and burn, though she knew she couldn't look away. The spindrift was thick, hiding the telltale cross ridges and depressions that marked the openings of the crevasses. She had to watch the ground carefully to avoid them.

The runners of the sledge were outfitted with circular frames of flat metal paddles—she thought of them as flippers—that slapped out in front of the sledge as it moved forward and then drew back underneath as it traveled on. They were a safety device, a sort of makeshift cantilever designed to carry her over any fissures she happened to encounter—or at least any fissures no more than six feet wide. Several times, she had felt the sledge plummeting forward suddenly and then lifting and righting itself before it moved on and she knew she had crossed over another crevasse. She felt as though she were driving a car down a crumbling road. The supporting ice of the glaciers had been decaying for decades, and rifts as deep as subway trenches could open in a matter of hours, sealing themselves off just as quickly. If she slipped, she wouldn't be discovered until the ice finished melting sometime in the middle of the next century. But she had been trained by years of city driving to recognize every bump and jar she felt as just another flaw in the road. If she was leaning forward in her seat and a particular sort of lurch went through her body, she naturally assumed that she had hit a pothole. It was a form of muscle memory.

Muscle memory. Mussel memory. Alive, alive-O!

The storm continued for the next few days. She had to trust to her compass and the few flickering signals that registered on her GPS monitor to maintain her bearing. She knew when she had reached the ice stream that connected the land mass to the bay by the number of knolls and ridges that appeared in her path, and also by the generally brashy quality of the ice, but she had no idea how long it would take her to make it through the pass onto level ground.

The snow fell heavy and fast. Sometimes she didn't see the obstacles that lay ahead of her until they were only a few feet away. She had to drive very slowly to avoid them. She was lucky to cover a mile or two in an hour, ten or fifteen in a day. The runners of the sledge dipped, lifted, and dipped again as she made her way through the drifts, and the snowflakes clustered together like stars on her windshield. By the end of the day, when she lay down in her sleeping bag and closed her eyes, her body would seem to rock back and forth inside itself, and she would see streamers of white light slanting across her vision. Even in her dreams, she felt herself sledging across the ice and the darkness.

She was working harder than she ever had in her life, and she was exhausted. She had chopped wood before. She had mixed concrete. She had even helped the Coca-Cola Homes for Neighbors Club build a row of apartments on the side of a hill, clearing the stumps and brush, laying the foundations and everything. But this was nothing compared to the effort of keeping a two-ton sledge on course through the center of a snowstorm. Whenever she stopped to rest, for even a few minutes, a stabbing pain would tear through the muscles in her calves and forearms, and she would have to remind herself to breathe. It was not so much the amount of exercise she was subjecting herself to, but the way she was holding her body at tension for so long. It took an hour or more of total stillness before her muscles would begin to go slack, followed by a comforting numbness that made her want to drift off to sleep.

She was too tired to cook at night, and she was tempted to leave the metal pots and the Primus stove in the back of the sledge, but she carried them into the tent with her so that she would be able to heat her coffee in the morning. The temperature sometimes dipped to forty or fifty degrees below zero, and she would have to spend a good half hour shivering in her coat and gloves before the tent truly began to warm up. She ate two or three multivitamins and a handful of dehydrated biscuits as she waited, and sometimes also a protein bar, and sometimes also a piece of chocolate, and she allowed a few chips of ice to melt on the surface of her tongue. Then she stripped to her long johns, tightened the drawstrings of the sleeping bag around her, and listened to the side wall of the tent going taut and slack and taut again, bellying in and out as it took the wind like a sail.

On the eighth day of the storm, she was traveling on a downhill slope when a spur of rock came rearing up out of the snow and filled her windshield. Her heart rose up in her chest. She swerved to avoid the rock, but it was too late.

She rammed into the spur at the rear corner and heard the solid crunch of something breaking. The sledge spun around twice and gradually drifted to a stop. She let go of the steering mechanism. Her skin was covered in sweat, and her stomach had tightened into a knot. The droning sound of the sledge slowly died away, and its runners settled into the snow. She checked herself for wounds. She seemed to be okay—no bleeding, no broken bones—but she wasn't sure about the sledge. She climbed outside onto a half dozen chunks of rock and ice that had been knocked loose by the collision.

She made her way toward the back end of the vehicle, holding on to the upper rail with her gloves, the snow twisting around her in an obscuring shroud. She had heard stories about people who had become so disoriented in snowstorms that they had lost their sense of direction only a few feet from their front doors, people who went stumbling and weaving into the tempest with their arms stretched out in front of them like zombies. She knew better than to let go of the rail. She found the spot where the sledge had run into the spur. A long rent had been torn into the wood and metal, exposing the inside of the storage hutch. Her duffel bag was wedged inside the hole, so that only a thin crack of space remained open to the air, bordered with a row of jagged wooden teeth. She could hear the wind passing through it with a whistling noise.

She sank to her knees, probing at the snow around the runners to make sure nothing had fallen out. She couldn't feel anything—the bulge of the duffel bag seemed to have sealed the breach in the hutch. She risked a short walk uphill, heading directly toward the spur, but all she saw was a tapering strip of wood and a single, palm-sized lump of black rock. When she was satisfied that she wouldn't find anything else, she staggered back downhill. She turned the sledge around and continued along the channel of the ice stream.

It would be more than a month before she discovered exactly what she had left behind on the slope and the full consequences of her accident became clear to her.

~

That night, after she sealed the hole in the sledge with a strip of plywood, she found herself replaying a certain incident from her childhood. It came to her while she was pitching the tent, whirling and condensing in her memory like a tiny runaway planet, so that by the time she fastened the door it had returned to her in all its particulars. The incident was an inconsequential one—of no importance whatsoever, really. But then most of the things she remembered, most of the things anybody remembered, were of no natural importance—were they?—and that never stopped them from rising into the light.

In her memory she was seven years old, and her mother had just taken her out of school for a dentist's appointment. Only that morning, her mother had said, "Now don't let me forget, we have to get you to the dentist by two-thirty. What time do we have to get you to the dentist by?" and Laura had answered, "Two-thirty o'clock," and her mother had said, "There's no *o'clock* to it, hon. It's just two-thirty," which was why she remembered what time the appointment was supposed to be.

She buckled herself into the car seat and waited for her mother to finish talking to the woman with the orange vest who stood by the front door in the afternoons. Laura and her friends had made an I-Spy game out of the orange vests: whoever could spot the most was the winner. She had noticed that there were always more of them on the days when the sirens went off than on the days when they didn't.

Only recently had she grown tall enough to see out the window of the car without rising onto her knees. As her mother climbed into the driver's seat and the engine made the coughing and shredding noise it always made when it was turning over, she noticed an unusual thing. On the roof of the house across the street was something she had never seen before. It looked like a spinning silver pumpkin trapped inside a metal grate.

"What's that?" she asked her mother.

"What's what?"

"That thing," she said, pointing. "The silver ball on that roof."

"Oh. They have those all over the place. It's a—" Laura watched the motions of doubt appear in her mother's face as she began to answer the question and then realized she didn't have the words. "You know, I'm not sure what it's called. It's part of the house's circulation system. I can tell you that."

Earlier in the week, Laura had watched a TV program about the body's circulation system. She remembered the image of a man whose skin peeled away to show his blood pumping through him, a loose basketry of red and blue vessels surrounding a large, throbbing heart. The connection seemed hazy to her. "A circulation system like for blood?" she was about to ask, when another car came hurtling around the corner of the parking lot, driving backward, and punched into the edge of their front bumper.

The car scraped along their driver's-side door, not grinding to a stop until it had lined up with them window for window, rearview mirror for rearview mirror, pressed against them as though it were backing into a parking space. Laura saw the driver pause and shake her head before she reached over to apply the emergency brake.

Softly, as though she were simply commenting on the weather, her mother said, "Well, goddamn it." Her face usually had a strange, almost strict expression when she was driving, but for the moment, at least, it was completely empty. She was one of those people who truly became beautiful only when they showed no sign of thought or feeling on their faces, like bright, blank flowers unfolding their petals in the sun. Later, after Laura had grown up and moved away, that was how she would remember her mother—as a woman caught in a lovely thoughtlessness.

"Are you okay?" her mother asked her.

Laura said that she was fine.

Her mother lowered her window and motioned for the woman in the other car to do the same. The woman's window sank away, taking a dim reflection of them with it. She said, "I'm having an unbelievably rotten day."

"So am I," Laura's mother said. "At least *now* I am."

"Like you wouldn't believe," the woman said.

Laura's mother began working a muscle in her jaw, but almost immediately she became plain again. "Listen, maybe you should pull forward and let me open my door."

"I can't," the woman said. "That's one of the problems."

"What do you mean, that's one of the problems?"

"There's something wrong with my car. It won't pull forward. It will only go in reverse. That and my kid left his books at home, and the stationery store was closed."

"Then maybe you should *back up* and let me open my door," Laura's mother said.

"Oh. Okay." The woman released her brake and inched backward, scraping along the side panel of the car. She slowly drifted out of contact with them. She switched her motor off and rested her forehead on the padded arch of the steering wheel, lacing her fingers together behind her neck. It was then that Laura heard her moan—a low, soft animal sound that seemed to swell up from somewhere deep inside her.

"The cow goes moo," Laura said.

"Quiet, honey."

Her mother unlatched the door. It made a creaking and buckling sound as it swiveled around the crimp, and almost at once, the car's warning bell began to ding. The bell usually came on when the door was opened by even so much as a crack, though sometimes it didn't. It was something that Laura found impossible to predict.

"Wait here," her mother told her. She shut the door and strode over to the other car. Laura could hear what she was saying through the open window. "Do you want to call the police, or do you want me to?" After a few seconds she repeated herself. "Hello? Do you want to call the police, or should I?"

"You're not supposed to move a person with a broken bone. You're supposed to wait for the ambulance," the woman answered.

"Did you break something?"

She shook her head. "I was talking about the car."

"Oh, for crying out—" Laura's mother frowned and cocked her hand in the air. Laura thought that she was going to cuff the woman, but she allowed the gesture to go slack and in the end only slapped the roof of her car lightly with her palm. The noise was still loud enough to make the woman jump in her seat.

"Look, if your car doesn't work, you shouldn't be driving it in the first place."

"It was working just fine when I left the house. Then the stationery store wasn't open, and I dropped Eric's books off, and when I came back outside, it would only go backward." The woman leaned over to pick something up from the floorboard and she straightened back up with a phone to her ear. She pressed a few buttons.

"And to top it all off," she said after a moment, "it looks like my phone is dead."

"I'll make the call," Laura's mother told her. "You wait right here. Don't go driving off anywhere. Just . . . wait." She returned to the car, sat down, and fished the telephone out of her purse. Laura listened to her telling the police operator all about the accident: who had hit whom, where they were located, how many people were involved. "No, no injuries," she said. "But the other driver seems a bit . . . *off*, I guess you could say."

Laura could see the woman sitting in her car. She was still holding the telephone to her cheek. Her knuckles were as white as candle wax.

"Mom," Laura asked, "why is she squeezing that phone so hard?"

Then the woman began to cry.

As they waited for the police, the school's front drive became crowded with the cars of all the parents and child-care workers who were lining up for the three-fifteen bell. The sunlight reflected off their windshields, hubcaps, and bumpers, filling the air with knives.

After a while, Laura began to feel an ache in her muscles from the impact of the crash. She unbuckled her seat belt, rested her head on her mother's lap, and stared at the ceiling.

"Well, it looks like we'll have to reschedule your dentist's appointment, hon," her mother said.

"Oh, that's right," said Laura. "I forgot all about it."

And when the sirens came, she didn't know whether they were the police cars pulling into the lot or those other sirens, the ones that sounded when the bombs were going to fall, the sirens of the orange vests.

~

It took her six more days to make it through the pass onto the Ross Ice Shelf. Six days of continuously falling snow that spun through the air in nets and skeins and lashes. Six days of collapsing ice and stone embankments that rose up inside the storm like baited traps. She had been afraid that she would miss the gap altogether, veering off the path and dead-ending against the side of the mountain, but she woke up one morning to an unexpectedly full silence, and when she stepped outside she found a plain of unblemished white ice stretching into the distance before her. Her relief was immense. The weather must have cleared while she was asleep. She turned around to see a line of cliffs and the tongue of the ice stream behind her. Immediately she understood what had happened: she had cut through the notch the day before, without even realizing it.

She packed the sledge quickly in the rising light and set out again. If the weather persisted—and that was quite an "if" so close to the coast—she might reach the station before exhaustion finally took hold of her. But conditions could change at the snap of a finger, and she wanted to cover as much distance as she could before they did.

Soon the sledge was traveling so swiftly that twin arcs of snow shot out from beneath the runners, pattering onto the ice with a quiet slapping sound. As the noon hour approached, the sunlight shone from off the snow as if from a layer of pressed foil. Beneath the sledge was the ice, and beneath the ice was the ocean, and she was surprised that she couldn't feel the circulation of the water down there. She had thought that she would be able to. But the shelf ice seemed just as solid, just as anchored, as the continental ice had been. Of course, the continental ice wasn't nearly as impermeable as it had been a few decades ago, before the great melting began. And from the little—very little—geology she had studied, she knew that even the land itself was never as stable as it seemed. Beneath the glaciers, after all, was the stone, and beneath the stone was the magma, and no matter where you stood on the planet, you were always bobbing around like a cork in open water. Perhaps she had just gotten used to the feeling.

Every time she climbed out of the sledge, and every morning when she left the jacketing warmth of her tent, the vigor of the cold would make her catch her breath. How long had it been since she'd set out from the shelter? Two weeks? Three? Already the days had become colder. The string that bound the sun to the horizon had grown shorter. She would make it through six or seven hours of sledging before the darkness settled over the ice—maybe eight hours if there were a few low-hanging clouds along the skyline to reflect the final traces of the light. Then she would erect her tent and go to sleep. The GPS system was working again, and if she wanted, she could have driven through the night, guided by the khaki-colored markings on the monitor. But she was tired. And beyond that, she was afraid. She was afraid that she would reach the station and somehow fail to see it.

She kept thinking about the time shortly after she graduated from college when she drove home from a late-night party and woke up on the front lawn of the house she shared with her boyfriend. She had spent the night sleeping in her car. Its fuel cell was depleted, but the front lights were still burning, and a group of children were standing above her tapping on the window. "I'd get out of here if I was you," one of them said when she opened the door, a boy with a globe of frizzy red hair. "The guy who lives in that house is an a-s-s-hole." Which, as it later turned out, he was. She had spent the next few weeks wondering what had happened to her. She remembered struggling to stay awake, then turning onto her street with a sense of exquisite relief, but after that nothing at all. She was amazed that she hadn't folded the car around a tree or a streetlamp. Or a camper van or a swing set or a living room. It was possible to drift without thinking into what you were looking for, but it was just as possible to drift right past it into something far worse. She must have come to a stop on her own front lawn by nothing more than the purest luck.

Sometimes, as she traveled across the ice shelf, the sky would gray over and the snow would begin to fall again, but it never lasted for long. Though there were mornings when she woke to find the tracks her sledge had left in the ice obscured by a covering of fresh powder, there were just as many mornings when they were lit to a razor's sharpness by the brightening sun and she could see them extending into the distance like carvings on a wax tablet.

Once, after a night of soft but persistent winds, she found the ground outside her tent scattered with thousands of marble-sized balls of snow. They were lined up along the sheltered side of the ridges, and were so delicate that they collapsed into a heap of crystals the second she touched them. She had never seen anything like them. Even the vibration of her footsteps was enough to make them collapse, she discovered, so she tried not to step too close to them.

Tried not to kill them, was how she thought of it. In the past few weeks, ever since Puckett and Joyce had left, everything around her seemed to have developed a personality.

By the time she loaded the sledge, the breeze had changed direction slightly, lifting the balls out from behind the ridges. They went skittering away across the shining field like mice. She powered up the sledge and started out toward the northwest.

She knew that she must be getting closer to the rim of the ice shelf. Fissures and crevices were appearing in the ice more and more frequently now. She slowed down whenever she saw a gap approaching, easing over it until the flippers caught on the other side and she was sure she could move forward. Once or twice she felt the balance of the sledge tipping over and had to back up and change course until the break narrowed.

At the bottom of one of the fissures, she spotted a dark thread of water. A few minutes later, an egg-shaped opening appeared in the ice, and she stopped the sledge to peer over the edge. There was a sunken pool of water inside, some ten feet down, telescoped by the walls of the tunnel. She could see it rising and falling, lingering for a few seconds at either end like the pectoral muscles of a sleeping giant. It was the ocean. She was sure of it. She was at that margin where the shelf ice began to break apart into pack ice, separating into mile-long chunks that bumped into one another as the currents tugged them back and forth. The station couldn't be more than a day or two away.

She moved out again with a renewed intensity. The few clouds that had been in the sky at dawn were gone now, and the air was scrubbed clean, so transparent that it played tricks with her notions of distance. Late in the afternoon, she saw a faraway structure with the low roof and squared off walls of the station, and her heart began to race. She accelerated toward the building, but suddenly it was gone. She activated the magnification feature on her windshield, but still she couldn't see it. She climbed down from the sledge to take a look around. Half a dozen steps behind the left runner she found the object she had seen. It was a juice box. A juice box with the low walls and squared off roof of the station. The familiar red and white Coca-Cola wave was slinking across the front, and the C. C. Juice slogan was printed just beneath it: "The Great Taste of Cola . . . in a Juice!" Somebody must have dropped it traveling across the ice shelf. One of the scientists from the station, maybe. Or Puckett or Joyce.

For a moment she thought to pick it up and throw it into the sledge, but then a surge of irritation went through her and she backed up to take a run at the thing. The box made a wonderful popping sound when she kicked it, sailing across the ice in a long, straight line.

She climbed back into the sledge. The incident made her remember the story she had heard about the girl who was raised in a room with no horizontal lines. She couldn't recall whether the story was true or simply a thought experiment, but the room, as she remembered it, was decorated with a series of black vertical stripes on the walls, and the floor and ceiling were curved to give the illusion that the vertical stripes were continuous. On the child's first birthday, the story went, she was taken out of the room. She had learned how to recognize vertical forms, but not horizontal ones, so that if she was situated on a table, say, or a platform, she would crawl right off the edge, but she would never run into the corner of a wall or the leg of a chair. Her condition lasted for about a month before her visual sense finally corrected itself.

The experiment was supposed to have proven something about the development of human perception, though for the life of her Laura couldn't remember what.

As far as she could tell, the only thing it demonstrated was that babies were capable of being tricked, and who would be surprised by that?

That same day, as the last slice of the sun was sinking behind the ice, she saw another form taking shape in her windshield, a low-bodied object at the very corner of the horizon. It shone oddly in the fading light, blinking on and off as she bumped across the ridges. At first she thought it was just a mirage—or worse, another juice container.

But then she spotted the klieg lights standing on either side of it, two dazzling panels of honed white light. They showed the building in all its contours. There was no doubt about it this time. She had finally reached the station.

Five

THE HOMECOMING

Dying had changed Marion Byrd. She had been so weary back when she was alive: weary of talking and weary of eating; weary of thinking, remembering, desiring, anticipating; weary, most of all, of the prospect of seeing her life out to its natural end. She felt as though she had spent the last ten years of her life carrying a tremendous unshaped stone on her shoulders. The effort of keeping her legs upright and simply walking underneath it had nearly crippled her. She didn't know how to cast it off, or even where it had come from, only that she had to carry it.

But then the virus had appeared and she had died, and suddenly everything was different.

She began to appreciate all the things she thought she had forgotten how to enjoy, like music and dancing and the way the breeze felt on her neck when she pinned her hair up in back. The tension gradually worked its way out of her muscles. She looked forward to waking up in the morning.

And then there was the matter of her husband: it seemed only natural, with all the other changes she had undergone, that she would love him again.

She listened to him swishing his razor around in the sink, for instance, and then tapping it clean against the porcelain—*tap tap tap*—and she knew that he would clear his throat next, and then dry his face, and only after he had blown his nose into a tissue and carefully straightened the towel on the rack would he call out to her with some question or other. The whole unwavering performance used to fill her with despair, but these days she found herself charmed by it.

"Any sign of Laura yet?" he shouted, and she answered, "Not so much as a rumor. Maybe later today, Phillip. We'll just have to wait and see."

It happened like clockwork.

Laura was their only child. She had been on a prolonged business trip when the virus hit, conducting some sort of environmental survey on the opposite side of the world. The two of them had no idea what had happened to her. There had been little opportunity for them to say good-bye, not even enough time to place a phone call or send off an e-mail. Laura was only thirty-two years old—not yet married, not yet weary. When Marion was thirty-two, she had already abandoned a graduate degree, fallen in and out of love a half dozen times, met Phillip, and concluded that that era of her life was over. She had miscarried one daughter, given birth to another, named her Laura after Laura Ingalls Wilder, spent five years raising her, and then packaged her off to kindergarten and resumed working half days as a legal secretary. At the time she had imagined herself to be a woman, and the truth was that even in hindsight, when she remembered herself as she was back then, it was a woman she remembered, with a woman's wholly developed mind and a woman's full breadth of feeling. So why was it that when she thought of Laura she couldn't help picturing her as a little girl?

"I thought we would go to Bristow's today," Phillip offered from the bathroom.

"This morning or this afternoon?" Marion asked.

"Well, this morning, I was thinking, but if you'd rather wait a while . . ."

"No, this morning will be nice. Just let me pick out a good pair of shoes."

This was another thing she had forgotten how much she

enjoyed: shoes. She had collected almost twenty pairs since she had died, including a beautiful pair of laced leather rainboots and a pair of high heels with tapering green straps that wound up her ankles like jasmine vines. Her shoes made her understand, in a way that jewelry and sunglasses and the other trappings of so-called feminine fashion never had, why people dyed their hair or wore tattoos. It was for the same reason that birds wove bits of thread or vinyl construction streamers into their nests: for the sheer pleasure of ornamentation. After she had chosen her shoes—a comfortable but attractive pair of dark blue flats—she grabbed her purse and headed back out to the living room. Phillip was still using the bathroom, so she inspected herself in the mirror that hung by the front door, wiping the oil from beneath her eyes with her thumbs. She kept her face as empty as she could. She could never stand to see herself smiling or glowering, blushing or frowning. Expressions of any kind, in fact, always bothered her. They seemed to turn her face into some kind of Halloween mask. Sometimes, even when she wasn't examining her reflection, when she was just thinking quietly or talking with her friends, she would realize that her face was taking on the cover of some emotion or other and immediately she would feel a little wash of discomfort pass through her features, distorting them like a stone tossed into a puddle. She was never sure whether her face was cracking apart because she felt so uneasy, or whether she felt so uneasy because her face was cracking apart.

Soon Phillip was ready to go. The two of them set out through the lobby of the building. The clearing across the street shone in the light of the sun. The pattern of walkways covering the grass seemed to carve it up into a giant wheel. Phillip and Marion had moved into their apartment at the center of the monument district less than a week after arriving in the city, just like everybody else who had heard the gunshots. At first there were only several hundred of them there, but within a few days there were

71

several thousand, and soon nobody was quite sure how many of them there were. There had been talk of appointing a census-taker, but as of yet no one had taken on the position. A few of the long-term residents had told Marion and Phillip about what they called the evacuation—or sometimes the leave-taking—during which the city had so suddenly emptied out. But no one could say why the people who remained behind had not yet moved on, beyond suggesting that someone must still have been alive to remember them. Marion had seen the Blinks firsthand, though, and she found this theory hard to believe. Certainly she couldn't think of anyone she knew personally who might have evaded the virus. And when she realized that it would have to be someone Phillip knew, as well, and not only Phillip, but the flower vendor, and the newspaperman, and the man on the corner who begged for change, and the kid who poured pitchers of water over the dirt beside the pawn shop, gouging out lakes and moats and islands with a broken stick, and the old Italian woman who didn't speak a word of English, and the man she heard whistling morosely for his dog every evening—well, the whole idea seemed absurd to her.

Of course, any number of people might have survived the virus and remained alive to remember them. But Marion found *that* idea even harder to believe than the other. She had been there, after all, when the virus spread across the plains and into the heartland. She had seen what it could do.

Phillip took a deep breath, pounding his chest. "You know, I love this," he said. He swept his fingers through the leaves of a bay tree. "Just being able to walk wherever I want to go, when-ever I want to go there. After Number Two, I thought my walking days were over."

Number Two was how they referred to his second heart attack. In their last few years, Marion had nursed him through Number One, Number Two, and what they had taken to calling Number

72

Two-A, a minor stroke, after which their family doctor had told him that he should avoid all strenuous activity: swimming, bicycling, aerobic walking—anything that might overtax his heart. There were certain things you didn't have to worry about when your heart stopped beating, though, and one of them was heart failure.

"It's like you're born with all these blessings," he said, "only you don't realize they're blessings until you lose them. And if you're thick-headed enough, like me, you don't even realize you've *lost* them, not until they come back to you. You know what I mean?" He squeezed her hand as if to punctuate the question.

"I'm glad it makes you happy," Marion said. And she was, although of the two of them, he was never the one who had made a predicament out of his happiness. That had always been her territory.

"Yes, but I'm not sure you understand," he said. "It's not just the walking I'm talking about, Marion—"

But they were at Bristow's already, and the noise of the diner cut him short.

Bill Bristow had been a toll booth operator for nearly forty years—that was what he'd told Marion and Phillip—but he had never wanted to be. He had spent rush hour after rush hour, day after day, staring out at the lines of traffic and imagining himself as a successful restaurateur. It had been his lifelong dream. And so when he died, only a year or so before the virus hit, he had decided to open a diner—nothing fancy, just hamburgers, chili, and baked potatoes, the kind of place that would serve breakfast all day long.

It had been his good fortune, he said, to set up shop just a stone's throw away from the monument. Now his restaurant was the oldest one in town.

"The Byrd family!" he exclaimed when he saw them, and Marion thought, Or two-thirds of us, anyway. "My favorite customers, the Byrd family! Just like the real birds—they come and then they fly away, and you ask yourself, when will they come back again? I've got a booth by the window for you. Will a booth by the window be okay?"

"A booth by the window will be fine," Phillip said.

"Excellent!" He escorted them to their table and called a waiter over to take their drink order. Then he bowed and excused himself, saying, "Such a busy morning," as he backed away.

When he was gone, Marion whispered, "It's like eating in a burger joint with an overexcited French maître d'."

"I think it's charming," Phillip chuckled. "He's obviously playing the role he's always dreamed of. We should all be so lucky."

Four elderly Korean women were sitting in the booth behind them. Marion could hear their mah-jongg tiles clicking and see their small gray heads bobbing over Phillip's shoulder. A little girl, maybe three years old, knelt beside them with her legs folded underneath her, sucking on a peppermint stick. When she saw Marion looking at her, she bit the stick in half and crammed both ends in her mouth, crunching at them until she was able to swallow. She gave a triumphant smile. The smile meant that Marion couldn't have any.

Soon the waiter reappeared to take their order. Then he left and Phillip began stirring a packet of sugar into his coffee. Next he would take a slow, pondering sip from the oval of the spoon, make a face as he decided that the coffee was not yet sweet enough, and empty a second packet of sugar into the cup, watching it break the surface, just as he always did. Time had made a wreck out of his body, Marion thought—a wreck out of both their bodies—but he was still a little boy in some respects, marooned at that age when discovering his own habits was a sort of game for him. The game had to be played the same way every day, or the pieces would fall to the floor, the board would collapse, and the

74

illusion that you were shaping your own life—that you were in control—would break. It was one of the many things Marion had loved about Phillip at first, then somewhere along the way stopped loving, and now loved again.

The service at Bristow's was unusually fast that day, and the waiter was already laying their plates on the table when Marion caught a glimpse of her daughter out the window.

A hook caught in her stomach.

She tapped on the glass and was about to call out, "Laura, Laura," but then the woman turned her head and it wasn't Laura at all, just a stranger who happened to have Laura's self-contained stride and ginger hair, stopping at the curb before she crossed the street.

This wasn't the first such apparition Marion had seen. As usual, she was embarrassed by her mistake. Why did she keep expecting her daughter to turn up everywhere she looked? Perhaps because she had run across so many other people she recognized in the city: neighbors, friends, cousins, casual acquaintances, along with hundreds of faces she could not quite place but was sure she had seen somewhere before, plus a few that seemed to have grown out of faces she had known in much younger configurations.

Even her own mother, who had passed away almost twenty years before, was there, though not her father, who had died when Marion was still a teenager and had vanished from the city, it seemed, just as Marion was arriving.

It was only from talking with people like Bill Bristow, people she had never met before she came to the city, that she realized how unusual her situation was. Many of the people who remained behind knew very few of the others. And some of them, a couple dozen at least, who had died in the late phases of the virus, seemed to know none at all. They had simply closed their eyes and woken one day in a city full of strangers.

Marion turned to Phillip. "So what *are* we doing here?"

"What we're doing is enjoying a couple of ham-and-egg sandwiches."

Sometimes her distaste for him reared back up in her before she could stop it. She grimaced. "No. What I mean is why are we *here* as opposed to someplace else. Here as opposed to wherever everybody else is."

"I know what you meant, honey. But I can't give you an answer. I don't think anybody could. 'What are we doing here?' For that matter, what were we doing *there*? Why were we ever anywhere at all? I think the only thing we can do is stop asking impossible questions and just make the best of it," he said. "Go for a walk with your wife now and then. Sleep in occasionally. Eat whatever sandwiches come your way." He took a bite of his own, as if to illustrate the point. "Which brings me to what I was getting at outside—"

Two men were deep in conversation at the next table, and one of them said, "Laura," or at least Marion thought he had, and so she hushed Phillip in order to listen in. She only had to wait a few seconds before the word turned over again, like a piece of shingle caught in a heavy current, and she realized that it was actually "laurel." She caught herself sighing. In the sound there was an echo of the one long sigh that had been the last few years of her life.

She said, "My mind is playing tricks on me again. I'm sorry, Phillip. Where were we?"

By then, though, he had lost the thread of whatever he was going to say, or at least the inclination to say it. They finished the rest of the meal in silence.

The food was excellent. Marion could sense her bad feelings drifting away from her as she ate, and by the time she was finished, her mood had lifted entirely. She watched Phillip drink the last of his coffee and return the spoon to his cup with a tiny clink, pushing them both to the side of the table. Then, as an afterthought, he wadded his napkin into a ball and dropped it in after the spoon. Next he folded his two empty sugar packets together and put them in the cup, as well. She was pretty sure that if the cup had been just a little bit larger, he would have found a way to fit his entire plate in there. He reminded her of the little girl with the peppermint stick, forcing as much of the candy into her mouth as she could. Looking over Phillip's shoulder, Marion could see the girl still slouching down in her chair, playing with the ends of her hair as the mah-jongg tiles clacked into place around her. Marion winked at her, but the girl didn't notice. Phillip noticed, however, and, assuming the wink was meant for him, he winked back at Marion, a look of delighted surprise taking over his face. This was the funniest thing Marion had seen all day. It must have been half a minute this time before she realized she was smiling.

As they were leaving the restaurant, Bristow hollered out from across the room, "Come back soon, Byrd family!" Phillip tipped an imaginary hat to him, and Marion nodded, and then they were outside.

The weather was fiercely bright, as though a lamp had been lit behind the sky. A few birds could be seen following a seam of wind over the buildings, soaring in a straight line until they were too small to see. And way up there in all that blue a single well-shaped cloud slid past, its shadow moving slowly over the grass.

Marion didn't feel like going home just yet. "What do you think about sitting in the park for a while?" she asked Phillip. There was a time when she would have invented an excuse, any excuse, to turn him away so that she could be alone. She would have sent him on an errand, perhaps, or insisted that she had one of her own to perform, or laid claim to some last-minute doctor's appointment. Then, after he was out of sight, she would have found a bench or a fountain-ledge to sit on, someplace where no one else would join her but where anyone might—the sort of place where she could indulge in her solitude, yes, but also in the possibility that something wonderful, something she never could have expected, might come along to break it. For a long time that had seemed to her to be the key to life: life—*real* life— was really just a solitude waiting to be transfigured. If Phillip was with her, the solitude she needed would be shattered, and along with it whatever wondrous thing might have come her way if she had been alone. Now, though, everything was different. Phillip was part of her solitude, just as he had been so long ago, when they were first getting to know each other. They could wait for the world to change together. Both of them were aware of the transformation, and both of them were secretly gratified by it, though modestly and never out loud, for fear that it would go away.

"What time are we supposed to be at your mother's?" Phillip asked.

"Sixish, I think we said."

"Then I would *love* to sit in the park for a while," he told her.

They had taken to inviting Marion's mother over for dinner a few nights every week, but recently she had begun needling them to come to her place for a change, and they had finally promised to join her for an evening of drinks and gin rummy. It was bound to be an awkward affair. In many respects, they barely knew each other anymore. Who was this woman, Marion found herself thinking when they visited her, who lived all alone in her small apartment in the heart of the city? With the row of strange African sculptures on her shelves? Who chewed her fingernails and cried all the time? Marion and Phillip had come to the conclusion that Marion's mother was in mourning again for Marion's father. The woman had died when she was not much older than Marion. She was still not much older than Marion, and it was obvious that she had not expected to lose her husband a second time. Her home was filled with mementos from the latter phase of their marriage, the phase that had commenced after they both died—photographs, theater programs, and handwritten notes that she turned over and over in her hands like small deposits of precious minerals. Marion never quite knew what she was thinking at such moments—or at any moment, for that matter. Christians always talked about the possibility of being reunited with their loved ones in the afterworld, but no one ever seemed to consider the idea that after twenty years of separation or more those loved ones might have pared themselves down into mere sticks of what they used to be, that they might have changed into utter strangers. Marion hoped the same thing wouldn't happen to her. If too much time passed before she saw Laura again, they might barely recognize each other. She didn't know if she could handle that.

The sun and the mild air had brought half the people in the city out to the clearing. There were men and women, teenagers and geriatrics, parents and children. There were people on their way to work, people heading to stores or restaurants, and people who simply had nowhere else to go. Marion was watching them flow around her, drifting by in slow-moving pairs and clusters, when she heard it again, her daughter's name, coming from somewhere over her shoulder. "Laura Byrd," a voice said. This time she was certain.

Phillip gripped her elbow. He had heard it, too.

She interrupted the two men who were walking behind her. "Excuse me, did I hear the two of you talking about a Laura Byrd?"

"That's right," one of them said. "Friend of yours?"

"Laura Byrd is my daughter," and she gestured to Phillip. "Our daughter."

"Laura Byrd with the red hair?" he said doubtfully. "Who used to work for Coca-Cola?"

Breathlessly she said, "Yes, yes, that's her."

"Go figure," the man said, grinning. "I was her boss."

Marion was stunned. There was a long moment of absolute silence during which she must have been staring at the second of the two men, because he shrugged his shoulders and remarked,

"Sorry to say, but I was just *his* boss. I didn't know Laura Byrd from Adam. That's what I was just telling him."

"And I was about to say, 'Antarctica? The environmental impact specialist?'"

"Oh, *that's* right," it dawned on the second man. "The photograph in the newsletter." He chuckled. "Now I remember."

"I thought you would. Well, she's another one unaccounted for."

The two men broke their look, and the second explained, "A lot of the old Coca-Cola gang are here in the city for some reason. We've been going over their names."

"A lot of names here," the first one agreed. "But no Laura Byrd."

Phillip broke the silence. "This is still quite a curiosity. Bumping into the two of you like this."

It was apparently an afternoon for such curiosities, for just then a woman who happened to be passing by seized short and tapped the man who had said he was Laura's boss on the shoulder. "I'm sorry. Did I just hear you say something about a *Laura Byrd*?" She stressed the name at all three syllables.

"You don't know her, do you?"

"Maybe. I mean, I'm sure there's more than one out there. But I used to live with a Laura Byrd back when I was in college."

It took Marion only a few questions—which college? when did you graduate? what did she look like?—to establish that the woman's Laura and their own were one and the same. She felt the first few threads of something cinching together inside her, some new way of seeing the world, but she couldn't quite make it come through. It was like a light flashing behind the leaves of a tree: barely visible through the branches, but there all the same, almost bright enough to identify.

Before long the men from Coca-Cola had to leave for an appointment. Laura's old roommate had no other plans for the afternoon, though, and she attached herself to Marion and Phillip as they went through the clearing conducting their survey. "Do you know a Laura Byrd? Does the name ring any bells?" A good number of the people they spoke to had never heard of Laura before, but more than a few of them thought they recognized the name and almost half knew her well enough to show some surprise.

How could so many people come together in an unfamiliar city and remember the exact same woman?

It was no simple coincidence, Marion was sure of that.

By the time they gave up for the day, it was late afternoon, less than an hour before they were scheduled to meet Marion's mother for dinner. The shadows at their feet were already stretching out to meet the horizon, and the crowds in the park had dwindled to almost nothing. They walked the last few blocks home and collapsed at opposite ends of the couch. Marion was as tired as she had been at any time since she'd first arrived in the city, when she had slept for seventeen hours straight. But for once she didn't mind. This was a different sort of weariness than the weariness she'd experienced when she was alive. It was a good weariness, that pleasant mental fatigue that comes from too much sunlight and too much expectation. She watched as Phillip closed his eyes and napped for a few minutes. He had always been like that—able to drop off to sleep in a matter of seconds, then rouse himself again twenty minutes later, his attention sharpened to a fine point. She found the ability too mysterious to be jealous of it. After he woke up, she gave him a moment to yawn and stretch, and then asked, "So what do you think it's all about?"

"You mean Laura?"

"I don't understand how all those people could have known her, Phillip. And I don't understand why she isn't here. Where is she?"

"You're just full of unanswerable questions today, aren't you?" he said. "Maybe she is here somewhere, but she just hasn't turned up yet. Or maybe she's changed so much that we can't recognize her. Or maybe she's still alive. Maybe there's a different afterlife for everybody, and this is Laura's, and we're all just waiting for her to die so that everything will make sense to us."

"Don't say that."

"Or then again, maybe the man who asked us for the match this afternoon was right, and God is just out there playing games with us to see how we'll react. Or maybe it's chance. In the end, maybe it's nothing but chance." He smoothed a crease from his pants as he stood up. "There's the long answer. The short answer is, I don't know. But I'm glad *we're* here, Marion."

He went to the sink to wash his face. She heard him running the water until it was hot enough for the pitch to change, then the rapid welling sound as he cupped his hands to the faucet followed by the sudden collapsing splash, like a tarp giving way, as he emptied the water onto his face. When he came back out, his hair was slicked back in mixed wet and dry strands, except for a thin loop that had come loose from the thatch to dangle over his eye. "*We're* here," he concluded, "and things are pretty good, and that's enough for me."

He sat down beside her on the couch. She was tired and so she rested her head on his shoulder.

"This is nice," she said after a while. "You didn't really help me with my question, but this is nice."

"I know it is. It's been a long time, hasn't it?"

"What do you mean, 'It's been a long time'?"

"A long time since we could just sit together quietly like this. A long time since you would let me, or since I would risk it. You know, sometimes I look back on the last ten years of our lives, and it feels like we were nothing but roommates. I was the bumbling roommate you had to pick up after, and you were the sensitive roommate I had to keep from upsetting. I don't know what did it to us. Maybe it was Laura's going away to college, the two of us being alone together after all that time. I don't know. But that's what we were, isn't it? The crazy thing is that I didn't even notice until it was all over. It took dropping dead, of all things, for me to see things so clearly."

It sounded as though he were about to laugh, but the laugh turned into a spasmlike inhalation, and he sneezed loudly, jarring her head with his shoulder. "Whew! Excuse me. I wasn't expecting that. Anyway, *that's* what I mean by 'It's been a long time.' I mean I'm glad I'm your husband again. I'm glad you're my wife. If my vote counts for anything, I say we keep it that way. I must have tried to tell you that a dozen times today, when you haven't been so . . . frustrating."

As usual, his speech had cracked apart into a mass of springs and cogs at the end, the parts of a statement rather than the statement itself. He had left her with the impression that he was about to clarify himself but had decided to opt out at the last second. Still, she knew what he meant, even if she wasn't quite sure how to respond to him. Finally she just gave up and said what she was thinking, which was, "I didn't know you'd realized anything was wrong."

The look he gave her was as old as time. He leaned over and said, "I'm going to change out of these clothes before we head back out, okay?"

Then he stood up and disappeared into the bedroom, shutting the door.

It was a mistake for her to think of him as innocent, uncomplicated. She knew that. But there was something about his fussiness, his obedience to certain long-established routines, along with the carelessness with which he presented himself to the world, that made it easy for her to imagine him as a child. She had imagined, for instance, that he was the one who had never seen their marriage clearly—or seen himself clearly, for that matter. That he was the one who was half-broken by every little sickness that came his way, and by nostalgia for the way he used to be, and by worry over what had happened to Laura. But she was beginning to suspect that it had been her all along. She was the innocent one. She was the child.

She felt for a moment the child's guilt and panic that she was to blame for something—for finally getting to know him, maybe. She knew that it wasn't the *getting to know him* part that would convict her in the end. It was the *finally*.

She cast the feeling aside and forced herself up from the couch. It was five-thirty, almost time to leave. She had to get dressed. Outside, the sun had all but disappeared, and the apartment had filled with those textureless blue shadows that were just a few degrees darker than the sky. She could hear Phillip snapping his jacket together in the bedroom. Each snap locked into place with a satisfying little click, much louder than it ought to have been in the falling darkness. She went to the door and prepared to knock, lifting her hand to the wood. It was an interesting sound.

Six

THE STATION

The bulges in the snow were graves.

At first Laura had mistaken them for natural formations, like the terraced ridges that sometimes appear on beaches or deserts when the wind blows just swiftly enough to carve its own patterns in the sand and just slowly enough not to disturb them. She had even—shamefully, she now realized—climbed on top of one of them, balancing herself at a flat spot along the crest to look out over the ice toward the bay. But as the days passed and the station remained deserted, the truth gradually dawned on her. The zoologists and technicians who had manned the station were dead. She had read their names on the duty roster that was tacked to the bulletin board: Armand Koen at the top, Nathan Sayles at the bottom, and between them eighteen others. Twenty names for twenty graves, strung out along the back side of the building like a row of beads.

One of them must have stayed alive long enough to bury the others—but *who*, she wondered, had buried *him*? What had killed them all in the first place? And how long ago had they died? She searched the station carefully, but it offered her no clues: no journal, no voice recording, not even a message inscribed on a post somewhere, a single cryptic word like the settlers of Roanoke Island had left: "Croatoan."

Croatoan. Cro-Magnon. Caveman. Cave painting. Graffiti. Confetti.

Confetti. She had been in elementary school when the last of the manned space shuttles had exploded over the launch gantries of Cape Canaveral. The footage had shown a million fragments of plastic and aluminum tilting and floating in the coastal wind, catching the sunlight in a great mass of sparks before it rained down over the spectators in the stands. At the time, when her teacher turned on the television, Laura had thought—all the children had thought—that they were watching an old-fashioned ticker-tape parade. They had laughed and whispered, and some-one at the back of the room had even applauded. Then Ms. Ter-rell had told them that they ought to be ashamed of themselves. "I can't believe you children, celebrating tragedy like that. It's terrible, that's what it is."

Soon enough, the image on the television screen had cut to the exact spot of the explosion, a strangled black cloud in the robin's-egg blue of the sky, and they had all realized what was going on. The silence that had filled the air was so complete that it made the classroom seem empty, she remembered, just the skeletons of a few dozen desks and chairs packed together on the carpet. It was the same silence Laura had heard the evening she arrived at the station. The sun had almost vanished by the time she drove the sledge into the center of the encampment. She was exhausted, of course, but she was also elated. She parked beneath a wooden overhang and slid out onto the ice. The wind was completely still. Surely someone must have heard the sound of her engine cutting off, but no one came outside. She would just have to surprise them at the door. The snow around the building was unbroken—no footprints, no sledge tracks, only a few small holes where some icicles that had fallen from the edge of the roof stuck out of the ground like fence posts. She had to punch through the crust with her boots in order to clear a path to the front door. When she got there, she banged on it with her fist. No one answered. What was going on?

She tested the lever and found the door unlocked. "Hello?" she called out as she stepped inside.

The lights were still working, and so were the heating panels. She could even hear the receiver crackling on a table in the corner. But there was nobody in the station.

Her heart sank. She had journeyed untold miles across the cold and the darkness and the broken ice, and for what? She walked through the sleeping quarters, the bathroom, the kitchen, and the dining room, expecting at every turn to find someone reading a book, eating beans out of a can, or shuffling a deck of cards in that noiseless way people had of sliding them back and forth in blocks between their palms. As far as she could tell, though, the building had simply been abandoned. There was no sign of recent human presence, no damp boots or sweating glasses of water. The rooms were quiet and undisturbed. It would have been obvious to anyone that they had been forsaken.

In the open space of the living room there was a couch. She discovered that it was long enough for her to stretch out on at full length. She propped her feet up on the armrest and stared at the ceiling. Slowly her skin began to prickle and flush as her capillaries opened up. The warmth from the heating panels wafted over her in tangible waves. It was only when she lay absolutely still that she realized how cold she had been.

She was too tired to figure everything out. Her back was aching, and all her muscles were sore. She had been traveling for God knows how many days, and she only wanted to rest.

She went to sleep on the couch and did not wake up until deep into the next day. Her first thought when she woke was that the members of the party must have left on some sort of scouting expedition. The emperor penguins whose migratory habits they were studying were supposed to begin tending their eggs at this time of year, weren't they? So maybe the team had set out to observe them, making camp on the other side of the mountains.

But she couldn't imagine they would leave the station entirely untended.

Maybe, then, they had been evacuated. Maybe there had been some sort of emergency and they had been lifted out over the ocean, all twenty of them, leaving their equipment behind so they could return for it later.

She sat down at the radio thinking that she might get in touch with Coca-Cola and then with someone who could tell her what had happened to the station's inhabitants, but when she tried to tune the headphones in, they greeted her with a mixture of shrill, discordant tones that cut through her head like a metal rod. The sound made her skull ache. The other frequencies she dialed were no better: all either perfectly silent or filled with the same terrible banshee's wail as the first. She tried to establish a web connection on one of the station's computers, but without luck. Then she found a satellite phone on a stack of books next to the transceiver. Though she didn't see how the thing could work so far away from a relay tower, she punched in the number for the Atlanta office anyway. To her surprise, following a few seconds of soft clicking and humming, the connection went through.

But the corporation's voice mail system must have been out of order.

The phone rang and rang. She counted the seconds off tick by tick, measuring them by the clock above the computer. After five minutes, she hung up.

When she dialed the number again the next day, she heard only an airy rattling noise that seemed to breathe and then suddenly fade away, muffled by the distance the way that bombs detonating on the surface of the earth must sound from the upper reaches of the atmosphere.

The station was fully outfitted, so there was no need for her to unpack the sledge. She found soap and shampoo in the shower, aspirin in the medicine cabinet, and a box of hundreds of red and yellow toothbrushes in clear plastic sleeves beside the bathroom sink. The food locker was filled with vegetables and cuts of meat stacked on top of one another in wrappings of crisp white butcher paper, and the pantry was stocked with several dozen cases of Coca-Cola and bottled water. She would stick to the water. She hadn't really been able to enjoy a Coke in years. It was that old adage about mixing business with pleasure: her days were somewhere between sixty and seventy percent Coca-Cola already, and she refused to give any more of herself over to the stuff.

At first she expected the station's team of scientists and technicians to come walking through the door at any second, shucking their coats and gloves, banging the snow from their boots in a parade of kicking and stamping. She had expected Puckett and Joyce to return to the shelter on the far side of the mountains in exactly the same way. But as the days passed and no one arrived, she grew accustomed to the station's capaciousness and silence. Sooner or later, she was sure, someone would come back for the equipment and find her there. Until then, she was content to wait.

She tinkered every so often with the radio or the computer or the telephone, tapping and dialing, listening for a human voice, but she never managed to reach anyone she could talk to. That was all right. Here at the station, after so many weeks on the ice, her solitude didn't seem to matter so much. For now, it was enough that she had a real bed, a warm room, and a diet free from jerky and granola.

There were still a few hours of indirect sunlight in the middle of the day, a single thin sheet of it straitened over the horizon. That was when she liked to go outside. The kliegs had been fitted with hoods so that they would direct most of their light to the ground, and her view of the sky was remarkably clear. It was a washed-out blue with wide streaks of red and orange in it, and there was a small peppering of stars there, so hot that they shone right through the atmosphere. Sometimes she could even see the trails of the satellites making their transit over the gap in the ozone layer. She would wait for the sun to vanish and for the rest of the stars to come out, and then she would go back inside.

It was during one of these outings that she decided to explore the terrain around the station. The wind was blowing so hard that her scarf flapped around her like a pennant, and she had to use a hiking stick to keep her balance among the drifts. The ground leveled out as soon as she reached the back of the building. She turned the corner and paused to catch her breath. That was when she found the bulges in the snow. They were packed hard, like outcroppings of stone. She climbed on top of one, looking out over the shelf toward the ocean. She could see a broken line of water in the distance, a trail of black dots and dashes at the very edge of the ice. It was like a message tapped out in Morse code. Certain patches of ice had been buffed to a mirrorlike polish by the wind, and they shone with the same red-veined blue as the sky. When the sun fell and the ice lost its color, she hopped down from the bulge and continued her journey around the building.

She was always shivering by the time she got back inside, which was curious to her. She had shivered so rarely on her trek across the ice field, and surely she had been much colder then than she was now. Maybe her body only shivered when she could anticipate being warm again: she knew there was a heated room waiting for her on the other side of the station door, and shivering was simply her body's way of reacting to that knowledge. Under such circumstances, it could even be considered a sign of hope. That was her theory, anyway. When she was trying to make her way through the blizzard, she had not exactly *lost* hope, but she had certainly not allowed herself to anticipate being warm again, and so her body had settled peacefully into its coldness, like a coin sinking to the bottom of a fountain, dropped by a little girl in a red cotton jumper who was only trying to make a wish.

She had been at the station for almost a week when she found the sheet of paper tucked under her mattress, a single folded leaf from a yellow legal pad. She opened and read it. It was a list, handwritten, of the twenty members of the emperor penguin party. There were notes scribbled in different shades of ink beside their names:

~ at least three a day
~ one in the morning, with breakfast, without fail
~ sporadically: "one every couple of days or so"
~ in the afternoon during radio sessions
~ at lunch—usually dinner, too
~ hates it, but might have a bit when there's nothing
  else around
~ no more than one or two a week

It looked as though the notes had something to do with the party's dining habits, but beyond that, Laura had little idea what they could mean.

In the printing margin on the left side of the page was a column of red X's, twelve of them, one beside each of twelve names. A thirteenth X had been partially completed, with one leg drawn and an apostrophe-shaped accent at the top that must have been the beginning of a second. The rest of the names were unmarked.

There was something about those X's. Laura stared at them, clenching her teeth in concentration. What could they mean? They reminded her of the crossbones that are supposed to be printed beneath the skulls on bottles of poison, or the sharpened tines on strands of barbed wire, or the vacant marks that cartoonists draw over the eyes of the dead. She was feeling sick to her stomach, though she didn't know why.

She ran her finger down the column and felt the impressions that the pen had bitten into the paper. It was at that moment, as she looked at the X's written alongside the list of twenty names, that she first began to suspect that something terrible had happened to them. And it was a short leap from there to her realization that the bulges behind the station were graves.

X's. Exes. Excess. Wisdom.

She put on her boots and the rest of her winter gear and made the hike to the back side of the station. She had to see the bulges again. She had to look at them with her own two eyes now that she had guessed what they were. Sure enough, they were exactly the right size, just long enough and just wide enough to cover a human body. For the first time, she counted them to see how many of them there were. Then she counted a second time to make sure. There were twenty graves. She touched each one with her hand before she went back inside.

She examined the note again and set it on the stand beside the bed, weighing it down with a coffee mug so that it wouldn't waft to the floor. If it was time to undertake a more careful inspection of the station—and she believed that it was—she might as well begin with the sleeping quarters. She lifted the other mattresses one by one, looking for a diary or another folded sheet of yellow paper, but she found nothing but a watch on a long silver chain and a couple of pornographic magazines. Most of the footlockers had been very loosely padlocked, their catches undone or their keys poking out like fingers. She opened them and sifted through the piles of clothing and toiletries inside. It was amazing how much you could tell about a person from what he concealed in the lower right-hand corner of his footlocker. Beneath all the underwear and reading cartridges and Bertelsmann devices, she uncovered multiple sachets of cocaine and marijuana, a box of sixteen porcelain Walt Disney figurines, an antique Bible with gold embossing and annotations written in Victorian-era English, a large tub of Vaseline with a spoon sticking out of it, bottles of antidepressant medication and steroids and serotonin, and a pacifier knotted onto a frayed piece of terry cloth that must have belonged to someone's son or daughter.

There was nothing, though, that might explain what had happened to the station's people, all those biologists and polar technicians who had eaten the food in the cabinets and rumpled the beds. Nothing that would tell her where they had gone or what, if she was right, had killed them.

The bathroom and the kitchen had even less to reveal—a jar of fine olives, a few containers of bathing salts, and that was about it. Everything else—the food, the dishes, the toiletries—she had already uncovered days ago. But she had explored the kitchen and the bathroom pretty thoroughly in the course of her daily routine. In the dining room, which she had rarely visited, she found a garbage bag stuffed beneath a wooden storage hutch and filled with curved pieces of broken glass and stoneware—coffee mugs and drinking glasses, from what she could tell. The only item that was still intact was a cream-colored mug with a pale brown ring around the inside of the lip, exactly the color of the secret messages she remembered searing into sheets of notebook paper using lemon juice and a lightbulb when she was a girl. She looked beneath the chairs and end tables in the living room and in the chink of space between the couch and the wall, but she turned up only a few buttons and paper clips, a broken yardstick, and a thin layer of dust. She pried the cushions off the couch and uncovered a wallet containing a photograph of a cocker spaniel, and a license with the name Lewis Mongno on it. She recognized the name from the duty roster posted above the transmitter.

Finally, in the bottom drawer of the computer desk, she found what she was looking for: a printed copy of the home page of a newspaper. The newspaper was out of Kansas City, Missouri—*The Kansas City Light*—and it was dated February 3rd.

Which was to say that it had been printed sometime between three and four months ago, if she hadn't lost track of too many weeks.

The headline was a single word, PLAGUE, with an outsized

exclamation point. The subheading read: DEADLY VIRUS SWEEPS MEXICO, UNITED STATES. TENS OF MILLIONS CONTRACT "THE BLINKS."

~

Laura's first lover had been a journalism professor at Columbia University, where she had spent the summer after she graduated from high school taking a ten-week college prep course. She was there to study environmental biology—her prospective major—but she chose the professor's Introduction to Journalism course as her one elective. Though she dropped the class after a single session, the two of them continued to see each other for the rest of the summer.

He was a tall, strikingly intelligent man named Luka, with the quiet wit and prematurely graying temples of a movie scientist from the black-and-white era. Every so often, when he had been drinking or engaged in heavy conversation, a mood would come over him, and he would adopt the habit of speaking entirely in headlines.

"Phone Rings Three Times Before Laura Answers," he would announce. "'It Was My Mother,' She Says."

Or, "Evening Winds Down. Fornication Imminent."

Or, "Sims Grows Bored with Discussion. Wanders Away to Bang Head Against Wall."

She still thought of him—she couldn't help it—whenever she read a newspaper headline that seemed to call a certain sort of attention to itself. DEADLY VIRUS SWEEPS MEXICO, UNITED STATES. TENS OF MILLIONS CONTRACT "THE BLINKS."

She hadn't seen him since the afternoon before she left New York, when they'd had sex and ordered Thai food and then stood looking out over the city as they ate, watching the lines of traffic cluster and spread apart between the fixed chains of the stoplights. It was midsummer, and though the days were already

94

growing shorter, the sun still would not set until eight-thirty or nine o'clock.

Luka lived on the thirty-third floor of the Future Building, in a two-bedroom apartment with a boomerang-shaped balcony that floated over the building's courtyard. The two of them liked to stand there at the rail and gaze down at the crowds. It was tempting to say that the people looked like ants from so far above. Tempting, but not quite true. The people came in brighter and more eccentric colors than ants, for one thing, with strange appendages like briefcases and grocery sacks and umbrellas. And they moved with far less order, far less mindfulness, than ants ever did. Their motion was more like the formless winding of water insects skating over the surface of a pond, she thought, though no one would ever say that the people looked like water insects.

She and Luka were standing side by side, their elbows propped on the ledge of the balcony. He asked her, "So this time tomorrow, are you going to miss me?"

"This time tomorrow, I'll be in an airplane somewhere over about Iowa." Laura dreaded the prospect. "I'll be sick to my stomach, with a splitting headache, and I'll miss everything that's not fifty thousand feet in the air."

"Including me, though, right?" Luka prompted.

"Including you, Professor Sims." This was what his students called him. "But it won't matter, will it? Because in a few months I'll tell my parents about us, and then I'll drop out of college and move back to New York, and we'll get married and live happily ever after. The end."

Laura was teasing him in one of the few ways she knew how. He gave the sort of shallow, wincing laugh that people who don't want to admit a joke has embarrassed them give. Both of them had understood from the very beginning of their relationship that they wouldn't see each other again after the summer was over.

But because he was so much older than she was, and also because he had been her teacher—if only for two hours—he felt a certain amount of guilt about the affair from which she herself was immune. "So much debauchery," he would joke sometimes, shaking his head as she lay in his bed wearing only a T-shirt. And though she knew he was only kidding and she would always offer up a smile for him, there was a germ-sized speck of truth to what he said, just enough to put a note of real self-reproof in his voice.

"That's right," she repeated. "Married and happily ever after."

"Well . . . I look forward to it," he said.

"I'm sure you do," she told him, and she patted his hand. "God, I hate flying," she said.

"I know you do."

And then, to lighten the mood: "Weren't we supposed to have teleportation devices by now? Didn't they promise us teleportation devices?"

"And rocket jet packs," he added.

"And moving sidewalks."

He pretended he was marching with a picket sign. "What do we want? Rocket jet packs!"

"Teleportation devices!" she added.

"When do we want them?"

"Now!" she said.

"The future!" he said, and something about it struck them as funny. They began to giggle, and then to laugh, catching themselves in one of those loops in which they realized how meager the humor of the original remark was, found the meagerness itself funny, and laughed even harder than they had before. Soon they were laughing at nothing more than the fact that they were laughing.

The terrorist warning beacons on the roofs of the city's buildings flashed on with their blazing yellow lights, then went dark again after only a minute or two. It hardly mattered. No one paid any attention to them these days, anyway.

"Must have been a false alarm," Luka said.

"Another one," Laura said.

Her stomach was pleasantly tight from laughing. Luka took her wrist between his fingers and began to rub it up and down with his thumb, a hard touch that sent a shiver through her body.

Then something extraordinary happened.

A child who was cutting across the courtyard with her mother (at least they thought the child was a girl—it was difficult to tell from so far above) lost hold of the balloon she was carrying. It went floating out toward the street, cleared the roof of the garage next door, and then a crosswind plucked it from its path and brought it sailing back toward the Future Building, where it came twisting and bobbing up the long row of balconies, a quickly expanding red sphere. Laura could see the girl yanking at her mother's arm, trying to pull her toward the balloon, but it was already far out of reach.

"I think that thing's going to pass right by us," Luka said, and sure enough, the balloon had hit some still corridor of air that ran up the side of the building. "You know," he said, "I think I might be able to catch it."

He tilted out over the ledge of the balcony, and Laura seized her breath. When the balloon soared past, he looped his hand out in one swift gesture, like a bear snatching at a salmon. Suddenly he was holding it by the string.

Laura looked at the balloon, and then at him, and then back at the balloon. "I can't believe you did that," she said. "Five dollars to the man with the golden hand."

He looked down into the courtyard. "They're still down there. Come on." He led Laura to the elevator and pressed the call button. The compartment must have been lingering just a floor or two away, because the bell sounded almost immediately. The doors slid open and then closed with a diminishing whispering noise, and as they dropped toward the lobby, Luka held the CLOSE DOORS button down with his finger. The balloon hovered at the ceiling. When the elevator reached the ground floor, he said, "Hurry," and took her by the hand. They rushed past the doorman into the courtyard.

The child and her mother were gone. A man was feeding cheese curls to his dog, which was eating them fastidiously, like someone trying to split a seed open between his front teeth. A group of teenagers was listening to music on a pocket radio.

"They were headed down Thirty-second," Luka said. "Quick. This way." Laura followed him down the steps that led past the garage, weaving through a cluster of old men who were talking about the races, and then sprinted beneath a line of trees and scaffolding. At the end of the block, they saw a woman waiting with her daughter at the crosswalk.

Luka caught up to them just as the light was changing.

"Excuse me," he said to the girl. He was out of breath from running, and he gasped a few times, his mouth opening and closing like a bellows.

It was just long enough for the girl to notice the balloon and say, "That's mine!" She turned to her mother. "I told you so! A man catched it on his porch. I told you so!"

"'Caught,'" her mother corrected her. And then the mother accepted the balloon from Luka and said, "Thank you. Thank you very much."

She stooped over and wrapped the white string around her daughter's wrist, making a knot. "I'm telling you, it would have been nothing but balloons from her for the next two weeks. What do you say to the nice man, Sarah?"

"Is this the first balloon you caught?" the girl said. "What's your job? Is this what you do?"

"Say thank you, Sarah."

"Thank you."

The crosswalk signal, which had been green, began blinking on and off. "Shoot," the woman said. "Look, we're really in a hurry, mister. Thank you again. I'm sorry."

"Thank you, Balloon Man," the girl said, and Laura was sure that's how the girl would think of him from now on, what she would call him whenever she told the story: *Balloon Man*. She and Luka watched the two of them dash across the street as the light changed, the bumpers of half a dozen cars nosing at the backs of their legs. They walked past a bookstore and an old movie theater, the girl's outfit, the same yellow-green as a firefly's bulb, flashing between the bodies of the other pedestrians, and they vanished into the crowd.

And then Luka said something that Laura knew she would never forget.

"You know, that may be the best thing I've ever done with my life," he said.

~

What was the best thing she had ever done with her life? she wondered now, as she listened to the wind moaning outside the station. She had never founded a charity or raised a family. She had never saved another person's life. Hell, she had never even saved another person's balloon.

The best thing she had ever done with her life was probably some small, half-conscious act of kindness she had long since forgotten.

"Laura Byrd Gives Wildflowers to Her Mother and Father."

Or, "Laura Byrd Offers Token to Man at Subway Terminal, Promptly Forgets."

Or, "Laura Byrd Flashes Headlights, Warns Other Drivers of Speed Trap."

When she had finished reading the article, she set the paper aside and put her head in her hands, closing her eyes and massaging her temples. If the paper was correct, a mutagenic virus had begun spreading through North America at the end of January, right around the time she, Puckett, and Joyce had fallen out of communication with the people at Coca-Cola. The virus was by all accounts lethal and had migrated by air and water from Asia and Western Europe. The nations of South America had attempted to establish a cordon to prevent its further spread, but pockets of infection had already been discovered in Brazil, Ecuador, and Argentina.

The paper referred to the virus as "the epidemic," but said that it was known in popular discourse as The Blinks, because the first sign of exposure was often a redness in the eyes that caused an uncontrollable blinking response. Whether the virus was manufactured or the result of natural mutation had yet to be determined. But it was widely suspected to be manufactured.

Laura spent the next few hours hunched over the radio transceiver, adjusting the dial by the tiniest of increments, pausing at every frequency to listen for an intelligible signal. For a long time she heard nothing but white noise. Then, late in the afternoon, when she switched to the highest band setting, she picked up a voice speaking in a tongue she didn't understand—a grinding, popping language filled with unexpected rushes and halts.

She gave a start. There was somebody out there.

She fed the signal through the computer's translation program. The message was being broadcast in Malay. She listened to the interpretation: . . . *no survivors, repeat, no survivors. I can feel the sickness coming over me. I know I do not have long. I can only hope that this recording will continue to run as long as the power holds out. I love you, Piah. You will see me again soon, my dear.* There was a clicking sound, followed by a high-pitched whir of noise, and then the voice began again. *This is a message to anyone who is listening. Stay away from the city, repeat, stay away from the city. There are no survivors, repeat, no survivors. I can feel the sickness coming over me . . .*

She listened to the message a dozen times before she switched the transceiver off.

That poor man, she thought. That poor man and his poor lover.

And then, though she tried her hardest to avoid the thought, Poor me.

Outside, the night was deepening. There were still a few minutes of hazy light in the middle of the day, a sort of false dawn that seemed to seep directly into the atmosphere. The sun no longer appeared on the horizon, though, and the light quickly faded back into itself. Laura walked out into the snow and took a few deep gulps of air.

The sky was all moon and stars now. She found herself wondering if she was the last person alive. It was something she had speculated about before—something everyone who had ever read a science fiction novel had probably speculated about. But in her case, she thought, it just might be true. Maybe the reason she hadn't been able to reach anyone on the radio, telephone, or computer was because there was no one left to reach. For the first time, it occurred to her that she might truly be completely alone. She couldn't quite believe it, though.

She had already explored the station pretty exhaustively, but she decided to commence the search again from scratch, ransacking the cabinets and lockers, overturning mattresses and cushions, and peering beneath the heavy furniture with a flashlight. She had to find out exactly what had happened to the emperor penguin party. She had to know what all those X's meant.

The work was exhausting, but it paid off. Late that night, about to fall asleep from fatigue, she discovered a loose panel behind one of the beds. She popped it out of its mounting to look inside. In the crevice between the wall and the insulation, she found a small, hand-worn book. It was bound in leather. There were black patches along the lower right edge where it had been stained by the oil of someone's fingers.

She wiped the dust off the cover and opened the book to the first page. *Journal of Robert Joyce,* it read. *First Entry, September 12.*

Seven

THE PATRIARCH

The wind stopped along with the rains, and the silence kept him awake for most of the night, and in the morning he opened the two doors and chose his sign for the day and shooed the Laura birds off the balcony, watching them drop like styrofoam balls to the benches and the dirty pavement. Their blue-and-gray tails twitched in the yellow light, and though the birds were demons, the light was good, and he took his sign and carried it out into the city. When he came to the gathering place, he shouted, "You, my brothers! You, my sisters! If you listen, you will hear, and if you seek, you will find!" and while most of the people brushed him aside, and some even derided him, crowing out their profanities, there were always a few who stopped to listen.

"Do you really believe that?" they asked him, and "Find what?" they said, and, "What does that sign of yours mean, anyway?"

Today what his sign said was, IF I WILL THAT HE TARRY TILL I COME, WHAT IS THAT TO THEE?, and it meant the same thing that all his signs meant: Jesus is returning, so you'd better prepare yourself. "It's John 21:22," he tried to explain. "The Lord is speaking to his disciples. Most people think that the verse refers to the Wandering Jew, but if you read it carefully, you'll see that it doesn't. The 'he' in question is actually the apostle John. Tarry means wait, and wait means live. So the verse means, 'If *I*, Jesus, will that *he*, the Apostle John, live till I come, what is that to *thee*, my disciples?' Which is to say Jesus's disciples, not mine. I'm not Jesus. Do you understand?"

It was a complicated question, and so he would repeat his explanation a second time, and then a third if he still saw a flicker of confusion on their faces, and sometimes a fourth if other people had begun to tarry nearby, and usually he would finish only to find that everybody had drifted away, shepherded from the true sound of his voice by the noise of the birds.

And so he would move once more into the crowds, and start over again, and wait for the people to gather around him.

The people were created in the image of God, and thus they were within the precinct of His grace, even the ones who did not know Him, the ones who withdrew themselves from His presence. It was something he had to remind himself of when they ignored him, or jeered at him, or parroted his voice, or even, as had happened once or twice in the other world, when they arrested him, handcuffed him, and confiscated his sign. Sometimes, when he sensed the spirit of God moving inside him, turning over like a soft bundle of clothing, he would feel so satiated that he would forget to feed himself, and late in the day his legs would buckle underneath him inside the swim of his own hunger. There was a mail carrier, a good man named Joseph, who would offer him a hot dog or a slice of pizza at such times and wait with him until he could stand again without feeling faint. Today, though, he had filled his pockets with bread sticks before he left for the city. He ate them sitting on an iron bench in sight of the obelisk, where he watched the shadows of the birds as they collided with the shadows of the clouds.

It was late in the day when he saw the two men—boys, really, no older than twenty—holding hands and kissing beneath the awning of a deserted hardware store. One of them was gripping a hank of the other's hair, and the second was squirming and rocking inside his blue jeans, and when the first one whispered into the second one's ear, they both began to laugh. He approached them at a rush beneath the awning, where he tried to tell them something about the Bridge of Jesus and the Translation of the Elect. But they struggled against him and would not listen.

"Fuck off," one of them said, and the other snapped, "Get your hand off me, you old cocksucker," and then they batted his sign with their arms and open hands and it lurched back and hit him in the jaw.

When he opened his eyes, he was lying flat on the pavement, and the boys were gone. He could feel something hard between his gums and his cheek. It was a tooth. When he rolled it over onto his tongue and spat it out, it came out dark red, like the stone of a cherry. On his way home he buried it in the soil of a churchyard, marking it with a crossed pair of bread sticks, so that when he died again and was gathered unto himself he would be made whole. And that was one day.

~

REPENT, FOR THE TIME IS AT HAND, his next day's sign read, and he inscribed it, YOURS VERY TRULY, followed by his name, which was Coleman Kinzler, Ph.D. He had conferred the Ph.D. upon himself the same day he finished reading his Bible, at the age of thirty-three, for he knew that though he had never actually been to college, he was a doctor now in the eyes of the Lord. At that time, his Bible was the same one he had been given as a boy, a pocket-sized edition with silver edging and fine white paper and a blue leather cover that wrapped around on itself and snapped together in the front. He had carried it everywhere with him until the day he met a woman who had never read it, a Hindu woman in a robe the color of bricks and dark coffee, and he asked her, "If I offer this book to you, will you study it and keep it sacred?" and she promised that she would, so he gave it to her, though it hurt him to let it go.

But he was convinced that he was doing what the Lord would

105

ask of him. The world was brimming over with Bibles, so many Bibles that they came spilling from the shelf of every drugstore and hotel room in the country, and he knew he could always find a new one for himself. As for the woman, though, he would probably never see her again. It might be her only chance to receive the Word of God.

He thought about the woman often after that, and also about his Bible, though indeed he never saw either one of them again.

This was the incident he was remembering as he toted his sign through the district. The sky was overcast with a dimensionless table of gray clouds, and the banners and traffic lights hung slack in the stillness of the air. Two of the Laura birds hopped from beneath a parked car into the path of his feet. They settled between his ankles, where they attempted to make him stumble, but he did not lose his balance, and he did not drop his sign. He yelled at them and whirled his arms around and stomped his heavy shoes until they flew away and landed down the block.

The newspaperman and his girlfriend were standing by the door of Bristow's Restaurant, as they did every morning, handing out the latest edition of the *Sims Sheet*. MORE EVIDENCE FOR BYRD HYPOTHESIS, the headline read, and when the newspaperman gave him a copy, he folded it into quarters and put it inside his jacket pocket. The girlfriend noticed the bandage covering his chin and asked, "Jesus, what happened to you?" She touched her own chin involuntarily.

"Yes," he said. "Jesus. I have been bruised in the name of the Lord." And he told her about his tooth and the breaking of his sign and the boys who had left him on the street to fall, and when he finished, she said, "Oh, you poor man," and gave him a second copy of the paper, which he folded into quarters and put inside his pocket with the first.

"The rich shall be made poor, and the poor shall be made rich," he answered, and he left the newspaperman and his girlfriend outside the restaurant and continued on his walk through the city.

On H Street, he stopped to talk with a doorman, and when he asked him if he knew the Word of God, a tiny smile creased the doorman's face. He removed the cross from the neck of his shirt and let it sway back and forth on its thin strand of chain. "God's blessings," Coleman wished the doorman, and the doorman offered his own blessing in return, and the small silver cross turned slowly between his fingers, stopped, and began spinning the other way, winking at Coleman as it caught the light from a nearby sign.

Coleman put the placard to his shoulder and continued on. He had forgotten to bring his bread sticks along with him, and though he was hungry, he did not stop to eat. He was thrust out of a home furnishings store by a pair of security guards, and afterward he gathered a small crowd around him when he climbed onto the lip of the fountain in the shopping plaza, and then the crowd scattered and he spent twenty minutes preaching to a woman who seemed to be listening to him with perfect transport until he asked her for her name and she answered in a flurry of Italian. Though the clouds kept rumbling with thunder, it did not rain, or if it did, the rain never reached the ground. There were times when the sky would growl and then his stomach would growl and then the sky would growl again, and he could almost imagine that the two of them were speaking to each other.

He was nearing his own apartment again when he passed a booth distributing T-shirts that read GOD IS LOVE, stacks and stacks of them, in red and white and black, and as the phrase moved in and out of his vision, it provoked a dialogue. There was one part of him that believed that God truly *was* love, that the equation was really that simple. But there was another part of him that believed that love was too small a force: too small for God and too small for what people needed of Him.

The first part said that the love of God was like sunlight and water to us: it strengthened us, filled us out, gave us color. It was only when we rejected that love, when we shut ourselves away from it, that we withered in on ourselves and lost our joy in Creation.

Foolishness! said the second part. It's not the *love* of God that nourishes us, it's the *hope* of God. It is hope of any kind. Hope and love are two separate forces, whether you're talking about God or whether you're talking about human beings.

But doesn't love offer everything that hope does and more? the first part asked.

Insofar as love generates hope, perhaps, the second part said. But love doesn't always generate hope. Anyone who has ever experienced love knows that you can have too much love or too little. You can have love that parches, love that defeats. You can have love measured out in the wrong proportions. It's like your sunlight and water—the wrong kind of love is just as likely to stifle hope as it is to nourish it.

Coleman let the two voices rumble on at each other, thundering back and forth, though which was the thunder of his gut and which was the thunder of his sky, he couldn't say. It was only when he noticed the other people in the elevator staring at him that he realized he was speaking out loud. He found a package of rice cakes and a jar of peanut butter in the cabinets of his apartment, and he fell upon them with great hunger, and that was the second day.

~

The verse that actually alluded to the Wandering Jew was not John 21:22, of course, but Matthew 16:28, THERE BE SOME OF THEM THAT STAND HERE, WHICH SHALL IN NO WISE TASTE OF DEATH, TILL THEY SEE THE SON OF MAN COMING IN HIS KINGDOM, and that was the verse that he carried on his sign the next day. The Wandering Jew, known variously as Ahasuerus, Carthaphilus, and John Buttadaeus, was the cobbler reported to have taunted Jesus, "Go on quicker," as he carried His cross through Jerusalem, to which Jesus answered, "I go, but thou shalt tarry till I return," thus condemning the cobbler to walk the world until the Second Coming. Coleman knew that the story did not appear in the pages of the Bible and that many Christians doubted it, but he himself had always found it persuasive, just as he was persuaded that the snake in the Garden of Eden was actually Satan and that St. Peter was crucified hanging upside down so that he would not die in the same manner as Jesus—two stories that also relied on the evidence of tradition rather than the evidence of Scripture, and nobody doubted them.

The blanket of clouds had drifted to the edge of the sky during the night, but the sun was tiny, and it had lost all its power. It was half the morning before the dew evaporated from the grass. Coleman took up a position on the verge of the road to proclaim the Good Word of God. Nobody on the path stopped to listen, but there was one man who settled on a nearby bench as though he wanted to eavesdrop. Coleman tried to cast his voice in the man's direction, for he knew that even the most reluctant listener might be swayed by the Truth of the Lord. But then he noticed the man feeding the birds, tossing cheese curls into their beaks from a plastic sack, and he leapt from the verge and crushed the cheese curls beneath his feet and he chased the man away.

He ate lunch with the mail carrier Joseph, who was his friend, and while they were throwing their wrappers away in the garbage can, Joseph said, "You know, when I was a kid I thought that everyone was born with three wishes. I remember using one of mine to wish that I would never have to go to the bathroom again. It didn't work, of course. I was mad at God for a long time about that."

To which Coleman said, "I think you're confusing God with a genie."

He meant it as a statement of fact, but something about it must have struck Joseph as funny, for he would not stop laughing until Coleman had taken up his sign and left.

The problem was that if the Wandering Jew was real, if he truly existed, the city ought to have been much more heavily populated than it was. Everyone seemed to accept that the people of the city were sustained there by the memories of the living, which was yet another story without scriptural provenance. But there they all were—that much was certain—and Coleman had no reason to doubt the explanation. So why, then, wasn't the city filled with all the millions of souls the Jew had encountered in the two-some millennia since the crucifixion of Jesus?

There were three possibilities, as Coleman saw it: either the Jew had died in the virus, in which case the virus had coincided with the Second Coming. Or he was still alive, in which case there must be other pockets of humanity in the city, or even other whole cities out there somewhere. And then there was the final possibility, which was that the Wandering Jew had never existed at all.

He could not decide which possibility was the most likely, an uncertainty that disturbed him greatly, and for the rest of the day he found his mind returning to the matter as he preached, his voice lapsing into silence while he listened to the wings of the question beating around inside his head. The people of the city flowed around him like water around a stone, and finally he gave up and went home and sat on the edge of his bed, and he watched the shadows as they shifted across the floor of his room, and he listened to a girl who was jumping rope on the street below his window. The girl was chanting a rhyme that went "Miss Mary Mack, Mack, Mack, all dressed in black, black, black," and he stepped through the two glass doors onto his balcony and called down to her, "You there, what's your name?"

The rope fell slack at the girl's feet, like a ribbon of seaweed bleached by the sun. She stared up at him without answering.

He called, "Aren't you even going to ask me *my* name?"

She hesitated for a moment, then said, "I know who you are. You're the Birdman."

"No, my name is Mr. Coleman Kinzler."

"That's not what we call you. We call you the Birdman of Alcatraz."

There was a heaviness to the girl's features that made him wonder if she might be a bit feebleminded. He used his gentlest voice to ask her, "Do you know about Jesus Christ?"

To which she said, "Yep. He died on the cross to save us from our sins."

"Good girl," Coleman said. If he had had a toy at hand—a doll, for instance, or a pinwheel—he might have thrown it down to her as a present. But the only items on the balcony were a rusted lawn chair, a spider plant that had gone crisp from neglect, and a stack of signs attached to white wooden pickets, including the one he was planning to carry tomorrow, which read, JESUS IS THE WAY, THE TRUTH, AND THE LIFE. So instead of a present, and because it was the best he could do, he held the sign up and showed it to the girl, waving it back and forth, until she shrugged and picked up her jump rope and went skipping away down the sidewalk.

And that was three days.

~

The birds were dinosaurs.

He had read about it in a book once—how in the time of the great dying the largest of the dinosaurs had been killed off by disease and starvation, but the smallest had survived, and over the centuries they had changed, and finally they had become the birds. So the birds were dinosaurs, and the dinosaurs were reptiles, and the reptiles, as everybody knew, were demons. It took a diligent eye to see through all the disguises that were in place.

He peeled the bandage from his chin to investigate the scrape he had gotten in the fall. Though the injury was shallow, it had not yet sealed over, and he carefully probed at the edges with his fingers to see whether a crust had formed there, and, if so, whether it had begun to curl away from his skin. Did people heal from the outside in or from the inside out? He wasn't sure. But he himself did not seem to be healing at all. He cleaned the scrape and replaced the bandage and got his sign from the balcony, and later that day, when he was eating lunch with Joseph, he said to him, "I'm no better today than I was yesterday," and Joseph said, "Well, I can't say that I find that very surprising."

"Why not?"

"I don't know that any of us ever gets any better. I have a hard time believing that people change at all."

Coleman disagreed. "We are all changed by the hand of the Lord. God gave Saul a new heart, the Bible says. Both Sauls, in fact—King Saul and that Saul who became the Apostle Paul. But I wasn't talking about my heart. I was talking about my chin."

"Oh. Well, I can't say I'm surprised by that either."

"Why not?"

"If I leave you to yourself, you eat nothing but starches all the time. You don't get an ounce of protein. Whatever happened to 'Your body is your temple' is what I want to know."

Four birds circled overhead, and Coleman realized that they were watching him again. He hushed Joseph and pointed into the air, and for the rest of the lunch hour, as they finished their hamburgers, he would not let him speak.

It had been only a few weeks since he had asked the Lord to reveal to him the names of the demons, whereupon he had felt a hand directing him into Bristow's restaurant. He had overheard two men talking about the birds. "So it all comes down to the

Laura bird," the first man had said, and the second man had nodded and answered, "Yes, the Laura bird, that's what it looks like," and ever since then Coleman had heard people talking about them everywhere.

The Laura birds. The Laura birds. The Laura birds.

It seemed that nobody could escape from them.

He followed the sidewalk past a vintage clothing store and an empty dance studio and then past the gaping mouth and long distended throat of a subway entrance. When he rounded the corner, the wind threatened to tug his sign away from him. He had to turn it sideways in order to keep his grip on it. The sun was showing on the windshields and silver trim of the cars parked along the street, a pearl-strung line of small white balls with thin spikes of light coming out of them. They were almost too bright to look at. A teenager with a halo of frizzy red hair skateboarded past him and said, "The Truth and the Life. All right, man!" and it took Coleman a moment to remember the message that was printed on his sign. He turned and shouted to the boy's disappearing figure, "You forgot the Way. Don't forget the Way," and the boy raised his hand to Coleman in a salute.

He spent the rest of the afternoon, into the early evening, circling the poorly distinguished boundary line of the district, that meandering belt of fenced-in lots and vacant buildings where the streets began to fade into the empty city. He was looking for people who not yet heard His message. By the time he reached his home, the moon was shining like a Wiffle ball in the highest portion of the evening sky. And that made the fourth day.

~

The rest of the night passed slowly, and in the morning he opened his eyes, and though the sun had risen and the hours had gone by, he could not say whether or not he had slept. He felt as though he remembered dreaming, but as soon as he tried to summon the dream to the front of his mind, it slipped away from him, vanishing into the shadows. The only thing he was certain he remembered was lying as still as he could for hours on end, waiting for that strange feeling of segmentation in his limbs that meant he was finally drifting off to sleep. But as to whether or not he had, at last, slept, he could not be certain.

It was yet another thing that God knew and he did not, though perhaps one day it would be revealed to him.

The Laura birds had landed on his balcony again, and he frightened them away, opening and closing the two glass doors with a sudden loud bang that sent them flying down to the street. Then he put his shoes on and selected his sign and carried it out into the city. There was a little grocery store at the corner of the block, and he stopped there and picked up a bag of peeled baby carrots for the vitamins and a small styrofoam tray of dried sausage fingers for the protein. Joseph was right—his body was, after all, his temple. He put the carrots in one pocket and the sausage fingers in the other, and he found that he could feel the packages on his thighs as he walked, swinging back and forth, their weight almost perfectly balanced. It was a good weight, like the weight of God's attention, which held all things to the earth and prevented them from vanishing into atoms.

The morning was cool and sunlit and peaceful, and hundreds of people were already out roaming the city streets. He raised his voice as he drifted between them, calling out, "Brothers and sisters! My many friends! Hearken to the Word of God, for His Word is true and His Word is just!" And he held the sign he was carrying high above his head, steadying it with both his hands so that everyone who approached him could see it without obstruction. It read GOD IS LOVE in bold black letters, though on the other side he had also written GOD IS HOPE, just in case.

Several hours had gone by and the sun was hidden behind the crown of a building when he passed the clockmaker's shop on the west side of Park Street. He knew it was noon by the chime of the clocks in the window. There were dozens of them, carefully synchronized. He stood there watching their mechanisms turn for a while before he moved on—their second hands sweeping across their faces, their minute hands ticking forward by tiny, almost imperceptible degrees. He left when they touched 12:05. He followed the shadows of the clouds through the gathering place. He stopped to preach to the line of people that had formed outside one of the coffee shops, and when the manager ran out waving his broom at him, he tucked his sign under his arm and fled, and shortly thereafter, he came to the churchyard where he had buried his tooth.

The bread sticks he had joined together in the shape of the cross were missing. Though he examined the ground carefully, he could not find the patch of soil they had marked.

There were birds all around him, though, pecking at the grass, and it took him a moment to realize what they were doing: they were searching for his tooth so that they could swallow it. They had already eaten the bread sticks, concealing the place where the tooth lay buried, and now they had decided to eat the tooth as well, to pry it from consecrated ground and take it into the dark furnaces of their stomachs so that it would never be returned to him.

They had not yet uncovered it, though, and with the guidance of the Lord, they never would.

Coleman found a rake leaning against the wall of the church, and he took it up and left his sign in its place. He shouted, "Get out of here! Go!" as he pursued the birds through the church-yard, swinging the rake from side to side and then across his feet and then down from over his head like a mallet. The tines rang and clattered as they hit the ground. Only once did he actually make contact with one of the birds, clipping its tail so that a little spray of feathers burst into the air and drifted lightly to the grass. The creature squawked and went flapping away, land-ing on the neck of a lamppost across the street. He kept chasing the others, following them from one hopping point to the next until finally, after much screaming and beating of the grass, the last one flew away. The churchyard was empty. His tooth was safe for now.

A crowd had gathered along the property line, but when he let go of the rake and looked up at them, they dropped their eyes and strode off in a dozen different directions, as if they had been headed somewhere else all along.

He found two sticks and crossed them at the transverse and then knotted them together with a thread from the hem of his jacket, planting them in the ground to mark the spot where he thought his tooth might be. And he leaned the rake against the wall, and he picked up his sign, and all that day he walked the streets delivering the Good Word of Jesus, struggling to make himself heard through the hoarseness of his voice. When he got home that evening, he put the sign away on the balcony and sat on the corner of his bed, emptying his pockets into his hands. He ate all of his sausages and most of his carrots. And that was five days.

~

FOR THOU SHALT BE IN LEAGUE WITH THE STONES OF THE FIELD, AND THE BEASTS OF THE FIELD SHALL BE AT PEACE WITH THEE. It was the great message of God's mercy upon the suffering, from the fifth chapter of Job, God's great book of suffering. Ever since Coleman had died, he had carried the verse on his sign at least once a week as a reminder of God's grace and His mystery. Of all the books of the Old Testament, Job was the one he found the most puzzling, and also the one he most venerated, and he had often wondered when he was alive if that particular verse, Job 5:23, wasn't both a promise and a forecast of death. It seemed to suggest that God's mercy upon the suffering lay precisely in the fact that He allowed them to die. What could it have meant to the

Israelites to be "in league with the stones of the field" if not that they would be buried finally among their ancestors?

It meant that they would be at peace upon the earth, not at peace beneath it, one of his voices said.

And the other voice said, But in death God created for His people a new earth.

And the first voice said, Tell me then, oh Wise One—which earth is this?

And the second voice did not answer.

Midway through the afternoon Coleman was addressing a crowd of people from the bench outside a fitness club when he saw the two boys who had knocked his tooth out. They were carrying tennis rackets and gym bags, and one of them snapped a towel at the seat of the other's pants, then reached around the back of his neck and playfully tucked his shirt tag into his collar, his fingers tickling over his skin. Coleman leapt down from the bench and shouted after them, "God loves you. He loves you and will heal you if you give yourselves over to His care."

The boys seemed embarrassed. They refused to meet his eye. The first one muttered something into the other's ear. It looked like "It's him again," though it might have been "On the count of three" or even "Whose turn is it this time?"—Coleman had never been very good at reading lips—and then the boys started off at a sort of galloping walk. He tried to keep up with them but lost sight of them in the shopping plaza, and then he banged his shoulder as he was running around the edge of a wooden kiosk, and before he knew it he was sitting flat on the ground, his sign resting dead in his lap.

"Are you all right, Mr. Coleman?"

There was a girl standing over him, no older than twenty, with a wide-open look of sympathy around her eyes. But how, he wondered, did she know his name?

"You wrote it down," she said. He realized she was reading his sign, to which he had once again attached his signature—Coleman Kinzler, Ph.D.

"Here, let me help you up," she said, and when he was on his feet she added, "My name's Sarah."

"Abraham's beloved wife."

She shook her head. "You must be thinking of someone else. I'm not married yet."

" 'And the Lord visited Sarah as He had said, and the Lord did unto Sarah as He had spoken.' "

Suddenly she seemed to think better of introducing herself. She spent a long quiet moment staring at Coleman. It was as though he were a jack-in-the-box whose lever was winding down, and she was just waiting for the clown to pop out of his skull. Then she said, "Are you sure you're okay? I've got to go meet my mother."

Briefly he remembered the Bible he had given to the Hindu woman so many years ago. He said, "I miss my Bible."

"Your Bible is there in your hand."

She was right—he was indeed carrying a Bible—but it was not the Bible he had been thinking of, the one he had bent his heart toward for so long.

Still he said, "I thank you very much for your kindness," and she said, "All right then," her voice climbing an extra notch as she spoke, as though she were asking a question, and he watched her move slowly off across the plaza.

He waited until he couldn't see her anymore, and then he lifted his sign up and turned toward the nearest person he could find and began preaching the Gospel again. He explained how Job's afflictions were a test of Satan—yes—but also a test of the Lord. He asked the man who was stapling flyers to the kiosk if he had heard the News, the Good News of Jesus Christ, and when the man blew a puff of blue-gray cigarette smoke into his face and walked away, he asked someone else, a woman in high heels who was hurrying into a bookstore, and when the woman tossed a handful of change at him, he asked somebody else again.

And so the day passed by.

That night both his legs and his tailbone were sore. He took his shoes off, filled a bucket with warm water, and carried it out through the two glass doors onto his balcony. As he sank his feet into the water, a wave of pins and needles rolled gradually up his body, tapering off somewhere around his shoulders. He sat in his rusted lawn chair watching the light from the sun embering out.

And that was the sixth day.

And then he rested.

Eight

THE VIRUS

So Puckett and Joyce had made it to the station. They had followed the same path Laura had, sledging over the western edge
of the continent's land mass, then down the ice stream and
across the frozen sea. According to Joyce's journal, the weather
had been good to them, with a brisk wind and a steadily slack-
ening snowfall. By the time they reached the fissures and jags of
the ice stream, the few remaining wisps of cloud had dissipated
entirely. They had lost a day or two repairing a broken runner.
They had come across a few crevasses that were too wide for
them to cross. And of course they had bickered, as they always
had, about when to rest at night and when to start out again in
the morning. But for the most part their journey had been an
equable one.

It wasn't until they pulled up to the station that their troubles
truly began.

~

SEVENTY-FIRST ENTRY, FEBRUARY 25. *Arrived. Finally
arrived. We slid into the camp around noon, made our way
down the short path to the station door. So wonderful to see the
impressions of boots stamped into the snow, rather than all that
endlessly smooth white ice. Made me feel like Robinson Crusoe
standing on that island beach of his. P. beat on the door, expect-*

ing someone to answer. And after a while someone did, but not from inside. The crew were all around back. There were six of them. They came scrambling around the corner of the building, carrying picks and shovels. Saying things like "You finally came," and "We didn't hear the engines," and "We almost missed you." Who they thought we were, I didn't know. I told them our situation and asked if we could use their equipment to contact the Atlanta office. They looked absolutely crestfallen. Said we were welcome to try the equipment, but—. The "but" must have meant that it wouldn't do us any good. Which it didn't. The radio worked, and the satphone, and the computer, but no one was picking up. One of the men said they hadn't been able to get in touch with anybody for weeks, not since their last supply shipment was dropped off. P. asked the man his name. He said Meatyard. He tapped the duty roster, where it was spelled out. There were twenty names up there. "Where are the rest of you?" I asked, and Meatyard said, "There is no 'rest of us.' We're all that's left. We just buried Mongno out back. You don't want to be here." They told us about the whole ordeal. The story was that some sort of virus had invaded the station, making its way into the building along with their last supply shipment. Puckett: "What was in the shipment?" Another man (Turner? Dykstra?): "Food, soft drinks, cleaning fluids. Nothing out of the ordinary. We asked for a plasma crucible, but they neglected to bring it." Me: "And when did people first start getting sick?" Turner (or Dykstra?): "Nine days later. That's when we saw the first signs. It was just Washington initially. And then ten days later [note: I think he must have meant the next day, i.e., the day following the ninth, but not for certain], he passed away." And then it was Meatyard again: "The six of us might as well be clanging our bells and shouting, 'Unclean, unclean.'" He told us that all the reports said the virus germinates pretty quickly. P. asked what reports, and they showed us the articles they had downloaded from the newspapers. A clean *dozen of them. London, NY, Bombay. Apparently the virus is part of some worldwide epidemic. I have to say the situation looks pretty dire. People are dying by the hundreds of thousands, if not the millions. Jesus. I wondered about Karen, Jessica, Marcus, my mom and dad. Fuck. Fuck. Jesus. My mom and dad. So many people. I should remain professional here. I'm sorry. No wonder we never heard anything from Coca-Cola. I'm sure we'll manage to get in touch with somebody sooner or later—they can't have forgotten about us completely, can they? Sooner or later. Sooner or later. Just a question of when. In any case, Puckett and I decided to stick with the food stores we brought on the sledge. Less risk that way. One of the men (Sayles was his name) spent the whole conversation wincing, swallowing, shivering, rubbing his eyes. Kept breathing in this funny way that made it sound like he was preventing a sneeze. Preventing one sneeze after another. What's wrong with this guy? I wondered. It turned out that what was wrong with him was the same thing that was wrong with all the others, the ones who had been buried out back. He died late this evening. Which makes fifteen. Somebody once told me that more people die while the sun is setting than at any other hour of the day. Sunset and dying, night and the grave, one ending and another. Is this true?*

~

True—every word of it.

Laura remembered exactly where Joyce had been when he'd heard this particular fact. She remembered the loosely hanging red and white streamers, the high-pitched whistling of the sound system, even the table where he had been sitting at the time. She remembered it all quite distinctly, because she had been there as well.

It had been last July, during the annual Coca-Cola Employee

123

of the Year banquet, just a couple of months before she and the others were scheduled to be shipped off to Antarctica. Puckett and Joyce were sitting at separate tables, each with his own division of the company, and Laura was sitting in the other corner of the room with hers. She could see Joyce talking into his telephone, nodding wearily. Puckett was harvesting something from between his teeth with the nail of his pinkie, covering his mouth with his fist as he worked. The three of them had already been assigned to the polar operation, and she, for one, was dreading the ordeal. Her eyes couldn't help but pick the two of them out whenever they were in the same room together. Between the tables and the streamers and the vases stuffed with flowers, between the thousand other people dining at the banquet, there they were, Puckett and Joyce, flashing and smoking in her attention like beacons on distant hilltops.

The three of them were victims of a common disaster—that was how she saw it—though she never could have imagined how vast that disaster would be.

One of the waiters bent over Laura's glass with his pitcher of water, and she laid her hand across the rim and told him, "No more for me, thanks." The woman sitting directly behind her, the wife or girlfriend of one of the accounting executives, slapped her table and snorted at some joke someone had offered. The banquet's custodian, who was wearing a shirt and tie so that he would blend in with the crowd, crouched over, as though to inspect his shoe, then sopped a spill of wine up from the carpet. He tucked the napkin surreptitiously in his front pocket, straightened his tie, and stood back up.

The recipient of that year's Employee of the Year award was Lindell Trimble, the vice president in charge of public relations, who had boosted sales of the company's primary soda line by one quarter in metropolitan areas and one third in small towns with what he called his ambient graffiti campaign. The idea was to hire graffiti artists to paint Coca-Cola advertisements on sidewalks, walls, picnic tables, trees, and buses—any surface where they might attract attention. There were men and women drinking Coca-Cola products and saying, "Aaaahhh!" There were still lifes autographed with only the Coca-Cola wave and the initials C. C. There were short phrases written in black spray paint so that they looked like gang slogans: "Try Coke!" or "Coke Rocks!" The corporation had to pay a cleanup fine, of course, and occasionally also a small nuisance penalty, but such fines were prefigured in the publicity budget and were minuscule compared to the cost of advertising legitimately on such a wide array of public spaces. Several of the graffiti artists were arrested, and one, in the small town of Rison, Nebraska, was beaten by the police and hospitalized with a dislocated kneecap and two broken ribs. "And that was an unfortunate incident. Definitely you would have to put it on the debit side of the equation," Lindell Trimble said when he was at the dais accepting his Employee of the Year plaque. "But on the credit side, the campaign has caught on in certain communities—Dallas, Miami, Detroit—and we've got people *we didn't even hire* painting our ads for us. Kids who just think it's the cool thing to do. Disaffected teenagers and the like."

He took a sip of red wine. "I'm sure the rest of the PR and advertising gang will join me in testifying that kids that age are the hardest demographic to reach. Absolutely the hardest. So it's been a good year for us. But that doesn't mean we can just kick back and take it easy. On the contrary. It's exactly when you kick back and take it easy that all the energy, all the momentum, drains right out of you, and for a business like Coca-Cola, loss of momentum equals death. A body is more likely to die at sunset than at any other hour of the day—that's a fact. The trick, then, is to keep the sun from setting. That's what we're looking for at Coca-Cola, and what we in the PR division have been fighting so hard to achieve: a sun that never sets. A perpetual noon. Thank you."

He waited for the applause to dwindle to a few last popcorn-like claps, and then he lifted his glass again in a sort of silent toast and drained it, tipping it up and over like a canteen, before he stepped down from the dais. Just then the automated security field sent its planes of intersecting light sweeping across the room, scanning for armaments or explosives. Lindell Trimble stumbled and dropped his glass as the light cut across his eyes. "Damn it," Laura heard someone whisper—the building's head of security, she presumed. "I thought I told them to turn those goddamn things off for the night."

When Lindell Trimble recovered his smile, he said, "Uh-oh. Caught in the cross fire." What Laura remembered best about the evening was the way a single syllable of laughter rose up from somewhere in the room, then stopped dead when nobody else joined in.

~

SEVENTY-FIFTH ENTRY, MARCH 5. *Only two left now. Meat-yard and Weisz and that's it. This morning P. and I helped them bury Turner out behind the station. Difficult work. We went down two feet, then heaped the ice back on top of the body. Had to round the entire mass into a sort of hummock before we were finished. Didn't want the wind to rip it apart. I pointed out that the ice there was shelf ice. I.e., beneath the graves was the ocean, not solid land. To which Weisz said, "At this point I can't see that it matters very much, can you?" And he was right. In another century, when the glaciers have melted, there will be a long row of bleached skeletons resting on the bottom of the ocean, and who will ever know? Or if the climate repairs itself somehow and the ice stays firm, there will be eighteen frozen bodies packed inside, fully dressed in their flesh and their cloth-ing. Eighteen and counting, I should say. And again, no one will care because no one will ever know. P. and I spent a good twenty hours this past week trying to contact Coca-Cola—or*

anyone else, for that matter. Failed, failed, failed. The news-
papers have all stopped posting. Radio signals are scattered.
Phone lines gone dead or diverted to answering systems. There's
every single indication that the virus has taken a global toll.
What's the word I'm looking for? Not an epidemic, but a—?
Can't remember. I wish I was a dictionary. Or an encyclopedia.
Or better: I wish I was a camera, one of those news cameras you
see hovering and darting around at traffic accidents. How else
to know what's going on? I spent this afternoon arguing with
Puckett about what we should do next—whether we should stay
or go, whether we should prepare for the effects of the virus. So
far we're symptomless. "But we won't be for long," Puckett said.
"We were dead men the moment we knocked on that door." Me:
"You can't know that for sure. Maybe we weren't exposed to the
infection. Or maybe we're immune. Someone has to be immune,
for God's sake." Puckett thinks I'm just being naive. So do
Meatyard and Weisz. One of the downloads we read suggested
that the virus can be spread through simple human contact, or
even through indirect exposure in a shared environment. The
old cover-your-mouth-and-don't-touch-the-doorknobs scenario.
Pandemic. *That's the word I want.* Pandemic. *Apparently*
there's an emergency radio by the penguin roost on the other
side of Ross Island. "The knoll," Meatyard called it. "It's
a powerful little thing," he said. He claims there's a slim
chance—but a chance notwithstanding—that it will be more
help to us than the radio inside the station. Says we might be
able to find a different tunnel through the reception. Should we
try to reach it? If things get any worse, we might not have a
choice. It's becoming colder all the time. Winter and the vanish-
ing sun. The rifts and crevices freezing back over. The ocean
receding. I keep thinking about Shannon and Ken and all the
others back in Pennsylvania. I wonder how they're doing. No,
let me tell the truth. What I wonder—what I really wonder—is
if they're doing. P. and I were supposed to have made the return

trip days ago. The trip back to the hut, I'm talking about, not the trip back home. Though for that matter, we were supposed to have made the trip back home days ago, too. Tried to radio Byrd this morning on the off chance that she had repaired the transceiver, but no success. She must think we're never coming back.

~

Not long after she found the journal, Laura resumed her routine of counting and pacing, numbering off her steps just as she had in the hut on the other side of the mountains. It occurred to her that maybe she was trying to walk away from everything. The station's rooms were arranged in a ring, with doors on each of the connecting walls, so that she could keep going for hours without ever reaching a dead end. Sometimes she would find herself counting into the thousands and the tens of thousands, taking one step after another in the same sort of blind compulsion that drives suicides to the edges of buildings, crossing through first the front room, then the kitchen, then the dining room and the bedroom and the living room, over and over again, until finally she would stop without thinking by the couch or one of the beds and collapse backward onto the cushions, falling with her legs rigid and her arms stretched out like a child playing catch-me.

It was one of those mind-emptyingly repetitious activities that people take up in order to suppress their anxiety. Some people rocked back and forth, or danced, or drummed their fingers on a tabletop. Some people exercised with heavy machinery. Laura paced.

Her walk was quick and steady—a march, almost—and it always cleared her head. At least for a while. But as soon as she stopped to rest, she would begin thinking about her friends and family again, begin thinking about even the most glancing acquaintances. She would remember her smallest interactions with virtual strangers, people who were very probably dead now. She would hear all the things they had said to her, bumping around inside her head like flies against a window. Bump—and Martin Campbell, the boy she used to baby-sit, would hop onto her lap and say, "Can a lion beat up a tiger? Can a shark beat up an alligator?" Bump—and her mail carrier would knock on her door (this was during the week she came down with the flu) and say, "You can't just let your letters pile up like this, Ms. Byrd. I won't squeeze anything else into that box until you empty out what's already there. Oh, and God bless you." Bump—and her boss would tell her, "I don't care if you think you got suckered into it. You can't back out on me this late in the game, Laura. You're our woman, you're going to Antarctica, and that's the end of it." Bump—and she would hear them all at once, not only her boss and her mailman and Martin Campbell, but everybody, a tremendous crowd noise, as though all the people she had ever encountered were clamoring to her in their millions of voices.

She had been at the station for three or four weeks already, and her body had slowly repaired itself. She was no longer sore when she got out of bed in the morning. The hitch in her back had vanished, along with the ulcers in her mouth and the rivery tingling sensation in her toes and her fingers. She could almost feel her muscles knitting themselves back together, becoming strong again, bending and firm, like a suit made out of chain mail. True, there was still a bruise on her left leg from the time she had stumbled against the corner of the sledge, but it was gradually yellowing out and losing definition. She could barely even feel it anymore.

The food locker was fully stocked, with hundreds of boxes of vegetables and hundreds of cuts of meat. The pantry was stuffed with containers of rice, beans, and milled grain, alongside dozens of cases of soda and bottled water. She could easily stay in the station for another year without eating all the food, but she wasn't sure if she should. If Joyce's journal was correct, and the virus had infiltrated the station along with the last delivery, there was every chance in the world that the food was contaminated, as well. Unfortunately, without the equipment to test for the virus and some better idea of what she was looking for, she had no way of knowing for sure. No way other than by weakening and dying, that is, and she had been eating freely from the station's food supply for weeks now without any sign of infection. In fact, she was healthier than she had been when she arrived.

So maybe the virus had already died out. Maybe it needed sunlight in order to propagate, multiple hosts in order to survive. Or maybe it was simply biding its time, incubating in her blood, leaving glistening silver slug-trails as it slowly crawled toward her heart.

Whatever the answer, she didn't see that she had any choice in the matter. She would have to keep feeding herself from the pantry and the locker. The food she had brought in the sledge was down to a few last bags of granola and a half-dozen hardened biscuits. If she was going to get sick, she was just going to have to get sick.

Bump—and she heard her mother saying, "Honey, if you sleep with the fan blowing full blast on you like that, don't you know you'll catch fever?" Bump—and then her ex-boyfriend said, "You do realize 'communication' has the same root as 'communicable,' don't you?" Bump—and the man sitting next to her in La Hacienda Mexican Restaurant said, "Sweet fabulous Lord, I'm hungry!" tucking his napkin into his collar like a bib. She did not think she knew the man, though she must have met him at some point. She began to walk the floor again.

It was the first entirely dark week of winter. Occasionally she would become restless, bored with her circuit of pacing, and she would open the door and walk outside for a while, though never without donning her protective clothing—snowsuit, boots, mask, and gloves. She would look at the moon and the stars, or at the tattered layer of cirrus clouds, or at the scarves of the aurora—which, because of the scrubbed transparency of the air, seemed to rest just a few yards above the ice. The klieg lights ticked every so often. The station's vents gave off clear rivulations of heat. The weather was cold enough to flash-freeze the moisture in her breath, and on those rare occasions when the wind was perfectly still, she could hear a thousand particles of frost falling to the ground as she exhaled, chiming like tiny bells as they hit the ice.

Even after all the time she had spent living in the Antarctic—and how long had it been? six months? seven?—she still patted her clothing down for a key whenever she headed back to the station. She would experience a split second of panic when she realized her pockets were empty. Then she would remember that the door was not locked, was never locked, and her heart would grow still again. This happened countless times.

She wondered how many other useless habits she was carrying around with her. Without even trying, she could think of at least two: she still left a spoonful of soup in the pot after she was finished cooking, so that no one would accuse her of taking the last serving, and she still coughed quietly before she opened the bathroom door, which was something her father had taught her to do in case anyone was sitting inside. She believed she had managed to cast aside most of the rest of her useless social habits—habits she had accumulated over a lifetime of living with other people. But there were almost certainly a few others she remained unaware of and was unable to put aside, habits she had no need of here at the bottom of the world.

The bottom of the world. Despite all her years of education, that was still how she thought of this place. When she was a girl, she used to believe that if she began digging a hole in her backyard and kept digging until she passed through the center of the earth, she would eventually emerge upside down on the bottom of the world. She had imagined it as a place where everything was wrong, topsy-turvy, where everything was exactly the opposite of what it should be. The clouds were like mountains, the sky like a blue lake, and the stars were like smooth white pebbles resting beneath the water. The people who lived there crept across the ceiling of the earth like spiders. She had pictured them clinging to the grass in a strong wind, holding fistfuls of it in their hands, struggling not to tumble into space. The idea frightened her. She had decided then and there that the bottom of the world was a place she never wanted to visit.

She could never have guessed that she would live there some-day—and not just at the bottom of the world, but at the *bottom* of the bottom of the world. Could never have guessed that she would almost certainly die there. But then, she could never have guessed so many things. That she would fall out of love with the man she dated in college and never speak to him again. Or that a degree in environmental biology would send her to work for the Coca-Cola Corporation. Or that her father would live through two separate heart attacks and a minor stroke without dying.

"You and your mother," she heard him saying. "It could be ninety-eight degrees outside, and as soon as the air conditioner comes on, you both complain that you're freezing."

Bump.

~

SEVENTY-EIGHTH ENTRY, MARCH 11. *And then there were none. "Ashes, ashes, they all fall down." Or how did it origi- nally go? "Atishoo, atishoo, they all fall down." About the Black Death, right? Though I can't remember who told me that. The "ring around the rosie" part was for the red marks on the skin of the infected, the "pocket full of posies" part for the flowers they were buried with, and the "atishoo, atishoo" part for the sneezing that came over them before they died. I suppose the "ashes" version would do just as well, though. "Ashes." I* feel like the survivor of a volcanic eruption, one of those poor wasted souls who come stumbling out of the char when the whole damned thing is over and done with, saying they climbed down a well or ran into the hills to wait out the catastrophe. *Weisz died yesterday. We buried him this morning. He was the last to go.* The man was in pretty bad shape these last two days. I suppose I should say that it was a blessing he finally went, but none of this feels like a blessing to me. It feels like a curse. A goddamned curse. Jesus. What a waste. Now it's just Puckett and me. Managed to find one more bit of information on the Web—part of a diary or personal log by some high school kid. Said that the incubation period was a matter of hours or days at the most. Here's what he wrote: "A few of us are still asymptomatic. We're holed up in the high school gym, away from everybody else. If it wasn't for the stupid quarantine, we'd be long gone by now. But it looks like there's no way out. As soon as one of us comes down with the Blinks, the rest of us are done for." Is this true? If so, I don't understand what P. and I are still doing here. Why we're alive at all. Maybe the freezing temperatures have slowed the development of the virus. That's all I can imagine. We tried to radio Byrd again, but we didn't have any luck. What can she possibly be thinking right now? We were supposed to be back already, weren't we? I'm so sorry, Laura. I just hope you don't decide to follow us. You're better off where you are, believe me. I was sharpening my knife a few hours ago when Puckett interrupted me. "Come here, you've got to see this." "What is it?" I asked. Puckett: "Just come here, will you?" He had found a Web site broadcasting real-time images from orbiting satellites. This means two things: one, that the satellites are still working. And two, so are the relays. The images weren't detailed enough for us to see individual people, or individual bodies, but we could make out roads, buildings, and stalled lines of traffic. This is what we've left behind, our legacy to the rest of the universe—a world full of wrecked cars and empty buildings with the lights of ten thousand satellites blinking overhead. Surely there must be others like Puckett and me out there. Recluses who've managed to escape the virus somehow. Sherpas. Mountain men. Hermits living in desert caves. The scattered survivors who are always left after any calamity to tell people what went wrong. But then, there are no people left for the survivors to tell, are there? Just two—Michael Puckett and Robert Joyce. Or three—Laura Byrd. The food we brought in the sledge is gone, and we've begun eating from the station's supplies. No other choice, unless we want to starve to death. It's good to have meat again, and soft bread, and vegetables. At least something is good. After we found the satellite images, we spent half an hour or so arguing about whether we should try to reach the other side of Ross Island. Puckett: "It's the only sensible thing to do. If the radio there is as good as Meatyard said it is, we might be able to make contact with somebody." Me: "Or we could head back to the hut for Byrd. We can't just leave her there." P.: "And then we'll do what exactly? Bring her back here? What's the point? I say we make for the penguin roost. At least then we'll have some hope of rescue. We can try for Laura afterward one way or the other." Me: "All I'm saying is the longer we leave her there, the worse off she's going to be." But Puckett is right, for once. We would be absolute idiots not to try for the other radio if there's even the tiniest chance it will work. We've used up the last few hours of the day restocking the sledge. Food, tools, camping gear, toiletries. The trip to the penguin roost shouldn't be nearly as difficult as the trip to the station was. The sky, even at this hour, is the deep red color of autumn leaves, with enough light still to see by. And according to the maps the terrain is mostly shelf ice. In other words, flat traveling, if not necessarily smooth traveling. We're setting out tomorrow morning. Eleven o'clock. We'll cut through Fog Bay, *directly to the south of the island. I'm going to use the rest of the night to get some much needed sleep. My head is pounding. My eyes are killing me.*

~

This was the last entry. Laura read the journal eight times over the course of the next three days, trying to determine what she should do next, whether or not she should leave the station, how likely she was to get sick. Had she been coughing more than usual lately? Had her eyes been watering? She seemed to remember waking up to sneeze the night she found the sheet of X's in the station, then swooning into sleep again before she could roll over or adjust her pillow. Was that a sign of the virus?

Also, what had happened to Puckett and Joyce? Had they made it to the other radio? Where were they right now?

She was worried about them.

When she finished the journal for the last time, she shut it firmly and held it in her lap. She sent the nails of her free hand across her scalp, a motion that her high school English teacher had once referred to as her "thinking gesture." Then she went to the pantry and began selecting the food she would take with her when she left the station.

Puckett and Joyce were right. If there was a chance she could use the radio at the penguin roost to communicate with somebody—any chance, with anybody—she would have to take it.

It didn't matter how slim the chance might be. It couldn't be worse than no chance at all, which was what she would have if she remained at the station.

And then, too, if she set out for the roost, she might be able to find Puckett and Joyce.

She had never unloaded the sledge, so the only supplies she needed to gather were food, clothing, and a few odds and ends such as aspirin, toilet paper, and a spare aerial for the transceiver at the penguin roost. She put the folio of Joyce's journal in the duffel bag, slipping it between her long johns and her spare day socks and bookmarking it with the newspaper article she had found beneath the computer, the one about the virus's spread through North America: PLAGUE! DEADLY VIRUS SWEEPS MEXICO, UNITED STATES. TENS OF MILLIONS CONTRACT "THE BLINKS." Then she carried the entire bundle to the front door, along with the ditty bag of soap and toothpaste she had packed and the chest of frozen food.

The darkness outside was constant, with no trace of sunlight, so there was no reason for her to wait until morning to get under way. Morning wouldn't break for another month or so, anyway. A night so long made the sunrise seem imaginary—like Atlantis, or the Heavenly City, or the Garden of Eden. A pipe dream, she thought. Or maybe she should say a daydream.

The stars were nearly motionless. The moon was a brilliant white wedge, emerging from behind a thick bank of clouds. She packed her new equipment into the sledge's storage hutch, slipped the latch into place, and took one last walk around the building. One of the klieg lights, the one directly above the graves, shone hard and straight onto the twenty mounds, so that they cast heavy foreshortened shadows that pooled against the wall of the station like oil puddles. The wind shifted, and she heard the scraping and buckling sound of the sea ice. She headed back out to the courtyard and started the sledge.

She was worried that the fuel cell might have chipped in the freezing weather, breaking the circuit, but as it turned out, she had no reason to be. The engine engaged with a muffled hum that slowly grew louder. First the headlights brightened, and then the runners lifted, and then the internal GPS monitor flickered on, which meant that at least one of the polar relays was still working.

But the rest of the relay system must have been down—or large patches of it, anyway. The display indicated that she was at

2° S, 39.4° E, just south of the equator, somewhere around Kenya.

She took a long, broken breath, closed her eyes, and rested her head on the steering column. She was trying to decide whether or not she should laugh.

Nine

THE NUMBERS

How many people was any one human being likely to remember?
A thousand? Maybe if you were cursed with a particularly slip-
shod memory. So then—ten thousand? A hundred thousand? A
million? Of course, if you ran out your life in some small village
deep in the Himalayas, the number would be greatly diminished,
but Michael Puckett wasn't thinking about Himalayan villagers.
Or monks, or nuns, or kids who never lived past that falling-
down-drunk stage of toddlerhood. He was thinking about himself, his own life, and by extension he was thinking about Laura.
She was the common element, after all, the link or what have you.
After all the discussion he had heard in the city, that much was
obvious.

He had spent the better part of a week trying to come up with a
good solid number, one that took his entire forty-three years of
life into account. At first he tried to make the calculations men-
tally, sorting through the great crowd of people in his head as he
listened to the stereo or rested in bed at night. But when he realized how complicated the whole matter was turning out to be, he
pulled out his #2 pencil and a blank pad of paper and settled
down to work.

He began with his immediate family—his mother, his father,
and his two sisters, plus the older brother who had died at the age
of eleven when he snapped his neck jumping his bike into a
creek-bed. Then he added his extended family into the mix: both

sets of grandparents, his aunts and uncles, his great-aunts and great-uncles, his cousins, including his second cousins, the husbands, wives, and children of his cousins, the second husbands and second wives and in some cases the second children of his cousins, and so on. Next he counted off his schoolmates and teachers, from kindergarten through graduate school, and then the schoolmates and teachers of his sisters, tagging on the occasional college friend that the two of them had brought home for a visit. There were his neighbors to remember. There were the people he knew from work, beginning with his first job sliding pizzas into ovens at Pizza D'Action and ending with his sixteen years at Coca-Cola. There were the members of his church, though when it came to church, he had never been what anybody would have called devout. He was more of an Easter-Christmas-and-whenever-someone-managed-to-drag-his-ass-out-of-bed-on-a-Sunday kind of guy. And then there were the thousands of loose friends who kept jumping into his memory—people who didn't fit into any obvious category, but nonetheless there they were, like acorns that came popping out of the grass as he mowed his lawn. There were the friends of those friends, and sometimes there was even another tier of friends beyond that. He added his girlfriends to the list (there had been seventeen of them), and his girlfriends' families, and then his first wife and her family, and his second wife and her family, and of course there was his son and his son's classmates and his softball team and his other friends from the block and whatnot. And there were all the people he had met at plays and dinner receptions and parties and weddings over the years. Oh, and then there were what he supposed he might call his personal commercial acquaintances, as opposed to his professional commercial acquaintances—his business contacts and such—though now that he thought about it, he guessed he would have to take them into account, as well. He was thinking of all the clerks and salespeople he knew by sight and sometimes even by name: the people who worked at the grocery stores, pharmacies, tool shops, garages, department stores, restaurants, and movie theaters he frequented.

Any number of times he imagined he was finished with the list, but he kept uncovering new clusters of acquaintances: his Boy Scout troop, the other guys at his gym, the twenty-some faces he remembered from his one disastrous AA meeting. He would go to the kitchen to rinse off a plate, and he would remember the plumber who had repaired his faucet for the past ten years, and the rotating lineup of plumber's assistants he had employed, and the son he had been forced to bring on call with him that one day when the schools closed down, who had put a deck of playing cards in Michael's toaster and almost set his kitchen on fire. Everything he saw, touched, or listened to seemed to remind him of a few more people he had neglected to write down. A woman he had seen at the library once and for some reason had never forgotten. His dentist and his dental hygienist. The guys he used to play pool with when he was in college. Finally, when he paged through his notes, he realized that he had forgotten somehow to list his sisters' extended families: their husbands and in-laws, his nephews and nieces, and on and on through the great cascade of additional people who seemed to be connected to everyone he knew, excepting only his brother, the one who had died, who was a broken thread to him and had no such connections.

When he tallied up the list he had made, the number he came up with was forty-two thousand, but for the next few days he kept discovering little pockets and byways of extra people—where did they all come from?—and if he had to guess, he would say that the number was probably closer to fifty thousand, or maybe even seventy.

"I can't believe it would be that high," Joyce said when Puckett showed him the list. "You must be imagining you remember people you don't really remember."

"I was thinking it was probably too low, actually."

"I doubt that." He gave the dismissive little stiff-palmed wave of his fingers—nothing more than a twitch, really—that he always used when he wanted to drive Puckett crazy. "Underestimation has never exactly been your defining characteristic."

Puckett ought to have buried him when he had the chance.

Joyce had succumbed to the Blinks just a few hours after they set out for the penguin roost. He had taken on a sagging posture that Puckett had mistaken for sleep until the sledge rounded a curve and Joyce tipped over sideways, striking the window with the side of his face. All at once, Puckett knew the truth. He cut the engine and felt Joyce's neck for a pulse. His skin was still warm, but there was nothing moving beneath it—no air, no blood. Even the muscles had lost their tension. It was the seventh death Puckett had seen in the past two weeks. He was getting used to the signs.

It had occurred to him that he ought to try the old breath-on-the-mirror test he was familiar with from so many movies. But then again, he reasoned, it was hardly necessary when the person in question was so obviously dead.

He and Joyce had never known whether to treat each other as friends or antagonists. Or maybe it was just that their antagonism and their friendliness had been so inextricably tied up with each other that it was impossible for anybody to tell the two apart. It was through their arguments, their bickering, that they expressed their fundamental goodwill toward each other, and they both took a particular pleasure in pretending they disliked the other more than they did. It was part of the game. For Puckett to admit that he was upset over losing Joyce, then, would have been a violation of the rules.

To tell the truth, though, he wasn't as upset as he had guessed he would be. After all, there was a part of him that had known this was coming for a long time. He only wondered how long it would be before it came for him, as well.

It would have taken him the rest of the day and a good portion of the next to break into the ice and lay a respectable grave for

Joyce, and it seemed more important to cover some more ground before the horizon swallowed all the good light, so he decided to bury him after he made it across the bay to the second transmitter. He started up the sledge and began following his compass over the ice. It wasn't long, though, before he felt himself becoming feverish and began losing awareness of his surroundings. It was the virus coming on—he knew it. His skin seemed to be coming loose from his skeleton, like a star casting off its final wobbling shell of gas. His eyes watered over and gradually lost their focus. The last thing he remembered was waking for a few moments some indeterminate time later and watching as a great wall of ice and black rock slowly grew larger in his windshield. Then he fell asleep again, and there was the pinwheel of gold and silver light, and when he tried to touch it, the petals folded together into a single enormous pillar, as tall and wide as a redwood tree. It was only through a supreme effort of his will and imagination that he was able to compress the pillar into a small rod the size of a #2 pencil—which was indeed a #2 pencil, the same pencil he would later use to prepare his list.

Joyce was the first person he saw when he arrived in the city. Immediately he knew that he must be dead. Puckett took a step back, stumbling over his shoes.

"What are you doing here?" Joyce asked him, and Puckett asked the same question, "What are you doing here?" And then they argued about something for a while. And then they went their separate ways. And it felt good, it felt right, it felt just like old times.

Puckett had made no particular effort to stay in touch with Joyce, and he was pretty sure Joyce would say the same about him if anyone asked. But then staying in touch had not demanded any particular effort. Wherever they went, it seemed, they were destined to meet. Puckett could hardly walk into a bar or restaurant without finding Joyce at one of the tables, clicking the salt and pepper shakers together or making lean-tos out of the cardboard coasters, and if he was not there already, inevitably he would arrive within the next few minutes. He could not step out for a quick stroll, could not go shopping at the grocery store, without suddenly coming upon him at the deli counter or the back end of the soup aisle. They had run into each other at the movie theater, the gym, and the drug store, and at the random intersections of a thousand different streets. More than once Puckett had stepped out of a stall in a public restroom to find Joyce buckling his belt only one stall over. They were no longer surprised to see each other, and it was with a certain sense of fatality that they would take up whatever conversation they had left unfinished the last time they met.

Just one day after he told Joyce about the list he had made, for instance, Puckett ran across him on the ground floor of an office building. Puckett was dashing in to take a quick drink from the water fountain, and Joyce was walking across the black marble tiles of the lobby toward the elevators, and they saw each other and realized their paths were going to cross again. After a short pause Joyce said, "I would wager I remember about two thousand people total."

Puckett shook his head. "No, I'm telling you, it's much higher than that. I'm not talking about the number of people you can call to mind without any effort at all, you know. I'm talking about the number of people you're capable of remembering when the right chain of associations occur. Sit down and figure it out sometime."

"See, the difference between us is that you imagine your own memory is reliable, or at least reliable enough to offer up a basically trustworthy accounting of your life. And I don't. Not for a second."

"I doubt my memory is any more reliable than yours. I just happen to know mine a little better."

"Riddle me this then," Joyce said. "If everybody in the world remembered—what? fifty thousand people, you said?—then how would they all fit into a city the size of this one? This place is pretty big, but I don't think it's that big."

The next day they bumped into each other again, as they were cutting across the southwest corner of the square. Puckett said, "First of all, do you have any idea how extensive this city actually is?"

"Do you?"

"No, but I have a feeling it's a lot bigger than you imagine. A lot bigger than this one district, that's for sure. I did some asking around, and nobody seems to know how far the streets go. The closest I came was a guy who used to dabble in cartography. He said in almost ten years of mapping he had never once seen the end of the city. He said—and I quote—that if the city had a boundary line, it must have gone tearing off like a blue streak whenever he came around."

"Okay. Maybe. And what's your second of all?"

"How's that?"

"You said 'first of all.' Implying a second of all. So what's your second of all?"

"Well, second of all, when I say that we each remember fifty or a hundred thousand people, I don't mean fifty or a hundred thousand people that nobody else remembers. There's bound to be a lot of overlap. Both of us remember Laura, for instance. We both remember the folks from the office. And not that it makes any difference, but we both remember Meatyard and Weisz and Turner and those guys, too."

Their next encounter took place in a burger joint where they had both happened to stop for lunch. Four gray-haired Korean women were playing mah-jongg at one of the tables, and a couple of IAS officers were sitting at the counter silently scanning the room. They were still wearing their yellow collars, for some reason, though what damage was left to be done Puckett couldn't imagine.

Joyce began with, "I think it *does* make a difference, actually."

"What does?"

"The fact that we remember Turner and Meatyard and the others. You said it didn't make a difference. I say that it does."

"I didn't mean that it doesn't matter at all. But it can't change what happened to them, can it?"

"*Really?* You don't think *Laura's* memory has changed what's happening to *us?*"

"Of course it has. But Laura is still alive. Or at least we presume she is." He took a sip of his coffee. Even after ten years of sobriety, he was still tempted to order a beer whenever he was eating a burger and fries. But, as always, he resisted the urge.

"Yes. And as long as we were alive, we were keeping some part of the rest of them alive, as well. Think about it, Puckett," Joyce said. "Think of all the people who must have vanished from this place after we died. Surely there was somebody who existed on this side only because you existed on the other. Can you really say that that doesn't matter?"

As usual, Joyce was missing his point. But also as usual, he was not entirely wrong. Of course it mattered; Puckett had no doubt about that. Still, he answered, "All I'm saying is that we're powerless to affect what happens over there from over here. The arrow goes in one direction, and in one direction only."

"I'm not sure everybody would agree with you on that," Joyce said, but Puckett was too tired of the argument to ask him to elaborate.

It was much later in the day and he was walking home through the quiet, blue-lit streets when he realized that his older brother—the one who had died when he was only eleven, when Puckett was only four—must have continued out his days in the city until very recently, when Puckett himself had died and the memory of him had finally vanished from the face of the earth.

My God, Puckett thought. That was almost forty years.

He had already figured out that his parents, his grandparents, his wife, his son, the entire roster of people he had known over the course of his lifetime had remained in the city until the very moment he had died. He would even say that he had reconciled himself to the fact, though it was hard when it came to some people, he would admit: his son, for instance, who was only fifteen, after all, and just coming into the prime of his youth. But somehow the idea that his brother, who had been gone for such a long time, was one of those people had never occurred to him. It made him feel as though he had wandered into some strange empty building where a door at the end of a twisting hallway opened onto the bedroom he had slept in as a boy. He was almost afraid to step inside, but he knew he would regret it forever if he didn't.

By the time he got home, he had made up his mind. He would have to search out the city for any traces of his brother.

~

The investigation, as it turned out, was not as difficult as he had supposed it would be. His first thought was to track down some of the city's old census records and look for his brother's name inside. There was a vacated library around the corner from his building, the front door of which had been removed from its hinges and carted away by vandals at some point. While he knew that the shelves inside were mostly bare, it still seemed like the most obvious place to start. In the Archives Room, on the third floor, he found a cabinet labeled, miracle of miracles, CENSUS RECORDS—PAST FIVE YEARS. He used a metal ruler to jimmy off the lock. The cabinet had already been emptied out, though, and the only thing that remained inside was an old Vaseline jar filled with red rubber bands. He was about to leave when he saw a row of phone books stacked beneath the information counter. The books were almost ten years out of date. Still, though, he was able to find his brother's name inside, with an address listed on the outskirts of the monument district.

He tore the page out of the book along with a map that was folded into the back cover and took it along with him. There was a chill in the air as he navigated the streets. His ears began to ache, and so he pulled his collar up and pressed the fabric against his temples until he could hear the workings of his own body, that distant rumbling sound that always reminded him of logs rolling down a hill.

The map from the phone book seemed to be some kind of interpretive cubist diagram of the city rather than an actual map. A number of small streets—streets that were not displayed on the map at all—had been wedged in between others that were supposed to be directly adjacent. And some of the streets that were on the map had been disarranged slightly, intersecting at the wrong places, as though some careless shopper had taken them out to look at them and then put them back on the first shelf that came to hand. In one case, a weedy, half-dead golf course stretched over what ought to have been—but was not—four city blocks named for the great cities of Southern Africa: Kinshasa, Nairobi, Lusaka, and Johannesburg.

More than once Puckett had to retrace his steps and ask for directions. The sole of one of his shoes came loose and began to flap against the pavement.

All the same, he managed to find the building he was looking for.

He rode the elevator to the fifth floor, gave a precautionary knock on the door of the apartment listed in the phone book, and then took hold of the doorknob. He had expected the apartment to be empty—he didn't know why—but just as he was getting ready to open the door, a lanky middle-aged man answered. The man's glasses were smudged with some kind of transparent grease, and a feather duster of limp yellow hair trailed over his eyebrows. He was eating raisins out of a dixie cup.

"I help you?" he said after a few moments of silence, and Puckett realized he had been staring at the man like an imbecile.

"I'm sorry," he said. "I think I screwed up. I was looking for somebody who used to be at this address. Or maybe he did. At least I thought so."

The man popped a raisin into his mouth. "This somebody have a name?"

"Nathaniel Puckett."

"Mm-hmm. He cleared out—oh—about the tail end of the evacuation, I'd say. You knew him?"

"He was my brother."

"You Mikey?"

"Well . . . Michael."

The man nodded and stepped aside. "Come on in then. Your brother and I were roommates."

Your brother and I were roommates. It was that simple, apparently. Puckett could hardly believe it. He sat down on a sofa that had been upholstered in a pattern of blue and white stripes, an enormous beast of furniture that took up half the room. There were no other chairs around, and so the man with the glasses sat next to him. "I suppose you want to ask me about your brother," he said. "Fire away. I'm not armed." He had finished his raisins, and he crushed the dixie cup and began transferring it slowly between his palms, smoothing out the folds and bulges. Everything about him seemed to amble along at its own deliberate speed, the lone exception being his habit of snipping off the beginnings of his sentences, which was a way of making up for lost time, Puckett guessed.

Puckett's brother had always been a mystery to him, a ghost-like stranger with a dirt bike and a broken neck who had collected comic books and stayed up late watching television and

149

had once convinced Puckett to curl up into a ball at the bottom of his sleeping bag so that he could swing him in circles around the living room. That was all he remembered about him. But over the course of the next few hours, he learned any number of new things. Upon his death, apparently, Nathaniel had taken a room in one of the city's many orphanages, as most children did. He might simply have remained there—again, as most children did. But though he had never grown older than eleven, he had eventually decided to move out on his own. He continued to ride his bicycle for a few years, though it was a racing bike rather than a dirt bike this time. He was in three or four minor traffic accidents before he decided to sell the thing. Afterward, he became an afficionado of the subway system. On Sunday afternoons, he would ride the cars for hours at a stretch, taking them as far as the white clay district, while he stared out at the other cars and the dark tunnels and the aquariumlike spaces of the waiting platforms. For seven years he had worked in a hobby shop selling model airplanes and die-cast figurines to young men nostalgic for the childhood he himself would never lose. Then he had gotten a job pruning bushes at a greenhouse, and after that he had worked for a while as an assistant groundskeeper at one of the city's largest topiary gardens.

The man who was telling Puckett about him had been staying in the apartment's extra room for almost five years now. He and Nathaniel had met at a lecture on "The Comic Book as Literature," he said. The man had been an English teacher when he was alive, with a taste for what he called "illustrated novels." And as for Nathaniel, comic books still made up his main reading material. He had built up a sizable collection since he had arrived in the city. He invited the man to his apartment the day after the lecture to look at them.

"And I never left," the man said. "What can I tell you? I was brand new. Needed a place to stay, and your brother needed the company. It worked out just fine."

"Did he ever talk about me?" Puckett asked.

"You and your family both."

Puckett heard himself letting out a sigh. "I don't know why I should be relieved by that. I barely . . . and here I am . . ." He was stumbling over his thoughts. "You know, I really wasn't sure he would remember me."

"He remembered. You didn't get a chance to say good-bye, did you?"

"To say good-bye in person? No. Mom took me to his grave once, but I was pretty little back then. I basically just stopped thinking about him after a while."

The whole time the man was talking, he had been shaping the dixie cup slowly between his fingers, and now he was holding a nearly perfect sphere in his hands. "It's important to say good-bye. My family was at my bedside when I died."

"Were you sick?"

"Leukemia. A bad time."

"I'm sorry."

"No need to be."

"But your family was there?"

"They were. You want to hear about it?"

And with that he began his story.

He said that he had been sick for a long time before he was hospitalized. "Almost three years. People say they want to die in their own home. But me, I was ready for the hospital. The sterilized sheets, the machines, the whole bit. It just seemed easier there. Easier to cast myself off, I mean. There was less to let go of. You have to understand, I was in pain. Had been in pain for a long time. I was ready to die. Whenever I felt myself slipping away, though, I would see the pictures of my wife and my boys on the wall, or I would notice the chair by the dresser and remember where I was when I picked it up, or any one of a thousand other things. They were like these little knots that I couldn't unfasten. Finally I decided that if I was going to die I needed to be in unfamiliar surroundings. Maybe because I was getting ready to move into the most unfamiliar surrounding of all. Don't know. In any case, I asked my family to put me up in the hospital, and they did. They were real good about it. They visited a couple of times a day—even my oldest, who was in college at the time. One day he asked me—Clay, that's my oldest—he asked me if I believed in an afterlife. I didn't know what to tell him. You know those stories you used to hear about people who pass through the tunnel of white light and see Heaven waiting for them on the other side? Never knew what to make of them myself. But the fact that the people who survived to tell us about it were always by definition the ones who turned around and came back—well, it would be hard for me to explain why, but it made me doubt their reliability. Still, I kept thinking about it. People used to believe that you could look into the eyes of a dead man and see an image of the last thing he ever saw. Did you know that? I had always imagined the opposite myself. That your vision turned the other way as you died. That time flipped inside out and you saw what was coming next rather than what had come before. Anyway, I wanted to answer my boy's question if I could. I didn't know whether he would be in the room when I died. Didn't know whether I would be able to communicate with him even if he was. So I decided to write him two letters. One of the letters said that there was nothing at all after you died—just a big winking out, not even darkness. I sealed that letter up in a red envelope. And the other letter said that it was all true, everything you've ever heard—the tunnel, your loved ones beckoning you on through the light, and finally Heaven—or at least something like it. I put that letter in a blue envelope. There are other possibilities, of course, but those were the two that seemed the most likely to me. I wanted to keep it simple. I made up a rhyme so I wouldn't forget which envelope was which: 'Red is dead. Blue is new.' For days I kept repeating it to myself. *Red is dead. Blue is new. Red is dead. Blue is new.*

See, I was going to try to choose between them at the last second, when my vision flipped. But I started to worry that I wouldn't be able to talk when the time came. So I asked the nurse to put one of the envelopes in each of my hands. I held on tight to them. My room had a window, and I could see the sky passing over the top level of the parking garage. First the sun, then the stars, and then the sun again. That kind of thing. It was evening a couple of days later when I finally died. Like I said, my whole family was there. My wife, both my boys. I could feel it coming on. This time there were no knots to hold me in place. I let go of one of the envelopes, and I clutched the other one as hard as I could."

Puckett was fascinated. "Which envelope did you hold on to?"

"The red one," the man said. "Red is dead." The lower half of his face gave an awkward little twist. "Obviously I messed up."

Puckett laughed. "I'll say."

"If I had it to do over again, I'd pick the blue one, of course."

"Of course."

They both fell quiet after that. It was a good half minute before the man bent his head to the side and the light from the window touched the oil on his glasses, where it butterflied open in a dozen different colors. "What are you thinking about?" the man said.

"Why do you ask?"

"You were squeezing the bridge of your nose. That's your thinking gesture. You did it when I mentioned your brother's comic books, and then when I told you about my son, and you did it again just now. I'm good at spotting them."

Puckett put his hands on his knees. "I was thinking I should thank you for spending so much time with me. Believe me, it helped. But I need to be going now."

The couch released Puckett with a long creak of its springs. Before he could make his way to the door, though, the man said,

"You know, your brother was my only close friend in the city. It's good to have someone to tell your stories to. Which is my way of saying come back any time."

He reached out for Puckett in what Puckett presumed was a handshake. But when Puckett went to meet it, the man gave him the dixie cup instead: a small, round globe, worn smooth as velvet by his fingers.

"Would you mind throwing this out for me?" he said. "There's an ashtray right over there by the elevators."

~

So what was Puckett thinking about?

Mailmen.

Specifically, the number of mailmen he had known in his life.

They were yet another subset of people he had forgotten to take into account, though so far he had been able to remember only eight of them distinctly. There was the mailman who had always asked to see his driver's license when he signed for a package, the one he had spotted buying a case of wine in the liquor store, and half a dozen others.

He was sure he would remember a few more as he let the line of his thoughts play out. It must have been the story about the letters that had brought them to mind. As it had brought his son to mind, and his second wife, and his parents—the people who would have gathered around his own hospital bed if he had had one.

He was trying his best not to think about them. It was just too hard.

The air was colder than it had been even an hour or so before, and a thick blanket of clouds had emerged while he was inside. As he was walking home, he overheard two men, maybe thirty years old, hypothesizing about various ways they might contact

Laura. This was a popular subject of conversation in the city, though one that never seemed to produce any concrete initiatives.

"Has anybody thought about using a Ouija board?" one of them said.

"Well, maybe *she* could use a Ouija board to contact *us*, but it doesn't work the other way. See, I was thinking we could get everybody together and just try to, you know, project our thoughts or something. A harmonic convergence sort of thing. She believes in that shit, or at least she did back in the day."

"I don't see why we couldn't at least give the Ouija board thing a shot." The man made a rolling little high-pitched horror-movie note. *"They came from beyond the grave!"*

Puckett passed behind a clump of trees, and soon their voices faded away.

At the bus bench on the corner of Georgia and Sixty-fifth, a man with motor oil stains on his clothing was adjusting himself through the pocket of his pants. Puckett remembered some twenty car mechanics, though he was pretty sure he had already written them all down; he would have to check his list to make sure.

At the lower end of the golf course, a blind man was feeling his way down the sidewalk, tugging on the rigging of his beard. Puckett could remember at least six blind people.

He was almost home when he saw Joyce stepping out of a jeweler's shop, hunching his shoulders as the wind struck his face. He suddenly felt a tremendous weariness in his bones. Maybe it was the walk, or maybe it was his conversation with the English teacher, or maybe it was just the effort of thinking about his brother after so long, but the last thing he wanted right now was another pointless argument.

He ducked beneath an awning and waited for him to pass. Joyce was listening to his watch, shaking his wrist as he held it to his ear, and he did not see him. Puckett watched him cross the street at the corner. Then he moved out of the doorway, blew a long breath of warm air into his hands, and felt the first tingle of frost on his cheek.

He looked up into the sky, a loosely swirling motion of gray and white flakes.

Not this again, he thought.

It was snowing.

Ten

THE CREVASSE

Ice. Frost. Frosting. Crossing. Railroad crossing. Railroad train.
Fabric train. Wedding dress. Wedding ring. Ring of fire. Ring of
ice. *Ice.* Iceberg. Glacier. Razor. Stubble. Stumble. Fall. October.
November. December. Christmas. Xmas. X marks the spot. Trea-
sure. Gold. Silver. Silver Bells. Jingle Bells. Open sleigh. Snow.
Ice. Rice. Mice. Cats. Whiskers. Scissors. Paper. Paper angels.
Angel food cake. Nectar of the gods. Ambrosia. Ambrose Bierce.
Mexico. Mexican. Jumping bean. Jump rope. Rope bridge.
Chasm. Crevice. Ice floe. Iceberg. *Ice.*

As Laura strained at the sledge, the words snapped back and
forth in her head like a racquetball, a continuously rolling blue
whir that she made no effort to stop or control. She was trying to
find one word for every step she took, looking for that ideal balance of physical and mental locomotion that would keep her from
thinking too hard about whether she would make it to the penguin roost, and what she would find if she got there, and what difference it would make if all the reports she had read were true
and everyone, everyone in the world, everyone she had ever
known, was dead.

She did not know—did not want to know—the answer.

Answer. Question. Mention. Tension.

Her hauling stride measured slightly more than a foot—a foot
and four inches, say—which meant (she did the math) that she
could expect to cover one mile, roughly, for every thirty-five hun-

dred words she came up with. If her bearings were correct, she had eighteen miles and sixty-three thousand words to go. The sledge had shut down on her shortly after she crossed Fog Bay, sinking onto its runners on a flat stretch of perfectly ridgeless ice. The flippers had locked and the whole immense carriage had coasted slowly across the ice, razoring a full six inches into the snow before it scraped to a stop. She had tried everything she could think of to get the engine running again. She was no mechanic, though, and it quickly became clear to her that it was broken beyond her capacity for repair.

Which was not to say that it was broken beyond *any* capacity for repair. The problem might have been something as simple as a spent fuel cell or a snapped electrical connection. But without reliable tools, good lighting, and replacement supplies, she knew she was out of luck. She stood in the cold with her face in her hands. The snow beneath her boots was loose and high. The wind made the surface stir with thousands of tiny flexing snakes. She climbed back into the steering compartment of the sledge, where the heat was quickly draining away, and shut the door.

She had already traveled most of the way around the hump of Ross Island, and it made no sense for her to turn back now. She remembered that old joke about the man who swam three quarters of the distance across a river, decided he was too tired to go any further, swung around in the water, and swam back to shore. In the version she had heard the man was Canadian, though in certain areas of the country he was probably Mexican. And immediately across the border, to either the north or the south, he was almost certainly an American.

American. Yank. Tug. Tugboat. Engine.

There was only one option open to Laura—that was how she saw it.

She couldn't turn around, and she couldn't stay where she was, so she would have to keep going. She waited until she felt the last of the heat slip away, then took the harness and skis out of the storage hutch, clipped the skis onto her feet, and fastened herself to the front of the sledge.

She leaned into the harness and tried to pull forward. It was impossible. The sledge was a house, the sledge was a whale. She strained so hard that one of her skis pierced the snow, plunging through the crust with a sound like tearing paper. Her left leg sank down to the knee. She lifted herself out and tried again. This time she used both of her poles for leverage, leaning into the wind, her shoulders hunched and spread to give herself as much muscle as possible. She took one step, and then another, and then a third. Perhaps the traces were stretching slightly, but the sledge did not move. She decided she would have to lighten her load. She simply wouldn't make it otherwise.

The sledge came in two main pieces: the steering compartment and the storage hutch. She began by detaching the steering compartment from the runners, unfastening the couplings that joined it to the storage hutch and sliding it off onto the snow. It rested on the surface for a few seconds before its sharp edges punched through the crust, leaving a perfect four-by-four-foot square. Then she took the shovel out of the back of the storage hutch, which was still attached to the runners, and worked the snow loose from around the steering compartment's door. She filled the compartment with everything she thought she could do without: a few bundles of clothing, three thick pieces of plywood, her sunblock, of course, the second of her two cooking pots, and the chest that carried her frozen food, which she had already emptied into the storage hutch. Whatever she left behind, she reasoned, she would be able to pick up again on her return trip.

She shut the door, strapped herself into her harness, and yanked on the sledge's traces. Reluctantly it began to move—very slowly at first, then less slowly. After her first few strides, she fell into a gliding motion that carried her steadily but strenuously over the ice. The steering compartment disappeared behind her. The sledge was so much lighter than it had been before. It was half a house now, half a whale.

A whale. A wail. A good, hard cry. A gnashing of the teeth.

Laura remembered how she had begun grinding her teeth shortly after she started working for Coca-Cola. It was something she had done in her sleep, unconsciously and entirely without memory. She would wake up in the morning with her jaw aching and have no idea why, until the day her dentist noticed that her enamel had been worn down as smooth as pearl. "Frankly, I've never seen a mouth go so bad so quickly," he told her. "It looks like you put your teeth through a rock tumbler." He scouted around in her mouth for a while with a penlight, then switched the light off, looked her in the eyes, and said, "Have you ever considered therapy?"

For a while this had been her favorite dinner party story, the one she told whenever anyone mentioned teeth or psychiatry or the presumptuous suggestions of practical strangers.

But it had been months since she had thought about it.

And months since she had thought about her dentist.

Who was almost certainly dead now.

Dentist. Doctor. Braces. Eraser. Abrasive.

She could not expect to come across another shelter before she reached the sea. Once, not so long ago, hundreds of small, temporary settlements had dotted the plateaus of Antarctica, but that time had come to an end almost thirty years ago, when it became clear that the ice cap was beginning to melt. True, less glaciation meant easier access to the mineral resources of the land. But it also meant legal liability for the rising sea levels and climate changes the thaw was expected to bring, and most of the countries of the world had weighed the financial benefits against the financial risks and decided to relinquish their stake in the continent. The whole of Antarctica was purchased just a few years later by a trio of corporations—Coca-Cola, Bertelsmann, and

FCI—after both South Africa and Argentina, the last of the thirty-seven countries that had once held claim to it, suffered financial collapse. Immediately the number of polar and scientific expeditions had fallen to almost zero—in part, and undeniably, because the corporations had denied many of the scientists access, but also because the original settlements had not really been established as research stations in the first place. They were markers of a national interest that had now been exhausted, like the flags planted all those years ago on the beaten gray deserts of the moon. The shelters and heavy equipment were broken down and hauled out inside a fleet of cargo planes. The people were evacuated. Laura was aware of two other research parties that had been granted entry to the continent around the same time she was sent there by Coca-Cola. One of them was located on the far side of the Pole, toward Madagascar, and the other at the very tip of the Antarctic peninsula. But both had been abandoned before the onset of winter.

She would have to rely on her own tent for shelter, on her own momentum for warmth. When she first began sledging, the stars had been hidden behind a thick lid of clouds, so that even with her flashlight it was impossible for her to see more than a few yards in front of her. But by the time a couple of hours had passed, a broad patch of sky had become visible to the northeast. She could see hundreds of stars and satellites, and between them the shifting waves and folds of the aurora, in green and red and gold, flaring up, fading away, and sending out dozens of slowly extending streamers and ribbons. The ice was still dark, though, and there were few landmarks for her to steer by, only the occasionally discernible black rock of the mountain that lay to the east.

Every so often, when she sensed that she might have veered off course, she would fish her compass out of her pocket and check her bearings. She was so close to the Pole that the needle would drift and spin for a full minute before it came to rest, and even then only if she stood absolutely still. It was difficult for her to get moving again. She only had to pause for a minute and the sledge would take on the weight of its own stillness. The carriage would sink to its belly in the snow, and the runners would fix in place, taking hold of the ice like roots.

She had never known a person could be so tired. Sometimes she didn't see how she could possibly keep going. But she did, she always did.

The snow blew off the rises, leaving bald patches of slippery ice, but long drifts built up in the depressions and made the shelf seem more level than it really was. There were multitudes of people in her thoughts, multitudes walking behind her. Her mother and father. Her extended family. The friends she had known growing up, and in college and graduate school, and in her life as a working adult. Her lovers and all the close friends of her lovers. The people she saw every few days at the grocery store or at the bank, and the people who lived in her apartment building and the buildings surrounding it. The woman who sold the tickets at the movie theater. The man who worked the toll booth outside the Coca-Cola complex. The people she was used to passing on the street but with whom she had never actually spoken. She would think of them, and they would give her the strength to carry on, and then she would remember the virus and the newspaper article and the thousand cities of the dead, and her stomach would buckle, and she would start counting her words again.

Though she knew she was alone, there was a part of her that refused to accept it. Otherwise, she thought, why not just stop where she was, settle onto her knees, and let the snow accumulate around her? It would be so much easier that way—so much easier than all these exhausting footsteps, one after another, footsteps in their endless thousands.

But, she reminded herself, she was *not* alone, or at least she couldn't be certain she was. Somebody, somewhere, must have survived the virus. And what about Puckett and Joyce? They were still out on the ice somewhere, looking for her. For all she knew, she had already crossed paths with them on her way across the bay. The air was so black, and the wind so deafening sometimes, that they might have come within yards of one another and never even known it.

When the wind was blowing hard, in fact, it seemed to be the only sound in the world, but when it fell still, she could hear the snow creaking beneath her feet, the sledge shushing behind her, even the occasional shotlike report of distant slabs of ice contracting in the cold. The darkness made everything seem louder than it really was. And then there was the crushed-glass sound of her clothing moving against her body. Her sweat did not evaporate in the cold, but soaked directly into the fabric, where it quickly froze through. By the time she had been sledging for fifteen minutes her shirt and pants would be stiff with frost, and within half an hour they would be frozen into a thousand different angles and creases. It became difficult for her to bend her joints, and when she did, fragments of ice would come raining down her chest and legs, piling up at her beltline and the cuffs of her pants where she had tucked them into her boots. She made the mistake of taking off one of her mitts to reach for her compass once and ended up with frostbite on all five fingertips. At night, in her tent, she had to wait for her clothes to thaw before she took them off, and afterward she would watch as they lay on the floor steaming and collapsing fold by fold, rustling quietly as the heat softened them. They were not always dry by the time she woke up, and sometimes, when she stepped outside, the fabric would freeze together again. She made sure to take down the tent with her body already arranged in its sledging posture, a lesson she learned the morning her shirt hardened around her, locking into a position that left her head tilted awkwardly to the left for the rest of the day. There was no way for her to remove the clothing to adjust herself, and so she had had to walk that way until she stopped some eight hours later to set the tent up again.

The bay had been shaped and broken by the pressure of countless freezings. It followed the gradually rising and falling motion of a meadow cut by occasional streams. The streams were crevasses, and while some of them were narrow enough for her to cross, others were not. Each time she came to one, she would lengthen her trace and take her skis off and look to see whether she could make the leap. If she couldn't (and she often couldn't) she would walk toward the tapering end until the crevasse sealed itself off—sometimes in solid ice, sometimes in a bridge of packed snow.

The sound of these bridges beneath her feet was one she quickly learned to recognize, the hollow *thwud* of snow with nothing supporting it. She was always frightened that the ground would crumble away while she was trying to walk across. Somehow, though, it never did. Often she would put a leg or a foot through the snow, but she was always able to lift herself back out.

The sledge's flippers were fully extended, and it would slide over the gap on its own as soon as she began pulling again. It was becoming harder and harder, though, for her to draw the sledge at all. The strain of the cold, the twelve or more hours she spent between breakfast and dinner, between one meal and another, the neverending exertion of making her way over the drifts— it was all taking its toll on her. She was feeling weaker every day. Her knees kept buckling, she kept losing her rhythm of breathing.

It was on her fifth day of sledging—her eighth away from the station—that a dense, murky fog settled over the ice. Her flashlight was useless in such conditions, shining back against her hands off the motionless white wall. A small button of moonlight capped the fog, dull and lusterless, but its light was too weak to reach the ground. She wouldn't have seen it at all if she hadn't happened to look directly above her.

She spent hours walking blindly forward, trying to feel the changing shape of the ground through the soles of her boots. Was the shelf rising or dipping? How slick was the snow and how thickly was it packed? Was that the lip of a fissure she felt or simply the falling edge of a furrow? She checked her compass every few minutes to make sure she hadn't wandered too far off course. She tried to keep to a straight line.

She had been pulling for most of the day when a wedge of sky appeared ahead of her. First it was just a cup-shaped hole through which she was able to glimpse a few weak stars, but then the fog parted around it, spreading open as though someone had unfastened a giant zipper, and the moonlight came pouring through. She propelled herself forward with a dozen driving jabs of her poles, hurrying toward the light. The fog dissolved into clear air around her. The weight of the sledge seemed like an unnecessary burden. She would have thrown it off if she could have—just thrown it off and run. She saw the ice that lay above the crevasse, a thin sheet of brittle shining glass, a split second before she was on top of it. But there was no time for her to stop.

She said something out loud—"Wait!" she thought it was, though maybe it was "Shit!"—and then the ice made a splintering noise, shattering into a thousand fragments, and she felt herself falling.

She was caught by the straps of her harness. Her neck wrenched backward, the air rushed out of her lungs, and she heard a clattering sound. She saw white shapes like moths or butterflies floating across her vision in the darkness.

After a few seconds, she began to breathe again. She was dangling inside her harness. She kicked at the air, casting about for a ledge, a foothold, anything. The walls must have been ten feet apart. Her legs kept pinwheeling between them. Whenever she

165

managed to touch one, her feet would slide loose, and she would start swaying back and forth again. Finally she brushed up against what felt like a pressure cleft or an indentation, but before she was able to anchor herself to it, she began sliding down again.

It took her a moment to realize what was happening: the sledge was being pulled toward the fissure. She dropped five feet in a matter of seconds, then halted for a moment, spinning in her harness, before she dropped another two.

She waited until she was sure she had stopped. Then she looked up. The effort of craning her neck made her dizzy, but she forced herself to ignore the feeling. She could see one of the flippers projecting over the edge of the cut. It was outlined against the sky, a stream of stars contained between the solid black walls of the crevasse. The other flipper was not visible to her. The sledge must have lodged against a ridge or a snowdrift, twisting the runners off center. That had to be what was holding it in place. Temporarily.

Delicately, she reached for the wall. She was closer to it now by perhaps a foot. The rope held steady. The ice was hard and slick, with none of the snow that had given her traction when she was making her way across the shelf. She prodded it gently with her mitts. She could not feel any irregularities there. She was afraid that if she moved too suddenly, she would give the sledge enough momentum to skip off whatever obstruction it had lodged against and her weight would pull it into the gap. The walls were too wide for the flippers to be effective, which meant that the sledge would either crush her as it fell or go plummeting past her body and yank her into the void. How deep did the crevasse go? She wouldn't be surprised if it bottomed out at the ocean itself, that thin band of water that had somehow managed to remain liquid beneath the pressure of the ice: barely moving, home to absolutely nothing.

So she could freeze to death, or she could fall and break her neck, or she could drown. Those were the possibilities.

And then there was a fourth possibility, the only other one she could think of. She could climb the rope and lift herself out of the crevasse. She could save herself.

Or not. She had to admit she was tempted to undo the harness and simply let herself drop. It would be a thousand times easier that way. She would never have to pull a sledge again, never have to struggle or wish or remember again. She imagined death as a wonderful melting. The cold would pass out of her blood. She would be so much warmer. No one would ever find her or know what had happened to her, no one would ever see her again, and what difference would it make? The world was over anyway. She would never meet another living soul.

But in the end, she knew, she couldn't let herself do it, couldn't let herself fall. She had to keep struggling, for the same reason everybody else kept struggling, or at least they always had in the past. She felt that to let go of the rope would be cheating.

She looked up again. The flipper was still hanging over the edge of the fissure. She understood that if she was going to make it to the surface, she would have to start now, before she fell asleep and the rest of her strength drained away. She had given herself a fifteen-foot lead on the sledge, so the climb couldn't be any farther than that. She brought her hand to her pocket to put her flashlight away, but realized she was no longer carrying it. She must have dropped it when she fell. She looked between her boots to see if she could spot a pinprick of light twinkling somewhere below her, but there was nothing there to see.

The flashlight was gone. But she couldn't worry about that now.

She tried to take hold of the rope, folding her mitts stiffly around it. They crunched and crackled as the ice inside them snapped loose. At first she thought she had gained a grip on the rope, but as soon as she attempted to lift herself, her hands slipped free. She tried once more, and the same thing happened. Her mitts were too rigid. It was obvious that if she was going to climb out of the crevasse, she would have to use her bare hands. She took her mitts off, stuffing them deep in her pockets. The lining had adhered to her skin, and she had no choice but to leave it in place for now. She took hold of the rope again. Immediately, the tips of her fingers began to sting, as though she had plunged them into a mass of thorns, but within seconds they were numb. She managed to pull herself a few fists higher. Her muscles threatened to burst apart in a hundred limp strings, but the sledge stayed in place. So far, so good. She hoisted herself another few inches and then her strength gave out and she lost her grip again.

Once more, she was swaying at the end of her harness, her head spinning. She took the rope in her hands and began to climb again. All of the ice inside her snowsuit had cracked loose when she fell into the crevasse, and now, as she tried to lift herself free, she could feel the debris shifting around inside her clothing, two heavy bulges around her ankles and a third around her waist. They reminded her of the rings that formed around giant planets.

Which would make her the giant planet, she supposed.

Saturn, maybe.

She had heard somewhere that if you lowered yourself into a well, most of the sunlight would be sapped from the circle of sky that lay between the stones, and the constellations would shine through like steel rivets, even in the middle of the day. If only the reverse were true, she thought. If only the sun could burn through the sky in the middle of the night. When she gazed out of the crevice, though, all she saw were the same stars she had seen the last time she looked, along with the trailing thread of the aurora.

There was no feeling at all in her hands. She knew she had

taken hold of the rope only by the strain of the line against her bones and the dimmed-out evidence of her eyes. She made her way up inch by inch, refusing to let go. A great loop of rope went slack beneath her as she climbed. Once, halfway to the top, she made the mistake of placing her foot in the loop and trying to use it for leverage. The rope was yanked out of her grasp, and she slipped once more to the full length of the harness. She began climbing again. Every sound she made seemed to rattle around between the walls like a rock inside a tin can. She must have been on her fourth or fifth attempt when her foot grazed the pressure cleft she had noticed earlier. She worked at it until she could fit the toe of her boot inside.

It was a relief to feel something solid beneath her, no matter how precarious it might be. She paused there for a moment. Then she sank her weight onto her boot and gave the biggest leap she could manage.

The maneuver gained her almost a foot. The rope swung in a long curve that propelled her against the wall, and she almost lost her grip, but she held on as she waited for the line to fall still. The end of the climb was within reach. She lifted herself another few inches, took a deep breath, then lifted herself again. Five more handholds and she was at the lip of the crevasse, taking hold of the side. But before she could scramble onto level ground, the ice she was clutching calved off in her fingers. She dropped all the way back down into the fissure.

Again she lost her breath, and again she saw the white shapes meandering across the darkness, and she listened as the sledge sawed closer to the edge of the crevasse and then scraped to a stop.

She rested for a long time, slowly spinning in her harness. She didn't want to die there—she had decided not to die there—and so, limp and freezing and numb, she began making her way up the rope again.

Finally, after two more tries, and with the assistance of the pressure cleft, she was able to scale the rope and thrust herself onto the snow. She crawled away from the brink of the fissure before it could collapse again. Then she lay on her back and stared at the sky. She began to cry. The tears froze to her cheeks, but she couldn't stop herself. She was just so relieved to feel the ground beneath her. There was one particular star in the sky, fat and white, that burned like an electric bulb. She let her eyes trickle over its scores and bruises as she tried to catch her breath. She wasn't sure how long it took her to realize it was the moon.

She was about to pass out from exhaustion, which would have meant freezing to death. So she forced herself to stand up and stagger to the back of the sledge. She had trouble opening the storage hutch. The lining of her gloves had been shredded to ribbons in the climb. She bit a few of the scraps loose with her teeth. She didn't want to look at her hands, didn't want to know, but her eyes couldn't avoid them for long. The flesh of her palms had peeled and folded over on itself like the skin of a rotten peach, and the tips of her fingers—all ten of them—were black with frostbite. Jesus Christ. She fumbled at the latch and eventually managed to release it. The moon gave her just enough light to see by. She treated herself with the antiseptic cream and bandages she found in the first-aid kit, and then she slipped her mitts back over her hands and turned them over in the light, investigating the outline of each of her fingers to make sure they weren't crooked or doubled over at the knuckles. She couldn't feel a god-damned thing.

It took her longer than she would have expected to set the tent up. She staked it down, shut herself inside, and waited for the heat of the soft coil to fill the air.

After a few minutes, she felt the frost melting from her hair and eyebrows. Her pants and coat gradually softened and fell slack around her body. She knew that she should take them off before she got into her sleeping bag, but she didn't have the energy.

~

That night, the wind came howling down from the mountains, and by the time she woke up, the air outside was black with snow, a single surging mass of it that made it impossible for her to leave the tent, much less haul the sledge. She spent the next three days sleeping and eating, waiting out the storm. She listened to the gusting noise of the snow as it rode the wind. The blood slowly returned to her capillaries with a puncturing sensation that made her twist inside her skin, and her palms and fingers gradually began to heal.

On the third day, for reasons that were inexplicable to her, she began thinking about the small neighborhood park that was located just down the street from her apartment. In the center of the park was an area of red brick and iron benches, a gathering place carved out of the root-broken dirt where people liked to read books and walk their dogs and lobby one another to sign petitions. She had been through four winters in the neighborhood, but somehow she couldn't remember ever going to the park in the snow. It was a spring place—a summer place and an autumn place, too, perhaps, but mostly a spring place. The bricks and iron benches were constantly warmed by the sun, and the trees, a few dozen shadowy oaks and pines, always seemed to be leafing out.

The place was so different from this tent of hers in the middle of the ice storm, the only still spot for miles around. Maybe that was why she kept thinking about it: in the same way that the tent was a refuge from the weather, the park was a refuge from the present, a shelter she could rest inside while the cold and wind went rushing and swirling around her.

She remembered the rollerbladers she saw there, how they

would weave so swiftly through the crowd, separating and coming back together again in that graceful, nimble, impulsive way they had that always reminded her of a flock of birds. There was a group of four elderly women who played mah-jongg around a small brick plateau near her bench, sitting on picnic chairs they carried into the park themselves. They always yelled at the rollerbladers when the kids passed too close to them, shaking their fists and cursing in a foreign language. One of the women sometimes brought her granddaughter along with her, a melon-like baby who would happily spend the entire day sucking on a blank mah-jongg tile. Once, when Laura was leaving the park, she had leaned over the baby to untangle her blanket for her, and the baby had grasped Laura's finger in a surprisingly firm fist, bringing it to her mouth and working it between her gums.

"A little help here?" Laura had said to the women at the mah-jongg table. "Hello?"

But they had ignored her, hunching protectively over their tiles. Eventually, she had managed to extract the finger herself, and when she turned to leave, she found a man waiting behind her. He was canted over on his bicycle, propping himself up with his left foot. He appeared to be laughing at her. She laughed, too, and the man handed her a bandanna to wipe the saliva from her finger—"Here you go"—and when he asked her if he could take her out for a drink sometime, she said yes.

That was Mike Hargett, who became her final short-lived boyfriend, the one who had told her that the shade of lipstick she was wearing made him want to bite her lips off.

And then there was the time she gave a book of matches to a man she had never met before, a man in hiking boots and a business suit—such a little thing, but she had never forgotten it. "You don't have a light, do you?" the man had asked her, and though she did not smoke, she realized she was still carrying the matchbook she had picked up from a restaurant the night before.

She felt a tiny electric rush as she reached into her purse for it—delighted, the way she had been as a child, by her ability to carry out a favor for someone. "Keep it," she told the man, and he struck a match, cupped the flame to his cigarette, and walked away.

The latest war had just ended, and it seemed that the entire city had come together in the park. A woman was joggling a rubber ball from hand to hand. A man was walking his dog. There were a few police officers milling about, and here and there she spotted the yellow collars of the IAS operatives who could always be found in any large crowd. "Infectious Agents Squad," they would introduce themselves. "I need to search your bag, ma'am." A little girl was balancing clusters of pine needles around a twig she had poked into the ground, a jump rope slung over her shoulder. Two teenage boys were holding hands and whispering to each other. An old woman sat down on a bench, slipped her shoes off, and began muttering in Italian as she stretched her toes out. Laura watched a man pass by carrying a sign that read, JESUS IS COMING. DON'T BE DECEIVED. At the bottom of the placard he had written the word SINCERELY, as though signing a letter, after which he had printed his name.

Laura tried to remember the name the man with the placard had used, but she couldn't. Carter? Carlson? Carlsbad. Cavern. Stalactite. Stalagmite. Stalag. Gulag. Labor camp. Labor pain. Birth. Life. Creation. It was something unusual like that, she thought, something like Carter or Carlson—or Creation, for that matter—something with a hard *C*. But it wouldn't come to her. The tent belled out as the wind fell still and sank for a few seconds and then began gusting again. She lay back inside her sleeping bag, staring into the hollow darkness.

Carmen. Kevin. Kermit.

What on earth had the man written on the placard?

By the time she had stopped wondering, she was well on her way to sleep.

Eleven

THE CHANGES

Winter had come to the city, and the snow covered every level surface: the roads and the sidewalks, the fountains and the park benches, even the leaves on the trees, or at least the ones that weren't cocked over onto their sides. Lindell Trimble had to wade through a solid foot of the shit every morning just to make his way down the steps of his building, and there was more waiting for him wherever he went. On most of the district's streets and sidewalks it melted under the day's traffic, then froze again after the sun fell, so that a glasslike sheen of ice whose only visible effect was to slightly magnify the pavement would send person after person sprawling onto his ass. He stood at his door sometimes and watched them fall, one ridiculous tumble after another. They looked like monkeys or rag dolls, barely human, and the idea that he himself might cut so pitiable a figure, that some smug son of a bitch in a three-piece suit might watch him sliding around on the ice and cringe, was appalling to him. This was why he always walked through the banks of snow along the curb, despite the damage it did to his shoes and the cuffs of his pants.

That morning in particular he was squeezing around the side of an abandoned car when the motherfucking beggar came at him again, the one he could never seem to shake. He launched straight into his brother-can-you-spare-a-dime routine: "Got some change for me today? Hey, come on, buddy. You look like a man of wealth and power. I'm sure you've got a little change you can give to a fellow in need, don't you?"

And blah blah blah blah *blah*.

As usual, the beggar had appeared from out of nowhere, and when he realized Lindell wasn't going to answer him, he began shouting and waving his arms. "What's the matter with you, pal? Too good for me, is that it? Mr. Won't-Even-Look-Me-in-the-Goddamned-Eye. Mr. So-and-So-with-His-Leather-Briefcase-and-His-Hundred-Dollar-Haircut."

He followed Lindell across the street, the pair of them sliding around on the ice like a couple of jackasses, and when they reached the dirty snow heaped in the opposite gutter, he climbed over after Lindell and grabbed hold of his sleeve. Lindell shook him off.

"Whoa," the beggar said. "Whoa now." He held his hands out in a sign of contrition, wearing those fingerless black gloves that were the universal trademark of the urban poor. What, was Lindell supposed to believe that they couldn't afford to cover their fingers? Was that the idea?

"Hey, look, man, I'm sorry. I was just trying to get a rise out of you," the beggar said. "You know how it is. But you've got to understand I'm your friend, don't you, buddy? And friends look out for each other, right? So how about you check those pockets of yours again for me? I bet you've got some change you can spare for a good friend."

Lindell could see that his usual policy of fabricating a convenient distraction—pretending that he had spotted someone he knew down the block or that his phone had just gone off—and striding purposefully away wasn't going to do the job this time. He kept walking, though, plugging his feet one after the other into the hard crust of the snow. "Listen," he snapped out, "you're not going to chisel anything out of me, so why don't you just leave me the hell alone?"

Immediately the beggar fell away, giving a tight little laugh. "Yes sir, your highness," he said. "Right away, Your-Majesty-on-

His-Holy-Goddamn-Golden-Fucking-Throne." He made a saluting gesture. Lindell glanced back just long enough to see him looking around for his next target.

Sometimes he thought there must be something about him that attracted such people from an infinite distance. You know the way that certain wild animals will scout around for miles in search of the cleanest place to empty their bowels? Well, he was the cleanest place, and they were the wild animals. It was uncanny. In every railway concourse or shopping mall, he was always the guy trailing the long line of religious cultists behind him, a bright, exploding flare of bald heads, orange robes, and ponytails. The freaks and the con artists, the drug addicts and schizophrenics: inevitably, no matter where he went, they seemed to zero right in on him. Even here in the city he could not seem to avoid them, whether it was the beggar with his patchy beard and his hard-luck stories or that nutcase with the bird fixation and the Jesus signs.

He stopped off at the coffee shop for an espresso. It was a Saturday, or what everyone had decided to regard as a Saturday, and he knew that the Coca-Cola offices would be mostly empty. No receptionist waiting to hand him his messages, no marketing staff gathered for the morning meeting. He sipped his drink at a tall counter looking out onto the sidewalk and the alley and a snow-covered basketball court with two metal hoops dripping chandeliers of ice where their nets ought to have been. The ice would crack into a thousand daggers at the very first basket, he thought. *Swish, crash, boom,* and there would be a few less players on the court the next day.

When he was finished, he took the crosswalk to the building on the other side of Eréndira Street, unlocked the executive entrance, and closed it again behind him. Inside, the lobby was dark and quiet, with the weird theatricality and canyonlike feeling of spaciousness that all office buildings possess on the weekend. He rode the elevator to the seventh floor. The document he was looking for was in the top drawer of his desk. He had known for weeks that it would be best not to leave the thing lying around, but it was only the night before, while he was sipping a scotch and listening to some asshole broadcasting his jungle music for the whole building to hear, that he had finally decided what to do about it. So far, fewer than a dozen people knew what was what (or some of what was some of what, he should say, since despite their expertise nobody in the corporation had been able to piece together the whole story), and all of them had agreed that there was no earthly reason for them to tell anyone else. What was the use of drumming up trouble, after all, in a place where there was only peace and ignorance—a place where the peace, in fact, was the ignorance, and the ignorance was the peace?

To his last breath Lindell would continue to deny any responsibility for what had happened. It wasn't his fault. He couldn't have changed a single goddamned thing. Still, it was a fact that whoever had introduced the virus had done so only a few months after he and the PR department had initiated their white powder campaign, and the possibility that the whole chain of events was somehow inspired by the campaign—or even in answer to it— had definitely crossed his mind. The consumer affairs division had received any number of complaints during the high days of the congressional hearings and the media fuss, including at least one handwritten letter promising total world annihilation, but Lindell had learned from experience that there were cranks and failures beyond number in the world who blamed their lousy jobs and poor posture and the general lovelessness of their lives on some multinational corporation or another and who had nothing better to do than place angry phone calls and write menacing letters. Such people rarely if ever had the balls to act on their threats, for the simple reason that they were already defeated.

Yet somebody had decided to use Coca-Cola as the distribution nexus for the virus. That much was beyond doubt. The only questions to ask were who and why?

There were people in the PR division who were convinced that Islamic fundamentalists were to blame, or some group of anarcho-environmental zealots, or even, though it had been suggested mainly as a grim little joke, the Pepsi Corporation.

It seemed likely to Lindell, though, that whoever had devised the virus had no real grievance against Coca-Cola at all. They were simply looking for the product with the widest possible reach in the global marketplace, the one that would disseminate the virus with the most efficiency, and Coke was it.

Some ten years before, in response to falling transportation costs on one side of the equation and rising rates of water contamination on the other, the corporation had decided to centralize its processing operations in a single plant on the upper coast of Venezuela. It was cheaper to purify the entire soft drink supply in one location and then ship it the length of the world than it was to manufacture it in some fifty different noncontiguous locations and attempt to purify it on-site. Lindell had never been to the Venezuela plant, so he didn't know much about its layout, but his best guess was that someone had broken into whichever building held the processing equipment and introduced the virus directly into the syrup tanks. From there it had been mixed and bottled and carbonated, and then packaged and shipped around the world. And from there, undoubtedly, it had been consumed.

Of course, a lot of this was just guesswork on his part. He had sat in on the initial meeting between the CEO and the Infectious Agents Squad as the only delegate from the PR department. The one thing the IAS officers had been able to say for certain was that the contamination patterns suggested the virus was closely linked with Coca-Cola and that they intended to continue monitoring the situation.

The rest of the conversation had been very short. Lindell remembered it in its entirety.

"How many people are we talking about here?" the CEO had asked. "A few thousand? A few hundred thousand?"

One of the IAS officers had caught the other's eye, and they had both frowned.

"What? A few million?" the CEO said.

"We wouldn't want to guess, sir."

"More than that?"

"As I say, sir . . ."

"So what are we supposed to do? Are you asking the company to issue a recall order? I presume you people are working on a cure—an antidote or something."

"The virus is lethal. That's all we've been authorized to tell you." His voice shifted to a lower tone. "I can add that it appears to be spreading rapidly, and not only within the Coke-drinking population."

It was a moment before the CEO realized what the officer was implying—that it was too late to do anything at all. That the situation was out of their control. That they would just have to watch from the sidelines and hope for the best.

The CEO let out a sigh. "I'll be motherfucked," he said.

"That may be, sir."

And then the IAS officers had left, and the rest of them had sat around the conference table staring blankly out of their faces until someone broke the silence with a "Jesus H. Christ" and the CEO had pledged them all to secrecy.

Just a few days later, Lindell was working on a contingency press release disavowing any rumors of Coke's connection to the virus when the weblines began reporting that the thing had gone airborne and waterborne. And a day or two after that, he was preparing a crisis statement for the CEO to read to the board of directors when he heard that the epidemic had reached the shores of the United States.

He could hardly see as he drove home that night.

He had died early the next morning.

The document he was looking for now was exactly where he had left it, behind the files in the top drawer of his desk. It was a list of ten names, the ten people who had been present at the meeting with the IAS officers and thus knew about Coca-Cola's liability with regard to the virus, followed by a statement promising that those people would not reveal this knowledge to anyone else, including the many other Coca-Cola employees who were present in the monument district. Six of the ten had signed the document, the six who had so far completed the crossing—which was to say the six who presumably knew this Laura Byrd woman, though for the life of him Lindell couldn't remember her. The other four had yet to appear in the city, and enough time had passed for the six of them who *had* appeared to conclude that they probably wouldn't be coming.

It was the CEO's opinion, and Lindell agreed, that since the document was the only hard evidence of the whole situation, it would be wise to destroy it.

And though no one had plainly directed him to do so, he was fairly certain—more certain than not—that none of the others would mind if he went ahead and took the initiative.

So it was that in the darkness of his office, lit only by the desk lamp, he ran the little fucker through the shredder and watched as the strips of paper fell as a single loose curtain onto the plastic lining of the trash can. There was so much air trapped beneath the lining that the opening had tightened into a sort of sphincter, and the pieces rested on the surface like cheap flakes of goldfish food floating in the water of an aquarium. He had to swat at the bag, pressing the air out, to make them drop to the bottom. A few stray threads of shredded paper drifted onto the floor during all the commotion. He could make out a *Lind* and a *soev* and an *ola*. He was picking them up when he heard a shuffling noise behind him.

"Unusual to see anybody here on a Saturday."

A current ran through Lindell's back, and he straightened up. It was the building's custodian.

"Yeah, sometimes the work just follows you home," Lindell

extemporized. He was holding the trash can in the crook of his arm, pressing it close to his body like a large bird whose wings he was trying to keep from beating. "You know how it is," he added.

"I can't say as I do," the custodian said.

"Well, no." *Shut up and go away.* "I guess you wouldn't, would you?"

The custodian gestured at the trash can. "So do you want me to empty that for you?"

"Oh, no, no. No, I'll do it," Lindell said. "I can do it. But thank you. Thank you very much," and without thinking he brushed past the custodian's cleaning-supply carriage and went down the hall, where he waited for the elevator to carry him to the lobby.

~

So it was that two minutes later he found himself standing outside with a small metal trash can in his hands. What the hell was he supposed to do with it? He couldn't just leave it sitting on the street, where anybody with the curiosity, the patience, and a good bottle of adhesive could scoop it up and paste the document back together. And he was afraid to toss it into one of the city's hundred-some-odd Dumpsters for the same reason: who knew what kind of person might find it? If he brought it home with him, he would have to carry it past the doorman who wore the silver cross around his neck and always asked a thousand questions—*How's life treating you today? Can you believe all this snow we got last night? What's that you're holding there, Mr. Trimble? That trash can with the shredded paper? What's the writing on it say? Something about Coca-Cola?* And if he went back to the office, there was the custodian to deal with.

Perhaps it was only paranoia on his part, but in his experience there was never any shortage of people waiting for the opportunity to fuck someone else over, and he had decided long ago that he would do everything in his power—walk any mile, tell any lie—to ensure that he was always the person who did the fucking and never the person who got fucked.

He was standing in the middle of the sidewalk, which was still slick with ice from the freezing weather. He watched as one, two, three different people lost their footing and fell to the pavement trying to maneuver around him. It was as though he were participating in some kind of effortless carnival game. *Ding! Ding! Ding!* and one after another they went down.

Sooner or later somebody was bound to ask him about the trash can, and so he made his way gingerly onto the strip of snow at the curb and began walking. The cabs were not running. It was useless to try to drive under such conditions. The ice was still hard on the ground and the sun had not come out from behind the clouds all morning. What a totally shit day. Maybe later on, after the foot traffic and the rising temperatures and the first few dare-devil drivers had pounded a lane of slush down the middle of the road, the cabbies would clock in for the afternoon and begin patrolling the city. But until then he would just have to hoof it, trash can or no trash can.

He remembered what it was like when he was growing up and the salt trucks would invariably roll out to blanket the streets after the first couple of inches of snow had fallen. He wished that they were still around, those massive trucks with their massive drivers. But of course not. They were just another one of the millions of things that had been relinquished to the other world. He blamed Laura Byrd. She had never known any salt truck drivers, and so there were no salt truck drivers in the city. She had never known any software designers, and so there were no software designers. She had known plenty of petty little customer service types, and street people, and dirty screaming kids. But she had never known Lindell's wife or his girlfriend or his poor dead mother, and so he had to make do without his family.

Instead, look what he was left with—what they were all left with. There across the street from him, for instance, a woman had taken up a slumping posture on a cracked bus bench, where she was playing with a red rubber ball. Behind the window of her apartment, another woman was singing to herself as she slipped her arms into the kind of orange nylon vest worn by school safety officers. Inside a restaurant, a man was using a white plastic fork to eat what looked like a plate of tuna salad on iceberg lettuce, a paper napkin tucked into his collar like a bib. What a sorry lot.

Of the whole group of them, he was the only one who had had the good sense to muster everyone together in one place after the city emptied out.

What do you do when the world has dropped out from under you and you want to attract attention? You take a gun, and you fire it.

You would think that somebody else would have been bright enough to figure that out, but no.

Some guy was standing on the corner of the street handing out newspapers. Lindell tried to duck him, but the man stepped into his path.

"Some weather we're having lately, isn't it?"

Oh great, he thought. A weather conversation. "Yes, it is."

"So can I ask what you're carrying in the trash can?"

"Nothing important. Nothing unusual."

The man grinned and passed his hand through the air. "Headline: Man Lugs Trash Can Through the Snow, Refuses to Explain."

Just then, a woman came up beside the newspaperman with a couple of styrofoam cups in her hands. She kissed him on the cheek. "All they had was decaf, so I brought us some hot chocolate instead," she said.

Lindell chose this moment to make his escape. The newspaperman and his girlfriend didn't try to stop him. He crossed Park Street and climbed carefully into the snow-heaped clearing above the sidewalks, where a few scattered trees stood alongside the monument. It was surprisingly difficult to keep his balance carrying the trash can. Ordinarily, when he felt himself slipping, he would have thrown his arms out as a counterweight, but with the trash can in his hands he had to use his elbows and shoulders instead, jerking them this way and that. He must have looked like a complete fool. When he reached the top of the stairs, he ventured off the walkway into the grass. He could hear the satisfying crunch of fresh snow beneath his feet. The monument, rising above the white field and the black footpaths, looked like a pin stuck through a giant map—which in a way, he supposed, it was.

There were a few dozen other people in the clearing, including a guy who was trying to ride his bicycle through the snow, a couple of bird-watchers, and a ring of those parapsychology fanatics he had been noticing more and more often around the city recently, six deluded nitwits linking their hands together and attempting to beam their thoughts out to Laura Byrd. He managed to avoid them by skirting along the outside row of benches and picnic tables. He broke out through the opposite corner of the park, leaving a dotted line of footprints behind him, along with a dish-shaped circle where he had put the trash can down so that he could adjust his pants.

For the past few weeks he had been conducting long conversations about the end of the world in his head. They were simple discussions that, if he wasn't careful, quickly degenerated into savage arguments and then into swiftly moving imaginary debates in which various people, sometimes judges and prosecuting attorneys, sometimes just disembodied voices, accused him of bearing direct responsibility for the effects of the virus. They insisted that he ought to have done something to halt its spread, or at least to have warned people that it was coming. *Why didn't you?* they needled him. *Why didn't you do anything?* But it wasn't his fault. It wasn't. Fuck you. He was just a regular guy who happened to land a public relations gig with Coca-Cola. Public relations was all about generating or occasionally deflecting interest in your particular brand and then channeling that interest down the most appropriate pathway. Generating and deflecting interest: that was all he had done. What thinking person could blame him for it?

It was true that he might have broken his vow and told the press what was going on, announced that the virus was being disseminated by way of his company's product—*we're very sorry* and all that sort of thing—but what good would it have done? The virus had already spread beyond all its original vectors. Coca-Cola or no Coca-Cola, there was no way of stopping it.

He didn't see how anything he might have done could have changed what happened in the end. And that was what the accusers in his head really wanted from him, wasn't it? They wanted change—a change in the fate of the world—and they wanted him to be the one who brought that change about.

Well, it was too much to ask. They could all go to hell.

"You can all go to hell." He said it out loud.

He was going down an open set of stairs, on a side street that had been used so rarely since the weather changed that the individual steps were almost impossible to distinguish beneath the snow. He held the trash can in one arm and used the other to steady himself, stomping and sliding his way to the bottom. Then he cut through an alley between two high buildings and turned right onto what he could tell had once been a major avenue. He took the sidewalk past an automotive supply shop and a toy store and a real estate office, then past a newspaper kiosk, and then past a whole foods store and a coffee bar, all of them abandoned in the days following the evacuation. The farther he moved from the center of the monument district, the fewer people he saw. The snow seemed to be getting deeper and deeper.

He realized he was heading toward the river. Though he hadn't planned it that way, he figured that it would be as good a place as any to get rid of the trash can. He would let the current carry it out of the city, past the streets and the buildings, past anyone who might be expected to discover it, until it sank into whichever lake or ocean or larger river eventually swallowed the water.

As a boy, on empty afternoons, it had been one of his habits to hike to the creeks and rivers that lay within walking distance of his house. He would throw everything he found along the shore into the water: plastic spoons, baby dolls, pencils, sticks, pieces of waxed cardboard—anything that would float, basically. Then he would try to hit the things and make them capsize, using stones and chunks of dirt. He called the game Bombardment. He remembered the long marches he had to take through the strips of high yellow grass that ran along the highway to get to the river, and the way the water always moved more rapidly toward the center than it did along the shore, and he remembered the day he caught a minnow in the shallows and poured it out of his hands into a Coke bottle, screwing the cap on tight, then slung the bottle end over end into the quickest part of the current. The minnow kept trying to swim away, thrashing around so that the bottle rocked back and forth on the river's surface. Lindell felt a giant surge of horror and pity rearing up inside him—*poor fish*—and so he threw off his backpack and waded into the water and almost drowned trying to reach the damned thing. It was moving too fast for him, though, and eventually he lost sight of it. He must have coughed up half a gallon of green water when he finally reached the shore. He spent the next three days trying to smack the rest of the river out of his ears.

What a sentimental pussy he had been.

It was amazing the things you would remember if you let your mind wander.

This particular river lay at the bottom of a gentle slope. As he plowed through the drifts of snow, the trash can swung and rattled in his arms, the plastic lining breathing in and out as it caught the breeze and let it go, and caught and let it go again. He could see the suspension bridge that joined the two sides of the river together, its cables white on black with the snow that was covering the steel. He was only a hundred yards or so from the water now. It was obvious that the still places closest to the shore had frozen over. At first he thought that the whole enormous river had crystallized, but when he listened he could make out a quiet swirling and spilling sound. As he looked more closely, he spotted a dark channel of water flowing down the middle of the ice.

He walked to the end of a wooden dock and climbed down the ladder. The ice was thick enough to support his weight, and it did not groan or snap as he made his way toward the center of the river. He paused when he reached the gash.

There was nobody in sight. The wind was blowing softly.

He had walked so far that he imagined some sort of ceremony might be in order, but then he realized what he was proposing—a ceremony for the disposal of a rinky-dink trash can—and he thought, To hell with it. He threw the trash can into the current and watched as it rolled over, gulped at the water, and sank a couple of inches, but kept gliding downstream. A few shreds of paper drifted out of the bag and snagged against the ice at his feet. He was able to read the *worn* from "sworn" and the *cul* from "culpability." Then he kicked at the ice, and the river tore the pieces away. The trash can kept drifting on.

His sense of relief was immediate. He felt the way a dam must feel when its gates are finally opened, the way a bomb must feel when its pin is finally tripped. The document had been the last— and, as far as he knew, the *only*—piece of tangible evidence connecting him to the whole end-of-the-world affair. As long as he and the others kept quiet about it, no one would ever know what had happened.

And so, in a sense, nothing *had* ever happened.

That was the way it worked.

The trash can had already vanished downstream. He couldn't see it anymore, not the slightest trace or sign.

He had ended up at the river purely by chance, and he had no other business to complete there, so he turned around and climbed the ladder back onto the dock.

The snow was just as thick on the uphill climb as it had been when he was going the other way, but he found it much easier to make the hike with both his hands free. Why, it suddenly occurred to him, had he taken the trouble to haul the trash can all that way when he could have removed the bag from the can and simply jettisoned the rest? It would have saved him a whole lot of effort, that was for sure.

Well, there was certainly enough idiocy in the city. Maybe it was catching.

There was no sun for him to track through the sky, but it did seem to him that the light filtering through the clouds was slowly growing dimmer. By the time he caught sight of the monument again, evening had fallen over the city. The streetlights flickered on and made everything glow: the bus benches, the fire hydrants, and the millions of leaves on the thousands of trees, carrying their hilly little deposits of white snow.

He was almost at the door of his building when he heard the sound of footsteps stealing up beside him. "Well, if it isn't Mr. Cups-Runneth-Over again. How are you doing, my friend? Has this freezing cold day of ours taken any of the son of a bitch out of you? Tell you what, then, why don't you loan me a few dollars? Just enough for a hot meal and a cheap cup of coffee. And 'cheap' is the operative word here, am I right? Am I? Yeah, you know what I'm saying."

Lindell lowered his head and pretended not to listen.

It never failed. He could walk halfway across the city, accomplish everything he set out to accomplish, wear his soles down, tire his legs out, and wash his mind clean of any sense of culpability, and when at last he had made it home and was ready to take the keys out of his pocket, there he would be, the man with the black gloves, holding his hands out and begging for change.

Twelve

THE BIRDS

The spare tent was missing. Laura made a careful search of the supplies, raking through the tools in the back of the sledge, but it wasn't there. Several times she accidentally snuffed the candle flame out with her sleeve and had to light the wick again. The shadows twitched back and forth in the bound space of the storage hutch, swaying against the walls. She had not taken the tent out at the station—she was sure of that. And she didn't think she had unloaded it into the cache she left on the ice shelf, though she was so tired by then that she might have done anything, frankly. But she was damned if she could imagine where else it might be. Back at the hut? Inside one of the crevasses?

It wasn't until she slipped the latch back into place that she remembered the accident she had sustained traveling down the tongue of the glacier toward the station, the open gash she had dammed over with a piece of plywood, the way she had stumbled about in the falling snow feeling for anything that might have fallen out during the crash. She was absolutely sure, suddenly, that that was where she had lost the tent. She might have been observing herself through the lens of a camera, watching her hands as they probed at the ground, missing the tent by a matter of inches. That was how clear it all was.

Just a few days ago, when she was climbing the great curved slab of polished snow that connected the ice shelf to the penguin roost, she would never have guessed that a lost tent would be so

high on her list of worries. There had been so many other questions on her mind: What had happened to her skis? How would
she navigate her way around the bottom of the cliffside to get to
the knoll? Would she find the radio transmitter there? And even
if she did, who would possibly be waiting at the other end to
answer her?

But shortly after she topped the ridge, on her first night within
listening distance of the penguins, her tent's soft coil gave out.
She woke to find the walls rimed with frost, distinct blue-gray
swirls of it that sparked and glistened in the candlelight. The
sweat had frozen around the neck of her sleeping bag into a thick
manacle of ice, and she had to break through it with a few hard
jerks of her shoulders in order to climb out. Her clothing had
hardened into a single bloomlike mass. She spent an hour or
more pounding it loose and trying to fit herself inside. Then,
when she was finally dressed, she dismantled the tent by hand. It
took much longer than she would have expected. There was no
way for her to get to the soft coil without ripping the fabric
apart—and, in any case, she would have had no idea how to fix
the thing without a replacement coil anyway—so she packed the
tent away and used up the rest of the day threading the sledge
through the cracks, rockfalls, and pressure ridges around the
base of the cliff. Usually she was able to retain a little warmth
from her night's sleep, but not this time. She was so much colder
than she had been before. She would never have imagined that
such a thing was possible.

The next night was worse, and the night after that was worse
still. She had to rely on what little body heat she produced to
keep herself warm, along with whatever fire she could make by
burning the Primus stove, though she tried to use it no more than
a couple of hours a day for fear of what would happen when the
fuel was finally consumed. The coldest weeks of winter had set
in, and the temperature had dipped to seventy degrees below
zero—more than a hundred degrees of frost. Already the sweat

she had generated inside her sleeping bag had turned it into a rigid, icy box. She was not sure how long it took her to thaw her way into the bag each night, but it couldn't have been less than an hour. She would jam her feet through the neck and slowly work her way down, stopping every few minutes to rub the muscle pangs from her legs until she melted a tunnel into the ice. She was barely able to squeeze her body inside.

Finally she would fall asleep, though from exhaustion rather than comfort. It was a poor, patternless sleep, not shallow so much as fragmentary, and it lasted no better than six hours. She would wake numerous times during the night with the force of her shivering and with the cramping that seemed to grip her piece by piece: her legs, her stomach, her shoulders. Then a time would come which she would decide to call morning, and she would start the day again, climbing out of her sleeping bag and plugging the mouth with her spare clothing so that it wouldn't freeze back together.

It took her four days to reach the rookery from the edge of the ice shelf, which was three days longer than she had expected. The ground at the base of the cliff was riddled with pits and crevices, barn-sized heaps of rock, slopes that rose suddenly from flat ice to insurmountable angles. Every time she thought she was approaching the knoll, she would come to some impossible place in the ice and have to turn back.

Often, she dozed off while she was marching. She wouldn't wake until she tripped over her own legs, or bumped into the side of the cliff, or put her foot through a rift or a crevasse. It was a miracle that she didn't kill herself.

Occasionally, when the wind dropped, she would hear the hollering of the penguins, a harsh, braying sound like a thousand doors opening on a thousand rusty hinges. Sometimes it seemed as though the birds were only a few feet away. But then the ice would rise up in front of her or the wind would begin to sob again and the sound would vanish.

193

Finally, a few hours into her fourth day in the harness, as she was pulling the sledge deeper and deeper into a ravine she could sense was slowly drawing together (another dead end, she thought), she discovered a break in the cliff. It was roofed over with snow, but it was just wide enough, just high enough, for her to fit the sledge through.

A rabbit's hole.

She ducked through the opening, came out the other side, and suddenly she was in the rookery. She couldn't believe it.

The penguins noticed her before she noticed them. They began gabbling and beating their paddles against their sides. The noise echoed against the barrier. There seemed to be fifty or sixty of them, maybe as many as a hundred, calling out to one another and rocking from side to side like fat black metronomes. They did not approach her, but they did not move away, either. They must have been used to the presence of human beings by now, she thought. After all, teams of scientists had been studying them for more than a century. As she was watching, one of them scooted into the sea, a long, curved finger of which reached all the way into the cove. It leapt back out clacking its beak around some little piece of food it had caught and waddled over to the others. The breeze carried the high, brave stench of their droppings. The smell was only barely softened by the cold.

The last free-swimming whale had been sighted more than thirty years ago, around the time Laura was born, and it was the general scientific consensus that the creatures had all but died out, just like the elephants and the gorillas and all the other great mammals before them. It was possible that there were a few isolated specimens still living in those scattered sections of the ocean that had not yet been cultivated for food, but it seemed unlikely. Certainly Laura had not seen any there in the Antarctic, and it had been her job to look. The continent still hosted herds of leopard seals and immense flocks of skua—though not, apparently, here in the cove—but it was the penguins who were actually thriving, living off the krill the whales were no longer alive to consume. They were as large as Laura had always heard they were. She wouldn't have been surprised if some of them weighed more than a hundred pounds.

The moon was partially hidden behind an exposure of black rock, but the light was still bright enough for her to make out the landscape. She was tired and sluggish, an old woman suddenly, frozen into her stiff old body, and she wanted nothing more than to lie down and close her eyes. But she knew that if she did she would fall asleep, and she couldn't allow herself to do that. Not yet.

She set off with the spare aerial in her hand. There was unusually little drift inside the knoll. Maybe it had all been compacted into ice. Or maybe a shift in the wind had blown it out to sea. In either case, it didn't take her long to find the remnants of the hut—a heap of cracked plastic, wood fragments, and twisted metal tucked inside a shallow scoop in the rock.

It looked as though the building had been crushed by a serac or an avalanche, some great chunk of ice and snow that had calved off the side of the mountain and smashed to pieces. If that was the case, though, it must have landed pretty damn hard. She could see pieces of jagged ice stretching in a great concussion ring around the hut—a thirty-foot halo of rubble. It must have made a sound like the detonation of a bomb when it landed. She could only imagine the upheaval it had caused among the penguins. She pictured a hundred birds diving madly into the ocean.

She felt infinitely tired all of a sudden. Her eyes fell closed, and she forced herself to open them. What was she looking for? Oh yes, the radio.

She made her way carefully through the debris, picking around in the wood and plastic and metal. She couldn't find any real trace of the transmitter, only a beaten aluminum panel that might or might not have been part of the housing. No doubt the thing had shattered into a thousand pieces when the building collapsed. Which meant that her trip across the ice shelf—the crevasse, the frostbite, the days and days and weeks of hauling—had been utterly meaningless.

Meaningless. Pointless. Hollow.

Sleepy Hollow.

Sleep, sleep, sleep, sleep.

She tossed the spare aerial onto the sediment heap, then thought better and retrieved it. What could she possibly use it for? A depth measure? An ice gouge? She didn't know, but she hated to throw it away. In truth, she hated to throw *anything* away. She had been accumulating unnecessary objects around herself all her life: knickknacks, old magazines, twigs she had snapped off of dying trees. Occasionally she would look at them, pick them up, even turn them over in her fingers, and she wouldn't be able to remember where they came from. They were like those skeletonized images from her early childhood that sometimes flashed into her mind when her thoughts began to drift, disconnected from anything that might put them into context. Walking into a brightly lit room with her hair tickling her forehead. Her father lifting a heavy jar out of a cabinet. A dog with a red bow pasted onto its nose. These knickknacks, these memories—where had she collected them all? Her apartment back home was practically an abandoned city of worthless objects: acorns, plastic keys, and ten thousand other things she had no earthly use for. But she had to admit that she liked having them there. At some point, when you were fourteen or fifteen, before you reached adulthood or knew who you were, you had to determine whether you were going to be the sort of person who held tight to every single thing that passed through your life, no matter how insignificant it was, or the sort of person who set it all adrift. Life was easier on the people who were willing to relax their grip, but she had decided to be the other sort of person, the sort who wouldn't let go, and she had done her best to live up to that decision.

There was no sign that Puckett and Joyce had made it as far as the rookery—no abandoned equipment, no sledge tracks. She doubted she would see them again. But then she had guessed as much long ago.

She set the tent up on a patch of hard ice, unloading the sleeping bag, the Primus stove, and the rest of her cooking supplies. Her hands were so numb that she was unable to drive the stakes into the ground. Instead, she used four rocks she found lying in a pile at the base of the cliff, weighing down the tent's inside corners.

She couldn't help thinking of the secret fortress she had played in the summer she was ten years old. That was what she had called it, "the secret fortress," though it was really just a free-standing public restroom in a section of the riverfront that had been fenced off and sold to developers. For a few months, though, until it was demolished to make way for an office complex, she and her best friend, Minny Rings, had gone there almost every afternoon to talk about boys and hide from their parents and plot their lives together. Sometimes they would pretend they were grown women, mothers with jobs and families, sometimes spies or basketball players or marine biologists. Laura still remembered the day they had ducked through the loose corner of wire fence and found the bricks and tile and porcelain of the fortress flattened into a surprisingly small heap. The bits and pieces had looked so flimsy and pathetic there, as though they never could have sheltered anything at all, not even a row of toilets, metal sinks, and hot air driers, much less the enormously complicated worlds the two of them had imagined. They had looked, in fact, like the debris of the hut did now, which must have been why she was thinking about them in the first place.

But before the fortress was knocked down, she and Minny had walked there nearly every day for the whole of June and July, excepting only the week Laura spent at summer camp. Usually they would meet at Minny's house, cut through the woods in back of the grocery store, and follow the long gray band of the access road to the river, balancing toe by toe over the rocks that lined the water. The fortress was hidden from the sidewalk by a thick belt of mixed trees, and as long as they were careful not to be seen beforehand, they could slip underneath the fence and make their way onto the construction site without being spotted. They were just two girls playing by the river. No one would interrupt them. The fortress's door was unlocked along with the high, tilting windows, and they never had any trouble getting inside.

"Which do you like better: summer or winter?" Minny would ask once they were alone. This was her favorite type of question. "Say it's a clear day. It isn't raining or snowing, and the sun is out."

"I don't know. Winter, I guess. If you ask me in the winter, I'll say summer, and if you ask me in the summer, I'll say winter."

"I choose winter, too," Minny said. "Here's another one. Who do you like better: your mom or your dad?"

"That one's tough. It's like winter and summer, I guess. I like whichever one isn't around at the time." Laura boosted herself onto the rim of the sink. "I can tell you one thing, I like *your* mom better than *your* dad."

"Me, too," Minny said. "My dad is a jerk. Do you know what he did yesterday? He dumped the ashtray over on purpose, right onto the carpet, and he made me clean it up. I didn't knock it over, and that's what I told him: 'I didn't do it.' But he said, 'I didn't ask whether you did it or not. I told you to clean it up, young lady.' He's always doing stuff like that. One time—" Minny cocked her head. "Hey, do you hear that?"

"Hear what?"

"Listen."

Laura shifted her attention to the upper end of her hearing register. She heard it—a fine droning hum that beat rapidly at the air. She hopped down from the sink. The sound was coming from the skylight in the center of the room. She stood beneath it looking up, and Minny stood next to her. There was a wasp inside, bumping against the barrier of the glass. Its wings were a nearly invisible brown blur, and its stinger was floating beneath its body in the stately, motionless way of a diving bell on the underside of a boat.

"You're never going to get out through there," Laura said. She supposed she was talking to the wasp, though she knew better than to think that the wasp was listening. To Minny she said, "We should try to help it."

"*No way*. I am *not* touching a wasp."

"You don't have to touch it. You don't have to get anywhere near it. Just hold the door open, and I'll do the rest."

Minny glanced at the skylight. "If you want to get stung, I'm not going to stop you. I don't know why they put that thing in here to begin with. It's not like it lets any real light through." Then she went to the door and pulled it open, steering herself behind as she pivoted back toward the corner. Her voice came out from inside the closed triangle of space. "Okay. I'm ready."

"Chicken," Laura said.

"Fine by me," said Minny. "At least I won't get stung."

"Neither will I," Laura said. "I'm trying to help him." She knew she was being foolish, but she couldn't help herself. It was just that she felt so bad for the wasp: all it wanted was a way out, a way back into the sunlight, but the only thing it knew how to do was keep banging into the glass. She had to coax it away from the skylight. That was the first step. The problem was that it was too high for her to reach. She considered snapping at it with her T-shirt, but she was afraid that if she took the shirt off, the white skin of her chest and stomach would offer the wasp a target it couldn't resist. Instead, she took a paper towel from the bundle beneath the sink, worked it into a ball, and threw it at the wasp as gently as she could. Its wings buzzed, and its stinger curved angrily under its waist. She threw a second time, and then a third, aiming for the center of the glass.

After a few more tries, she managed to drive the wasp out of the skylight. It landed halfway across the room on the ceiling, dropped a few inches, and landed in the same spot again. She tried to reason with it. "Listen, I'm trying to help you. Just trust me and I'll let you outside."

From behind the door Minny said, "He can't understand you, you know."

"Yeah, well, most people say that cats can't understand you either, but you still talk to yours."

"Cats are smart. Wasps are morons."

"Not all cats are smart. Maybe not all wasps are morons."

But this one seemed to be. Laura kept trying to direct it toward the open door. Twice it settled on one of the windowpanes, tapping and vibrating and agitating from side to side until she was able to drive it back into the room. Occasionally it would make a dive for her and she would have to duck, covering her face with her hands. "Don't sting me, don't sting me, don't sting me!" The wasp always looped back up to the ceiling before it touched her.

The air carried a slight odor of ammonia that became much stronger above the grate in the center of the floor. It was the kind of smell that must have been like poison to a wasp—or to this one, at least, which steered carefully away from it. Whenever the wasp plunged toward her, Laura would retreat to the grate, and it would swerve aside.

Eventually, after what must have been dozens of paper towels, the wasp found the doorway of the building as if by accident. Suddenly it was gone.

The buzzing noise was pinched out by the breeze as it disappeared into the branches.

Laura sank against the wall, her face covered with sweat. "You can come out now," she said.

The door made Minny's voice sound unusually quiet. "Are you talking to him or me?"

"To you."

Minny shut the door. She walked over to Laura and leaned up against her, resting her arm on her shoulder. "That took just about forever," she said.

All these years later and Laura still remembered her answer: "Not forever, but long enough."

~

Which would make a wonderful epitaph, she now thought.

She was a world and a half away from the fortress, a world and a half away from everyone and everywhere she had ever been. The tent was impossibly cold. Tiny teardrop-shaped pendants of ice fell onto her chest and stomach as she shivered, and she had to brush them off before they melted against the heat of her skin. She could hear something rattling and cracking whenever she moved—either the sleeping bag or her own body. She was too tired, frankly, to tell the difference.

She knew that she had slept at least sporadically, because she could remember dreaming, and a person didn't dream unless she slept, did she? But she was so tired and so cold that the membrane separating her waking life from her sleeping life had become porous. Each side had begun to leak into the other. She found it increasingly hard to differentiate between the two.

She had dreamed that she was in her office at the Coca-Cola complex, for instance, watching a ribbon of sunlight slant across the floor, which meant that it must have been late afternoon, sometime in the spring. So why was she so cold, she wondered, and what was she doing in her sleeping bag? She wasn't supposed to sleep at work. It was the kind of thing that could get her fired. Maybe she was sick, she thought. Maybe she had been sent to the nurse's office at her high school, where the mattress crackled beneath her, gradually filling with ice. There was so much ice that the sheets crystallized in overlapping scales. She imagined that her mother was feeding her raisins as she lay in bed with a cold, dropping them one by one through the long straw that curved and dipped like a snake on its way to her mouth. "Open the tunnel," her mother said. "Here comes the train. Chooga-chooga-chooga-chooga—woo, wooo!" But the raisins were alive, and not actually raisins at all. Laura wasn't quite sure what they were. It was obvious, though, that they didn't want to fall. They put out dozens of black pincered legs to slow their descent. Thank God for the harness and the rope, she thought. The walls of the crevasse were so slippery, so steep. Who knew how deep it went? And the tent was like a hot-air balloon, barely tethered to the ground. She knew that she had to feed herself if she was ever going to get well again. She had to exercise and take better care of her body. That was what her mother had told her. Oat bran. Green vegetables. Bicycles. She dreamed that she was exercising on the treadmill at her gym, and then she felt something bulbous and hard shaking around in the bottoms of her shoes, and when she took them off and overturned them, her toes fell out like so many pebbles. And she woke up, and she was not surprised.

She had long since lost all feeling in her extremities. Even the nerves of her teeth had been killed by the frost. She would never have known she was clenching them together at all if it weren't for the spikes of tenderness she felt in her gums, thin needles of pain inside a surrounding aura of pressure. When she finally summoned up the resolve to check herself for frostbite, shortly after she returned from picking through the remnants of the hut, she discovered that the toes of her left foot were nothing more than ugly gray-black knots, beyond all promise of recovery. So were the fourth and fifth toes of her right foot. The tips of her fingers were in bad shape, too—terrible shape, really—along with her right cheek and the whole of her left ear. But she was able to treat them with a hemodynamic salve and bandages, and she had some small hope that they would get better in time.

How she would begin her trek back to the shelter, though, she couldn't imagine. She would never be able to make it over the shelf without help. And where on earth would help come from? The radio was broken, the sledge was broken, the entire world had been emptied out.

In addition to which she had taken no care to provide a return route for herself.

It was something of a miracle that she had made it as far as the cove in the first place. She wasn't sure she could find her way back onto the ice through the maze of cracks and pressure ridges that surrounded the rookery, much less to the far side of Ross Island. Hell, she was barely even able to find her way out of the tent at night. She would climb out of her sleeping bag sometimes in a high fever and grope for the opening as though she had never used her hands in her life.

Who was she? she thought. She was nobody special. When she died, there would be no one to remember her. The simple truth was that her strength—or whatever combination of muscle, luck, and willpower had driven her from the hut to the shelter and from the shelter onto the open ice and across the bay—was gone. Played out. Finished.

Finished. Finnish. Danish. Swedish. Meatball.

She gave a tiny, puffing laugh, but the effort hurt her stomach.

She could hear the emperors trumpeting beneath the barrier wall. The last time she went outside, to stake down a loose corner of the tent, they had been huddled together with their backs to the wind. Most of them were carrying eggs on the flaps of their feet, gripping them beneath the soft rounded bald patches on the undersides of their guts, which insulated the eggs from the cold. The ones that didn't have eggs were balancing egg-sized lumps of ice there, dead little worlds that they protected as avidly as though they were real. She had read about this behavior before, how the penguins were so desperate to incubate their young that they would seize on anything that even slightly resembled an egg. Stones, ice chunks, masses of snow—it didn't matter. Every so often one of the penguins nursing an actual egg would let go of it in order to dive beneath the water for food, and the others would drop their pieces of rock and ice and squabble over it until one of them had succeeded in tucking it under its gut. They always preferred the real eggs to the fake ones, which suggested that they were merely using the fake eggs as comfort devices, the way that mothers whose children have died will clutch the pillows they slept on or the stuffed animals they ported around with them, holding them to their faces and breasts in order to remember what it was like when they were alive.

Once, though, a behavioral scientist had placed a polished plastic canteen next to the penguins, a fluorescent orange sphere he filled with instant coffee, and they had abandoned their eggs—all of them, and all at once—to fight over it. They must have thought it was the most beautiful egg they had ever seen, the scientist speculated in his journal. The egg they realized they had always been waiting for. The egg of the future.

The rusty sound of the penguins' voices stopped suddenly, crested again, then slowly died away. Laura listened to the slapping of their wings as she lay shivering in the tent. She was hungry, or at least she knew she ought to be, but she couldn't steel herself to break out of her sleeping bag. The ice had frozen around the opening in a thick collar, and it would be a terrible struggle for her to push her way through.

If she didn't freeze to death, she was almost certainly going to starve to death, and she knew it.

Laura Byrd, the inscription would read, followed by the date she was born and the date she had died. *Laura Byrd. Not forever, but long enough.*

Filaments of frost and snow crossed the floor of the tent, blown into straight lines by the draft. Most of it had been swept inside when she opened the flap, but some of it was simply the accumulation of her own breath, which froze into a white powder as soon as it touched the air, settling on the floor in a long plume.

White powder. The Coca-Cola Corporation had initiated what they called their "white powder" campaign just a month or so before Laura left for Antarctica. The campaign had followed on the heels of the last big germ scare, during which a few thousand people around the country, mostly in small houses scattered along grayed-out highways, had found packages filled with the pale, almost colorless powders of smallpox, anthrax, and scarlet fever on their doorsteps. The deliveries had stopped after only a week, as suddenly as they had started, with no one imprisoned or apprehended. But soon after, people in their millions began receiving stiff cardboard envelopes in the mail that spilled a grainy white powder onto their hands when they opened them. Police departments, hospitals, and emergency warning centers were inundated with phone calls. Thousands of city and county governments activated their terrorism-alert beacons. The powder was quickly revealed to be a harmless laundry detergent with a coupon nested inside, which read, "Clean Up with the Coca-Cola Sweepstakes. Buy One Two-Liter Bottle, Get a Second One Free."

The corporation had been chastised for the recklessness of the sweepstakes by both Houses of Congress and the editorial pages of several hundred newspapers. They had released a statement apologizing for any disruption the campaign might have caused, and they had assured the public that such results were entirely unintentional. But sales of two-liter Coke bottles tripled in the weeks following the incident, and sales of all other Coca-Cola products doubled.

Guerrilla publicity, they called it.

Laura must have fallen asleep again, because when she opened her eyes she realized she was not listening to a discussion about the white powder campaign at all. She was not in the conference room that adjoined her office or anywhere inside the Coca-Cola complex. She was still lying in her tent. The glaze of ice had melted from around her eyes while she was sleeping, and the light was brighter than it had been in months. She could see everything with a remarkable clarity. The silver pan of the

Primus stove, crusted over with a light brown syrup. The fanlike patterns of frost on the walls. The double row of black stitches marching over the dome of the tent like a procession of ants. There was a half-eaten bar of pemmican in the corner, notched with the impressions of her teeth, and an unopened bag of granola beside it. A popcorn-shaped knot of ice had formed around the zipper of her sleeping bag.

She was taken aback not only by how much she could see, but by how much she could hear. It had never occurred to her that the light could improve her hearing as well as her vision, and yet undeniably it had. A penguin, for instance, was snapping delicately at its feathers. The fabric of the tent was booming in the wind. A vast tide of krill went swimming past beneath the ice.

Even her heartbeat was clear to her, regular and strong, as though she were holding her breath somewhere deep under water. The more closely she listened to it, the louder it seemed to become, until she could feel it keeping time throughout her body.

It was everywhere—in her toes, her stomach, even the tips of her ears. Amazing.

She shut her eyes and listened. Something unusual was happening to her. She was stretched around her heart, taut and firm like the skin of a drum, a perfectly sealed membrane that was beating, beating, beating. The heat of her blood was moving through her in millions of waves, more than she could possibly contain, and yet somehow she did contain them. She couldn't understand how she had become so big. She was as large as a forest, as large as a city. Her heart was the size of a lake, and she was swimming in it. She couldn't hear anything else. The sound filled her until she shook, and then it filled the tent, and then it filled the world.

Thirteen

THE HEARTBEAT

Once again Minny couldn't sleep. How many nights had she lain in bed beside Luka, barely touching his back with the side of her arm as she waited for the darkness to pull her under? Not every night, but often enough. She had tried all the various remedies people suggested—melatonin, red wine, exercise, chamomile tea—but none of them seemed to work. They made her body drowsy, but not her mind. And her mind, let's face it, was the problem. Her mind was a roulette wheel, rattling and spinning in endless circles, and there she was standing beside it, watching the bright silver ball of her consciousness as it bounced first one way and then another.

That was what insomnia was, after all—an excess of consciousness, an excess of life. Ever since she could remember, she had treated her life as an act of will, the you-can-do-anything-you-set-your-mind-to philosophy, but she couldn't *will* herself to fall asleep. The only way to fall asleep was not to care whether you fell asleep or not: you had to *relinquish* your will. Most people seemed to think that you fell asleep and then started dreaming, but as far as Minny could tell, the process was exactly the reverse—you started dreaming and that enabled you to fall asleep. She wasn't able to start dreaming, though, because she couldn't stop thinking about the fact that she wasn't already asleep. And anything that called her attention to that fact made it more likely that she would keep thinking about it, and a million little snowdrops of nervous tension would bud open inside her, and thus she wouldn't start dreaming, and thus she wouldn't be able to sleep.

What a mess.

She listened to Luka breathing in the slow rhythm of his own sleep. She had heard the sound so many times that she could have identified it in a police lineup. *Listen carefully, ma'am. Take your time. Is this the sound of the man you're looking for?* "Yes, that's him, officer. He says he loves me, but I don't know why."

Which was exactly what he himself had said the last time she pressed him for a reason: "I love you, but I don't know why. I just do. Shouldn't that be enough?"

And it should have been, but the question kept needling at her.

One, two, three—sleep, she said to herself, but of course it didn't work.

This restlessness of hers, the way her mind kept turning over on itself as she lay in bed—it was kind of like the city, wasn't it? The entire population was suffering from an excess of consciousness, an excess of life. That was her diagnosis. They were passing out their days in a place somewhere between life and death, in that drifting stage after the lights went out but before sleep came over them.

A city of people who were waiting to dream.

A city of insomniacs.

She moved her feet in slow, overlapping circles, a nervous gesture she had picked up around the time her parents divorced, when she was fifteen years old and just beginning high school. The friction warmed her feet, which were always a bit cold. She found the repetitive swaying motion comforting. Her mother used to pass by her bedroom and see her rocking back and forth beneath the blankets and shut the door, chastising her, "If you can't respect the other people living in this household, at least have some respect for your own body, dear," which always made

Minny laugh. She loved her mother and still saw her once or twice a week. Every so often, she even caught sight of her father, eating in some cafeteria or moving around on the far side of a crowd, maybe balancing a pack of playing cards on the rim of a glass in the back room of a bar. He always greeted her with the same look of surprise mingled with terror, then fled before she could say anything to him. Shortly after the divorce, he had put a gun to his chest and committed suicide. He must have imagined that he was escaping from everything he had ever known. Certainly he had never expected to see his daughter again.

She didn't blame him for running away.

She understood that she was better off than any number of other people in the city. Take Luka, for instance, who hadn't seen either of his parents since he had died, or at least since she had met him—just the two or three neighbors he had known and the handful of students he had taught during the one short summer he had spent with Laura.

Minny heard him mumble something in his sleep, and she turned over onto her other side. Her ear was resting on the palm of her hand, which was wedged between her head and the pillow. For a moment she thought she heard someone knocking on the door. Then she realized it was only the sound of her heart beating. And then she realized that it couldn't be the sound of her heart beating.

She had never been one of those people who went around the city with an invisible heart keeping time in her ears. She had always assumed that such people were undergoing some sort of mass hallucination. They had fixed their minds on something they either wished for or remembered (Luka would have teased the pun out: *something they had learned by heart*). And then, abracadabra, they imagined it was actually there.

But the beating she heard was unmistakable. *Ba-dum. Ba-dum. Ba-dum.*

She lay there listening to the sound for what must have been hours, and when finally she opened her eyes again, the light had risen outside her window and it was just as unmistakably morning.

~

The heartbeat did not go away. Several days passed and still Minny could not stop listening to it.

As it turned out, she wasn't alone. No one in the city failed to notice it. It seemed to fill the air like a soft rain of ashes—so abundant that it revealed the smallest motions of the wind, yet so light that it barely tingled as it touched their skin. Everywhere she went, Minny saw people reflexively putting their hands to their chests as they waited alone in the lobbies of movie theaters or sat talking to one another in crowded restaurants. She knew that they were feeling for that old familiar rhythm.

Luka wrote about the phenomenon one day in the *Sims Sheet*. He headlined the article, HEART BEATS, PEOPLE LISTEN. It was a man-on-the-street piece, profiling some half dozen people he had confronted with a pair of questions on the subject: What did the heartbeat mean? And, Where did it come from? As usual there was no consensus of opinion. A man who identified himself as Martin Campbell said that the pattern of the heartbeat was familiar to him, but he couldn't figure out where he remembered it from. He was only sure that it made him want to go to sleep. A woman named Linda Terrell said, "Don't you know? There's a giant heart buried beneath the subways. Take your shoes off. You can feel it beating in your toes." One man claimed that the heartbeat was his own, though he would not explain how he knew this to be the case.

"Whatever the answer," the article concluded, "this reporter refuses to believe that the sudden rise or recurrence of the sound is insignificant—though what its significance may be I leave it for you, the reader, to judge."

One thing was certain, and that was that everyone in the city was interested in the topic. For the first time since Minny had met Luka, they handed out every single copy of the paper that morning and found only a few of them balled up in the trash cans as they left.

Afterward, before they went home, they decided to share a late breakfast at Bristow's. The restaurant was full, and Minny left Luka standing in the lobby while she went to the restroom. When she came back, he was talking to a woman about the condition of the roads.

"I would say I've seen at least one traffic accident a day ever since the ice started falling," the woman told him. "Why, just on the way over here, I watched someone run smack into the side of a mailbox. That crumpling sound! Have you ever been in a car accident?"

He had, of course. The night they met, when they believed they were the only people in the city—the two of them and the blind man, that is—he had told Minny the story of how he had died in a highway accident. He said that he had lost control of the wheel and felt himself being jarred loose from his body. She had never forgotten the tingle that ran over her skin as he described it. But he answered the woman with, "Never. I guess I've been pretty lucky."

"See, for me it's been one accident after another," the woman said. "One time my accelerator went out, and I could only get my car to drive in reverse. I *literally* can't tell you how many traffic citations I've gotten. And *then* I rear-ended somebody once just trying to see how fast I would have to go to get a grasshopper to blow off my windshield. You know how sometimes you've got these questions in your head? Well, the police officer was sympathetic, but he said he had to give me a ticket anyway."

"I'm sorry to hear that," Luka said.

A table emptied out, and they left the woman waiting at the door. Bristow, the owner of the restaurant, showed them to their chairs and filled their water glasses. After they had placed their order, Minny asked Luka, "Why didn't you tell her about the accident?"

He stirred the ice in his glass. "She's a complete stranger, and mostly crazy would be my guess. I died, remember? That car accident was one of the three most important things that ever happened to me—probably a close second, right after my birth. I'm not going to tell just anybody about it."

"But you told me about it the same day we met. And I was a complete stranger."

"You were a complete stranger," he agreed. "And you're also mostly crazy. But you were never just anybody."

This was the kind of thing he would say every so often, a tight little knot of sentences, like the coil of rubber at the center of a golf ball, that would burst open in a spray of contradictory implications as soon as she tried to pick it apart. What did he mean? Did he have something serious in mind? Or was he just being cryptic for the sake of being cryptic, clever for the sake of being clever? She could never tell. He himself seemed to see such conversations as a kind of affectionate game. Sometimes she would try to play along with him, but she was not very good at it, and they both knew it. She felt clumsy, thick-witted. Usually, instead of joining in with him, she would try to come up with a topic that would shift the mood of the conversation onto a slower, steadier course, one she was sure she could follow. A walk instead of a dance, was how she thought of it. This was just one of the many reasons she couldn't stop asking him why he loved her.

"Or how's this?" he amended his answer. "You were a stranger, but you were never complete." He laughed.

"Did I tell you I saw the blind man yesterday?"

It had the effect she wanted: his smile sank back into his face, and his eyes took on a look of simple curiosity. "No, you didn't. Where was he?"

"He was having an argument with a ticket vendor. I stopped

and asked him if he was all right, and he said he was tired of remembering everything he wanted to forget and forgetting everything he wanted to remember. Those were his exact words: 'remembering everything he wanted to forget and forgetting everything he wanted to remember.' I think I might have been on the forgetting-everything-he-wanted-to-remember end of the spectrum. When I told him who I was, he said he was pleased to meet me."

"Yeah, he didn't remember me the last time, either. So that makes—what?—six for me and eight for you?"

"Nine for me, thank you very much."

"Nine it is."

The blind man had disappeared back into his solitude soon after they found their way to the monument district, and ever since then, they had seen him only in passing. They had made a bet that the first one to spot him ten times would win an unspecified favor from the other, collectible at any time. The blind man was something of a hermit, though, or at least he took a different set of streets than they usually did, and weeks would sometimes pass between one sighting and the next. Minny wasn't surprised that he didn't remember her. When she thought about those first few days with Luka, before they had heard the gunshots, it was tempting for her to imagine that the blind man had never been there at all. Luka had been the Adam to her Eve, the Friday to her Robinson Crusoe, the Master to her Margarita. None of them were stories that left room for anyone else.

On the other side of the restaurant, Minny saw Laura's parents, Mr. and Mrs. Byrd, eating a breakfast of what looked like scrambled eggs and toast. Mrs. Byrd was using her left hand, Mr. Byrd his right. Their other hands were concealed behind a salt and pepper caddy on the back side of the table, where they could lace their fingers together without anybody watching. They looked like two embarrassed teenagers on a first date. And, simultaneously, they looked like an old couple who had been holding hands so long that they no longer distinguished between the times when they were touching and the times when they weren't. It was sweet.

Minny had seen the two of them again and again since she had arrived in the city, had even waved to them every so often, but never once had they recognized her. This was understandable. After all, she had certainly changed a whole lot more in the years since she and Laura had been best friends than they had.

When she stopped to consider it, she realized that she probably hadn't thought about Laura more than fifteen or twenty times during the whole of her adult life. She had never been the kind of person who was haunted by memories of her past, or at least she hadn't been that kind of person before the virus and the news coverage and the sight of all those bodies propped up in the swaying green grass. But then she had died, and she had found out about Laura's fling with Luka, and all of a sudden she was thinking about her all the time. There wasn't much for her to remember, just a few stray images of the two of them playing house and pretending to walk a tightrope and then something about a butterfly and a fortress.

The man she was in love with and her best friend from— what?—third grade?

It was all too strange.

After they had finished eating and took care of the check, they gave up their table to a man in hiking boots and a business suit. It was snowing again, and Minny slipped her hands inside her pockets as they stepped out into the cold.

Luka hooked his arm around her waist and pulled her close to him as they crossed the street, his hand under the tail of her jacket. "Are you okay?" he asked.

"Mm-hmm."

"You seemed a little quiet back there for a while."

"I know. I was just thinking."

"About what?"

"About you. About Laura."

Luka put his fingertips on the hip of her dress, by which he meant to say, *You shouldn't worry so much.* Though what he actually said was "Man Loves Woman, Woman Loves Trouble."

"I don't love trouble," Minny sniffed.

" 'Man Loves Woman, Woman Loves Suffering,' then."

"I don't love suffering, either."

"Man Loves Woman, Woman Loves Coffee."

She bumped him with her shoulder, playfully. "I can't argue with that, I guess."

There were places where the snow had risen so far toward the roofs of the parked cars that they stretched down the side of the road in a series of identical, oddly shaped lumps, like the knots of someone's spine. The sidewalks were slippery with ice. Maybe it was just the banks of snow piled alongside every major lane of traffic, but sometimes it seemed to Minny that she was traveling through a city of tunnels, just another one of the mole people. The sensation was particularly strong on those gray, dismal days like today, when the sun failed to show itself behind the clouds.

She and Luka had established their own little circuit of stores, buildings, and restaurants soon after they decided to haul his newspaper equipment from his old office to his new one and move in together. It had been a long time since either one of them had ventured more than ten or fifteen blocks away from their apartment. But they had heard the same reports as everyone else. The snow had sealed the monument district off from the rest of the city. Luka had even written about it in a special double issue of the *Sims Sheet*. The district was framed by the river on one side and by a sliver of park and a pair of six-lane roads on the others. Beyond those borders the snowdrifts had become so high that the ground was almost impassable. All you could see were the corners of a half dozen billboards and the upper floors of a few tall buildings. It was as though the city were slowly digesting itself.

The man who always carried the signs with the religious messages printed on them passed by Minny and Luka with a placard that read, FOR OUT OF THE ABUNDANCE OF THE HEART, THE MOUTH SPEAKETH. He stopped and asked them if they had heard the sound.

He was talking about the heartbeat, Minny presumed. "I've heard the sound," she said.

"Yes," the man said, "we have all heard the sound, for it is the beating of His Sacred Heart."

"Is it?"

"He's coming soon. He'll be carrying my Bible for me."

"I'm glad," Minny said.

The man flinched when she reached out to pat his arm, so she put her hand back in her pocket. "You stay warm now," she told him, and she and Luka slipped around him and across the intersection and finally through the door of their building.

Luka spent the rest of the afternoon working on the next day's edition of the newspaper while Minny read a novel by the light of the table lamp in the living room. The days, unlike the nights, passed quickly, and before she knew it she had finished the novel, and he had picked up dinner from the Korean restaurant down the street, and the two of them were standing at the kitchen counter eating noodles and kimchi out of waxed cardboard boxes. He was a journalist, with a journalist's dining habits. And because she had never developed any firm dining habits of her own—cleaning habits, yes; reading habits, definitely; dining habits, no—she had been happy to adopt his when they moved in together.

"Which do you like better: the idea of the past or the idea of the future?" she said a few minutes later, as he was packing the leftovers away in the refrigerator.

"Not this game again."

"The idea of the past or the idea of the future?" she insisted.

"You sound like an optometrist testing lenses. This one—or that one. This one—or that one."

"You're not going to answer me, are you?"

"Well, the contest is rigged, in my opinion. But I guess I'll say the future. My real answer is the present."

"Me, too. The future. Which do you like better: this world or the other?"

"A real life-or-death decision, huh?" he joked.

"This world or the other?"

"This world," he said. "This world all the way."

He closed the refrigerator and winked at her, taking two big steps across the kitchen floor.

And then it was night, and she was in bed, and she fell asleep right away for once, though the next night she lay awake for hours thinking about what it would have been like if the two of them could have had a child (and here was a question: if she could have given their child a certain amount of each of the five virtues—health, kindness, intelligence, charm, and beauty— how would she have distributed them, and in what proportions?), and the night after that about the hotel where she had died, the quarantine at the edge of the parking lot, and the warm glow of the vending machine in the lobby.

~

She wasn't exactly sure when the heart stopped beating.

It might have been a few nights later, when she got up at two o'clock to walk around in the blue half-light of the apartment and heard a dripping sound that turned out to be the icicles melting outside the window. It might have been the next morning, when for the first time in weeks the sun came out burning hard and the birds reappeared from wherever they had been keeping shelter. It might have been the day after that, or the day after that, or even the day before. All she knew for certain was that there came a moment when she realized she could no longer hear the pulse that had accompanied her every waking moment for so long, and she felt as if something had died.

It happened like this: She was handing out newspapers with Luka when there was a short lull in the traffic, and suddenly it was quiet enough for her to notice the stillness in the air. She realized right away that something was wrong, something was missing. A fist seemed to tighten inside her stomach. "Listen," she said to Luka.

He fell quiet for a moment, then whispered, "What is it I'm supposed to be listening for?"

"It isn't there anymore."

"What isn't there?"

She gave him a hint: "Bump, *bump*. Bump, *bump*. Bump, *bump*."

His expression shifted through three distinct stages—first confusion, then dawning recognition, and finally, as the weights tumbled into place, full understanding. "Hey, you're right," he said. "It's gone."

"I know it's gone. I knew it all along."

"You 'knew it all along'? What does that mean?"

It would have been the easiest thing in the world for her to say that she had known since the beginning of their conversation— that that was all she had meant—but the truth was that she had something deeper in mind, something she couldn't quite pin down, and she didn't want to lie about it. "I don't know. Honestly. I didn't realize I was going to say that."

"Understandable," he said. "In fact, understood."

First she smiled, and then suddenly she found herself fighting back tears. She turned away from him so that he wouldn't notice. It had something to do with her sense that nothing was permanent, nothing would last. Hearts stopped beating. People put guns to their chests. There was no one and nothing she could ever know well enough to make it stay. It had been one of her chief preoccupations during the last few years of her life: the notion that there was not enough time left for her to really get to know anyone. Most people would say it was ridiculous. She understood that. She was only in her mid-thirties, after all. But whenever she would come into contact with someone new, someone whose stories she didn't already know by heart, sooner or later that person would start talking about days gone by, and she would get the sad, sickening feeling that too much had already happened to him and it was far too late for her to ever catch up. How could she ever hope to know someone whose entire life up to the present was already a memory? For that matter, how could anyone hope to know her? The way she saw it, the only people she had any prayer of knowing or being known by were the people who had been a part of her life since she was a child, and she hardly even spoke to them anymore. Just her mother and a friend or two from high school, and that was about it. As for everybody else she met, well—there were too many shadows behind a person and there was too little light ahead. That was the problem. And there was no force in the world that would remedy the situation. People talked about love as a light that would illuminate the darkness that people carried around with them. And yes, Minny was capable of loving, but so what? As far as she could tell, her love had never improved things for her or anyone else, so what good was it? She could never rely on it. It weighed no more than a nickel. It was only after she died and met Luka that the vistas of time seemed to open back up for her, and she began to think that maybe she could know someone else as well as she knew herself—that her love might be enough to make a difference, after all.

But sometimes she would start to feel the death in things again, and that old doubt would come washing back over her, and she would fill with the terrible familiar fear that nothing had changed at all. She could never be whole in the eyes of anyone else. No one else could ever be whole in her own eyes. She had known it all along.

"Are you okay?" Luka asked her, and when she nodded, he said, "You seemed to be someplace else there for a minute."

"I'm all right," she said.

She wouldn't ask him the question. She wouldn't let herself.

The traffic had picked up again, and there was no longer enough silence in the air for them to listen for the beating of the heart. They handed out the last of the newspapers. Then they walked back home over the wet sidewalks, the flattened grass, and the heaps of melting snow.

It was another day of reading and staring out the window for Minny, cut off entirely from the world. Usually Luka would ask her to come along with him while he scouted the city for reports he could use in the newspaper, but she had come to sense when he wanted to be alone, and today was one of those days. It could be a pleasure to walk the pavement with only your own thoughts for company. She understood that.

After he left, she opened the window to air out the room, and the trickling sound of so much ice and snow melting seemed to enter the apartment from all directions at once. If she had closed her eyes, she might have imagined that she was standing in the middle of some tropical cave, the moisture of the forest percolating down through infinite layers of stone to drip into a hundred little pockets of water. But her eyes were wide open. A few people were walking by down below with their jackets slung over their shoulders. Clumps of snow fell from the trees and the hoods of the cars, astonishingly white in the light of the sun. A couple of birds had landed on her ledge and then flown away. She could see the hieroglyphs of their footprints in the snow.

She must have gone back to the couch and fallen asleep after that, because soon Luka was standing over her with his hand on her forehead. Occasionally, in the middle of the day, when all of the pressure had fallen away, she would sit down to relax for a few minutes and open her eyes to find that she had dozed off for half the afternoon. It was one of the side effects of her insomnia.

She kept her eyes closed. She knew without thinking what Luka was going to say, because he had said it so many times before: "Wake up, Sleeping Beauty."

"What time is it?" she asked.

"Early," he said. "It was a light news day—just the heartbeat and the weather. Speaking of which, I thought we could go outside and enjoy the sun for a while."

She felt a breeze on her skin, and she propped herself up on her elbows to see where it was coming from. "I left the window open," she said. Then she turned to Luka. "Can I ask you something?"

"Uh-oh."

"No, no, it's nothing like that. You have birth and then you have the car accident, right? So what's the third most important thing that ever happened to you? You never told me."

There was a pause as he sat down, lifted her gently by the shoulders, and put her head in his lap. It was as though she had asked him her question again—why do you love me?—and he had decided to answer her as he always did, by not answering at all.

He spent a few moments stroking her hair with the back side of his hand, then flipped it over by the roots so that it covered her face in a thick curtain.

"Now you look like a caveman," he said.

It was so ridiculous that she had to laugh. He was always saying things like that—at the least expected times, in the least expected places. No one else had ever been able to make her laugh like he could. No one else had ever tried so hard. No one else had ever known her well enough.

Not a soul.

Fourteen

THE MARBLES

And the spring came, with the sun breaching the horizon and the wind lifting the snow off the ice and the bay popping and cracking like the frame of an old house. Shoals of fish traced the open water, and flocks of skua followed close behind them. Great chunks of glacier thawed and broke off into the ocean, carrying the blue-green ice of a thousand years ago. For a few hours each day the snow glistened like rubies in the drawn-out light of the sun, and for a few minutes, as the light grew stronger, it glistened like diamonds. No other spring in the world was anything like it.

It was a kind of twilight, though not the real one. The air was surprisingly warm, and for once Laura did not have to thrash around inside her sleeping bag to force her way out, because it had already melted down to the thinnest mesh around her. She lifted herself onto her elbows. Ten thousand loose threads slipped over her arms and shoulders and pooled together on the floor. They fell so softly that she could barely feel them moving over her skin. When she ran her hands through the threads, they rippled and separated, bending away from her fingers like water. A fish swam by beneath her. She had the notion that she could dive through the surface of the tent, parting the threads with her body, and wheel around to watch them close back together, that she could sink through the material until she forgot she was sinking at all, an anchor plunging deeper and deeper, but instead she opened the tent flap and stepped outside onto the crisp white snow.

The penguins were nowhere to be seen, nowhere even to be heard, though when she thought about it, she realized she could indeed hear them chattering hectically to one another, so they were somewhere to be heard after all, and she could see them huddled together at the base of the cliff, so they were somewhere to be seen. They had hatched their chicks and were warming them beneath the folds of their bellies.

The sun described a thin arch at the very edge of the sky, the moon a slightly larger arch at the opposite edge. The wind played softly over her skin. She was not wearing her jacket or her gloves, her boots or her socks, her pants or her undershirt—was not, as she understood it, wearing any clothing at all—and yet she had never been warmer or more comfortable. She wondered why she had ever been cold in the first place, why she had ever decided to be cold. Such a strange choice, she thought. And the world, this world, was all about choices.

It felt good to stretch her muscles. She flexed her fingers, combing them through her hair. There was still a trace of frost-bite on the index finger of her left hand, a small plum-colored circle as perfectly formed as an adhesive bandage, and she peeled it off by the tail of red string that protruded from the top, dropping it at her feet, where it sank immediately into the snow and disappeared. She held the finger up to the fading light. Much better.

Scattered over the patch of wind-polished ice that surrounded her tent were the same delicate little puffs of white snow she had seen when she was sledging across the ice so many months ago. Why she hadn't noticed them before, she couldn't say. They were the size of marbles, the largest of them no bigger than a quarter. Some of them even seemed to present the same whorled feather-ing pattern as marbles, spreading open into blurred segments inside the glass. She tapped one of them with her big toe and it fell apart, spilling into its nearest neighbor, which also fell apart. They seemed so insubstantial that she wondered how they had ever managed to hold together at all.

A light wind came twisting through the cove, and the marbles drifted lazily about before settling back into the snow. It seemed as though they were regulated by a weaker gravity. One good gust was all it would take to carry them away, she thought, and the thought alone was enough to do it, for it wasn't long before she heard the wind sighing down from the cliff, picking up speed as it worked its way toward the rookery. She watched the marbles shudder as the first few hairs of the breeze brushed up against them, and then they floated up off the ice and began to tumble forward. Within seconds they were on their way. They moved with the same strangely purposeful spontaneity as a flock of birds, tacking from one side to another, crowding together and then fanning apart, yet always pressing forward. Where were they heading with such deliberation? she wondered. Where would they come to a stop? She wanted to know, and so she followed them.

The marbles guided her along at a brisk walk. Soon she had left the rookery far behind. The metallic quacking of the penguins faded slowly away until she couldn't hear them at all anymore, just the dimmest rasping sound at the furthest limit of her perception.

The marbles were rolling out over the bay toward the sun, which was higher than she remembered, and in a different quadrant of the sky. Every so often they would shuffle positions, the ones in front sliding to the edge of the pack while new ones drifted forward to take their places. She assigned names to her favorites, and then abandoned the names and assigned them sizes, and then abandoned the sizes and assigned them colors. The red one overtook the green one as she maneuvered around a rise in the snow. The blue one was falling steadily behind. She realized that she had abandoned her campsite without any of her supplies, without even her tent, but she brushed the thought away.

She didn't need her supplies. She couldn't imagine she would ever need her supplies again.

The bay had broken apart into huge chunks and floes that bobbed loosely in the deep water, swaying on every axis like plates spinning on wooden poles. Tremendous gaps and scissures opened between them as they rode their weight through the water. Small waves lapped quietly at their sides. The marbles sailed over the rifts as if they weren't there at all. Laura walked carelessly along behind them, watching the cracks seal shut as she approached. The floes came together with a great heavy precision, butting up against one another with a hollow thump, like boats sliding into their berths. They lingered just long enough to allow her to keep her stride before they floated apart again. She went on like this for hours.

Eventually, the marbles hit some sort of pocket or eddy, spinning in place, and she paused to take a breath. She looked behind her. She had left only the most superficial string of impressions in the snow. The footprints at her feet were so shallow they displayed a hollow curve along the instep, something like a barbell in shape. There was a long empty gap between the thick part of the sole and the five tiny jellybeans of the toes. It was as though she had been walking over a thin layer of sand on a bed of the hardest rock. The sand was an unmistakable Sahara yellow. It gave off a continuous warm pressure that rose up powerfully against her bare feet, though her soles were no longer sensitive enough to detect the million-some punctures of the individual grains. They were hardened by her years of desert walking. She was a sort of nomad. A dry wind swept in from the flatlands. The air around her seemed to shimmer. She could hear the flapping of wings beneath the sun as she followed the marbles out toward the dunes.

There were ripples in the sand like the ripples in a sheet of tin roofing. Once, walking through the trees behind her apartment building, she had found a sheet of rippled tin draped across the path beside the tennis courts. Dirt and leaves filled the corrugations, with weeds like bundles of stickpins growing through here and there, all round heads and long thin needles. A year later, the sheet was completely buried by the soil. She was unable to make out even the slightest rib or corner of it. The only sign that it was there at all was the clunking noise a certain section of the path made whenever her foot fell across it. For a moment or two she was there again, in that patch of woods behind her apartment building. It was night, and the headlights of a car entering the parking lot were coasting through the branches of the trees, slipping from limb to limb. First they illuminated one of the oak branches directly over her head, and then they slipped off the edge, leapt thirty feet through the air, and came together again on the bark of a fir tree. There was no difference at all between here and there, or if there was, the lights didn't recognize it.

Then she saw the marbles rolling over the leaves and she blinked and she was back in the dunes. There was a formation of white stone in the distance, knobbed and hunched to one side, one of those tall desert pillars that had been bleached of all its color by the sun. The marbles turned toward it, and she marched along behind them.

Sweat was pouring down her face, down her shoulders and her back, dripping off her fingers and the tips of her breasts. It accumulated at her feet as she walked, an immense clear lagoon reflecting a hundred wiry kinks of sunlight. Eventually the pool spread past its own boundaries and the sweat trickled away, draining slowly into the yellow sand. She watched it disappear.

The wind was at her back, and she felt good, invigorated. She felt as though she could follow the marbles for days without tiring a single muscle. The desert was much cooler at night, and the scorpions and lizards lay for hours on the flat brown rocks that were gradually releasing their heat back into the sky, poised there like statues. When the sun rose, the lizards crawled back into the shadows, but the scorpions barely moved at all. The formation she had set out toward—the pillar of white stone—was actually an arch. It was only the sidelong view that had made her mistake it for a pillar. The marbles crossed beneath the inverted U of the arch and circled around one of the legs to cross under it again, and then again, and then again, like leaves caught in a back current. They were a bright quivering silver in the light of the sun, a color with a thousand worms in it, even the black marble and the green one and the gray one.

It was on their fifth circuit around the leg of the U that she followed them under the arch and through the sliding glass doors of the shopping mall into the parking garage, which was the frozen bay, where a broken mass of ice floes kept tapping their bumpers and sawing past one another with metallic grinding noises.

She hopped over a fissure and continued on. The sand was snow again. The confused noise of the car horns faded away behind her. She wasn't sure how far she had come from her original campsite, but it must have been at least a hundred miles, if not more. She veered with the marbles around an upturned shoulder of sea ice. The snow squeaked beneath her heels.

As far as her eye could see, the bay was a bobbing field of pack ice, interrupted only by the occasional small iceberg. It was jigsawed with bending cracks of ocean water that shone brilliantly in the red light of the sun.

She was close enough to the open water that herds of leopard seals lay sluggishly about on the ice, groaning and whistling and bubbling and grunting. They were calling out to one another or to the universe, she wasn't sure which. Their voices were so animated that she almost believed she could understand them.

Let the fish swim through the traces, one of them said.

Where has the moon gone? Where have the stars? said another.

All worlds are one world, said a third.

And then Laura forgot what she was hearing, and the noise

became exactly what it had been before, a din of barking. It was not the sort of barking that could ever be mistaken for the barking of dogs, but that was the thought that came to her mind. She thought in particular of the dogs that used to live in her neighborhood when she was a little girl. She remembered the way that when one of them, any one at all, would start barking—at a delivery truck, say, or a slamming door—all the others would take up the call in an expanding ring of yips and growls that made it seem as if there was nothing in the world but dogs: dogs that chased Frisbees and pawed at the dirt, dogs that charged after you as you rode past on your bicycle, dogs that stood over sprinkler heads on soft green lawns, lapping at the fans of water like puddles suspended in midair. The dogs didn't seem any larger than they had ever been, but it was undoubtedly true that she was weaving her way through their hair as she walked, hitching clumps of fur to the side as she marched over the ice floes.

Which meant that she and the marbles must have become smaller. Why was she always becoming smaller? she wondered. She put her foot down on a lump of ice that was also the ridge of the dog's spine and almost twisted her ankle. She would have to be more careful where she stepped in the future.

The fur along the dog's back, along with the great dented promontory of its head, blocked out most of the landscape. The sunlight came through in glints and flashes that took on the shape of the openings between individual shocks of hair, V-shaped windows that cracked apart for only a few seconds before they swung shut again. Every time she saw the light flickering out of the corner of her eye, she was compelled to jerk her head around. She was like a marionette. She couldn't help herself.

She thought of the blind man who used to stand in the atrium of the Coca-Cola building without a dog or even a cane, listening to the water as it poured down the wall of the fountain. He had jerked his head with the same instinctual twitch whenever something new caught his ear—footsteps approaching across the marble floor, the *ding* of the elevator coming to a stop beneath the mezzanine, trees rustling in the air-conditioning. He carried an old leather satchel that he used to set down at his feet, where it would spread its lips open like a dying lily, and whenever people dropped their coins inside, he would dismiss them with a wave of his hands, saying, "I didn't ask for that. I'm no beggar," before he emptied the satchel into the wishing pool. He was the kind of person she saw almost every day, then promptly forgot about until she saw him again.

The dog she was riding was not blind, though. It went racing after something it had spotted on the ice. She had to cling to its fur with both her hands to keep from falling over. The marbles trembled and bounced against its tallowy white skin, just visible between the roots of its hair.

Then the dog stopped, hunched over, and wrenched its head to the side as though it had caught a rabbit in its jaws. She slipped down its back and tumbled off onto the ice, landing on her butt.

She picked herself up and brushed the snow from her body, collecting the crystals in her palms and pouring them into the fountain over the thousands of silver coins, which shimmered in the light of the atrium. The still water reflected the scarves and curtains of the aurora. She watched them snap and flicker above the coins. Then she set off down the corridor that connected the atrium to the public relations building. The marbles were still rolling along in formation, though the air in the corridor was dead-motionless, even in the wake of her body, and she could no longer be sure what was driving them forward. Plainly it wasn't the wind.

There were doors to either side where she heard the routine sounds of business being conducted, sounds so familiar to her that they had long since lost all meaning. A woman was dictating a report into her computer's voice-recognition speaker. A man was pacing the floor of his office as he spoke on the telephone. A copy machine was processing a stack of papers, its armature sliding back and forth beneath the glass with a zippered halting noise. All the doors in the corridor were closed, and when Laura tried to open them, she found them locked.

She kept walking down the hallway. She passed by a bank of elevators and through an empty reception area where the water cooler beside the couch gave up a wobbling bubble of oxygen. It was hard for her to believe that she had spent so much of her life in this building, or in other buildings just like it, walking around inside rooms that were thirty or forty or fifty feet above the earth, whose walls and floors and ceilings had been constructed around spaces where no human being had ever set foot just a few years before.

The lead marble—she had forgotten its name—turned down a corridor that led toward an open flight of stairs, and the other marbles flocked around behind it. Without hesitation they took the stairs toward the roof, bumping from step to step like a colony of ants fording a stream across one another's backs. She began to climb up after them. It was twenty flights or more before she and the marbles reached the building's top floor, but she made the climb with surprising ease. She couldn't speak for the marbles, but she herself felt strong and vigorous, she might even say athletic. There was so much power in her body, more than there had been at any time since her adolescence. It was as though all her months in the Antarctic had never happened at all. She pushed at the fire door that was positioned at the top of the stairs and stepped out onto the roof.

The building beneath her was water. All its rooms were water, and all its hallways were water, and she was sailing across it on a great raft of ice. The fire door slowly shut behind her, drawing back with a long, hissing exhalation. She heard it lock into place. The marbles were all huddled together at the leading edge of the ice floe. They looked like passengers peering over the rails of a ship. Every so often, the wind would send one of its ligaments whipping up at them from the ocean, and two or three of them would go soaring up over the others to land at the back of the crowd.

Laura adjusted the sails on the ice floe and took hold of the wheel. When she spun it to starboard, the floe nosed out toward the stars and the open water, so she swung it back to port, and the floe drifted smoothly and slowly back toward the pack ice that skirted the land mass. It was several hours before she finally docked, sliding into the hollow between two loosely joined sheets of ice, at which point she let go of the wheel and walked off the end of the floe without dropping anchor. The new ice rocked slightly beneath her weight. But it remained afloat, and after a few steps, she found herself walking on a more solid foundation. The marbles were following her now, coasting and whirling over the snow, above and between the staggered lines of her footprints. Occasionally they would roll against the backs of her feet—a quick cold tap. And every now and then one or two of them would go slewing out in front of her in a fishhooking sort of curve, but they never ventured too far ahead.

The sun and the moon had been resting at opposite ends of the sky for so long that it was impossible for her to tell what time of day it was, but she decided she would call it afternoon, so afternoon it was. Late afternoon, she would guess. She had heard once that late afternoon—three-thirty or four o'clock—was when the human body temperature was at its coolest, and sure enough, when she pressed her palm to her forehead, she found that she was freezing. Her skin threw off the dry chill of a metal serving tray left outside on a winter night. She was cold enough to feel the contours of her skeleton inside her body. Yet she was perfectly at ease, peaceful even, with a wonderful looseness in her hands and toes and her blood completely still inside her. She felt as though she were sleeping in her bed at home.

When the ice sheet she was crossing fell off into the water, crumbling to pieces along the left side, she skipped over the margin onto the ice floe bobbing next to it. She was a dancer of sorts. She had always wanted to be a dancer. The gap where the ocean lay was an orchestra pit, and she could see the violinists sawing away beneath the water, the percussionist pounding on his big bass drum, the limb of the trombone sliding out, then consuming itself, then sliding out again. She rose onto her toes to leap over a chunk of broken ice. The music blossomed from the water to carry across the frozen bay. For a moment, she thought she was going to lose herself in it, in the sway of the strings and the reverberations of the horns—she had always known that she could lose herself in a piece of music—but then the breaking noise of a cymbal became the crack of a gunshot, and a flock of birds lifted noisily up from the ice, and she watched them take off and bank toward the ocean in a geyser of wings.

How long had she been walking toward the sun? It seemed like weeks since she had found the ruins of the hut alongside the rookery and fallen asleep inside her tent and then woken in a pool of red threads and shed her clothing and set off after the marbles.

Though perhaps it had been only a few minutes.

What was clear was that something had happened. Her sense of time had broken apart into two equal halves and fallen away from her like the shell of a walnut.

She found herself forecasting the colors the sun would make on the ice. A gold like the pollen of ragweed flowers. A pale green like the green of Easter-egg dye. At first the colors seemed to blossom open just an instant or two before she was able to put a name to them, but a little experimentation convinced her that the process was exactly the reverse: the thought preceded the color. It was a game. She pictured the creamy off-yellow of her bathroom walls, and a half second later there it was on the ice. Seven shades of blue poured into her head, and a moment later she was threading her way right through the center of them. She could shuffle the colors at will. It was like her word association game—one word, one color, leading inexorably to the next, by a process that was largely but not wholly within her control, a process of whim and chance and improvisation. Everything depended on the fluctuations of her mind, and her mind was not entirely her own.

Those were the rules. She was beginning to understand them.

When she looked up from the colors on the ice, she saw something standing in the distance, just to the left of the sun: a glittering city, with buildings of glass and stone and steel that rose high above the streets. She saw the clean line of a river cutting through the center, wooden docks piercing the water and grass and trees growing along the banks. A suspension bridge spanned the river from one bank to the other, resembling from this distance the torn silver web of a spider. She was too far away to see how much traffic was on the streets, or indeed whether there was any traffic at all, but the spokes of a railway station shone unmistakably beneath the blue sky. Parks and arcades lay sprinkled between the buildings. An immense cloud of birds wheeled in the air.

She lost sight of the city when she dipped beneath a hill. By the time she climbed to the top and was able to see to the horizon again, it had disappeared. She turned a full circle, but still she couldn't find it anywhere.

It must have been a mirage. She had forgotten about mirages.

The sun was bigger than it had been when she started her walk, a terrible white sphere that took up half the sky. It was so bright that she imagined she could hear it sizzling. It gave off the sound of an egg sputtering in a frying pan, an egg that was just beginning to go crisp at the edges, and because she was hungry she poured the egg off onto a plate and ate it with a knife and fork, but she did not eat the sun, and she did not stop walking.

The marbles were some twenty or thirty yards ahead of her now, a hundred teetering balls, so very small inside the sealed arc of the sun. Their shadows seemed to burn themselves into the air. They were right on the verge of disappearing.

How far she must have come to make the sun so large.

How close she must have drawn to the horizon.

Most of the ice had already melted away, and soon she was leaping from one chunk to another, resting barely long enough to feel the pieces bob beneath her. Then the ice was gone altogether, and she was traveling directly across the surface of the water. Plants with long green fronds composed slow figure eights beneath her feet. Small fish darted past in the crimped light.

She had finally hit her stride. She imagined she could walk forever.

Fifteen

THE CROSSING

It soon became apparent to the blind man that the city was changing. The birds had returned to the air in greater numbers than ever before, and at times the vertical space around him seemed to warp or shift in some way so that he imagined he heard them all calling out from the exact same spot, a great mass of voices clustered together in a tree or on the railing of a balcony. Though the phenomenon never lasted for longer than a few seconds, it was quite distinct. The notes the birds gave out were sharp, multiangular—sudden little whistles that cut across one another like thorns.

He had heard this sound before. It was the saddest sound in the world: the sound of something that thought it was free but had come bumping up against the walls of its enclosure.

The birds might have been the first sign of the city's transformation (they were definitely the first that he noticed), but there were certainly others. The last of the snow ran to water, and it ceased to rain. The wind picked up speed one day, then reversed directions, and finally stopped blowing altogether. Once, the blind man accidentally kicked a pebble through a subway grate and never heard it hit the bottom.

He knew, then, that the topography of the city was changing, but he didn't know how, and he didn't know why, until the first few people came back from the edge of the monument district and the word began to spread. The rest of the city, that portion of it that lay beyond the park and the river, was no longer there. It had melted away along with the snow.

The blind man heard the story from a man who was holding court in the center of the shopping plaza. "I was thinking I would just go for a ride, you know, really open up and see what kind of speed I could do." His voice was coming from a crouch. He was spinning the pedals of his bicycle, then yanking them forward to make the chain seize short against the sprockets. "Well, I got as far as the six-laner at the other end of Park Street, and then I had to turn back around. The road wasn't there anymore. No sidewalks. No buildings. I'm not talking rubble or an empty field, you guys. I'm talking absolutely nothing."

"Why didn't you keep going?" someone asked him. "You know, see what was on the other side?"

"That's what I'm trying to tell you—there *was* no other side. I tried to keep pedaling, but it was like climbing up the inside of a sphere. I could feel myself moving, I just wasn't gaining any distance."

There was a sudden firecrackerlike string of side conversations. Then a few more people came together in the center of the plaza, and the structure of the crowd tightened, and the man with the bicycle began repeating his story. The blind man had already heard enough, though, and he left.

Later that day, there was a similar report from a man who had tried to leave the district by way of the suspension bridge, and there was another a few hours after that by a woman who had taken the same route the bicyclist had. The woman said that the highway was missing now, too, and that the city dead-ended at the gray strip of concrete where the hazard lane used to be. "This was all I found," she said, and she let something trickle through her fingers—a few cigarette butts and some fragments of window glass, from the sound of it. By that evening, half a dozen people must have made the journey to the border of the monument district and back. And so began the pilgrimages.

The blind man himself walked to the border the very next morning. He took Tanganyika Street. The pavement was dry enough to clap beneath his hard-soled shoes again, and he did not have to listen so carefully for the conversations of other people and the carrying sounds of the traffic. He could hear his steps rising up off the ground, hear them echoing against the walls and the fences. That was all the guidance he needed.

He knew immediately when he had reached the margin of the city. Behind him some kids were listening to music, singing along with excited little whoops and hollers. A pretzel vendor's cart was perfuming the air, as were the thousands of blades of grass that had opened up beneath the treads of so many shoes. Before him, though, there was a total cessation of both sound and smell. It was as though a wall had risen up in front of him, but a wall with none of the usual physical properties of a wall. When he tried to touch it, he encountered no resistance whatsoever. Before he knew it, he was reaching across his own chest, his hand a full foot to the left of where it had started.

The same thing happened when he tried a second time, and again when he tried a third.

The wall was intangible but impassable.

No wonder the birds had come flooding into the air, he reflected. They had no place else to go.

He followed the same road on his way back that he had on his way out, though the walk went more quickly now that he knew the obstacles and could place his feet on the ground with more confidence. Soon he was back in his own neighborhood. He passed through the thousand dangling fingers of the willow tree that stood outside the abandoned library, and then past the upright mailbox, and then, after he had crossed the street, beneath the high rectangular buzzing of the movie theater's marquee. The theater showed only old silent movies—classics— which was why the ticket vendor always refused to provide him with a ticket, though the blind man had explained a thousand times that what he enjoyed was not the movies themselves, but the cool air and the quiet flickering of the film as it unspooled and the great sense of space above his shoulders, almost enough space for a sky to form there, he imagined, with clouds and wind currents and its own systems of weather. Or perhaps he had failed to explain it a thousand times, or explained it only in his head, or explained it to someone else altogether. It was one of the deficits of old age that he no longer remembered many of the things he would have expected himself to remember.

And then there were the things he remembered in spite of himself.

A girl was skipping rope in the courtyard across the street from him, for instance, chanting a crossbred version of a rhyme that had been popular when he was a child: "*Ham*burger, *fish* sticks, quarter pound of *french* fries. *Icy* Coke, *milk*shakes, on *Sun*days it's an *app*le pie."

He winced as the rope slapped the ground, involuntarily recoiling. It took him a moment to figure out why. At first he thought it might have been because of the way the sand had lashed at him while he was crossing the desert, hissing like a snake, which was itself a kind of rope, a living rope, which passed through his fingers like nylon and made only the barest rustling sound as it touched the grass. A rope was like a whip, and it was only natural for a person to wince at the sound of a whip, even a person who had never been beaten. He himself had been beaten once, though not with a whip. But that had been so long ago and he was so much older now that he found it hard to believe it could have anything to do with his reaction.

What was it then? Suddenly he knew—it was the girl who had lived at the other end of his block when he was growing up.

Mary Elizabeth was her name. He remembered listening to her as she skipped rope with her friends in the cul-de-sac that the kids in the neighborhood used as their playground. "Why are you *blind*?" the other kids would ask him. "Hey, why are you *blind*?"

placing a stress on the word that made it obvious they were taunting him. He had learned that they would keep taunting him no matter how he answered, so it was better just to keep quiet.

But Mary Elizabeth had never asked him the question at all—not once.

He couldn't have been older than eight or nine at the time, but he was in love with her—in love not only with how nice she was to him, but with the sound of her voice, and the way that her sandals flapped against the underside of one of her feet but not the other as she walked, and with the smell of cocoa butter that came from her skin whenever she was jumping rope and had begun to work up a sweat.

One day—he didn't know why—he braced up his courage to tell her so. He had been drinking warm Coca-Cola out of a thermos his mother had given him, tasting the way the rusty metal flavored the soda, and was still holding the cap in his hand. As she walked by with her friends, he said her name, "Mary Elizabeth."

But before he could finish with "I love you," as he had planned to, she interrupted him. "Here you go," she said.

He felt the weight of the coin landing inside his thermos cap before he heard it.

The other kids began to laugh, but Mary Elizabeth told them to shut up. "It isn't funny, you guys. Leave the poor thing alone."

The poor thing—that was what she called him.

He might have been angry with Mary Elizabeth, or so upset that he burst into tears. He was that kind of child. He might have loved her all the more for defending him. He was that kind of child, too. But instead he had just stood there embarrassed, his courage dying out inside him as the girls took up their jump ropes and began to chant again: "Big Mac, Filet o' Fish, Quarter Pounder, french fries, icy Coke, thick shake, sundaes, and apple pies."

It was amazing to think that he had constructed an entire lifetime out of moments like this. He had strung them together like beads, he thought, choosing only the ones that were the most painful to him, the ones that left a sandpapery grit on his fingers.

So intently was he remembering the incident that he did not realize he had come to the corner where the curb dropped off into a pothole, and when he stepped off the edge, his foot caught the side. He almost fell over, but he was able to stop himself with one quickly planted step. He could tell right away that he had twisted a muscle in his knee—not badly, but enough so that he should have taken his weight off of it for an hour or two. Still, he kept walking, so that no one would stop to ask him if he needed help.

He had gone another three blocks before he realized that he had already passed the door to his building. It was almost a quarter mile behind him now, just past the silent movie theater and the library with the willow tree on the front walk. Sometimes, like everybody else, he was afraid he was losing his mind.

~

The small section of Clapboard Hill Road that edged up alongside the riverbank before it curved away and rose into the city was the next block to disappear. It was followed soon after by the lowermost corner of the golf course, including holes nine, eleven, twelve, and fourteen. After that it was an old mattress-spring warehouse on the opposite side of the monument district, and then the bottom half of M Street, and then, a few days later, it was the river itself. The blind man began to think of the wall as a slowly shrinking bubble that was slicing away at the city from all directions. He had no direct evidence for the idea, but he couldn't keep himself from imagining it: a giant bubble, gradually drawing together along its circumference, rising up from below as it sank down from above. He wasn't sure what would happen when it finally shrank to a single point.

Sometimes, when his curiosity got the better of him, he would go to the park to listen to what other people were saying about the phenomenon. Nobody could see anything, ever—which was to say that they could see, precisely, nothing. Some of them said that they visited the outer limits of the district regularly, every day or every few days. Some of them said that they stayed as close to the center of the city—or what remained of the city—as possible. A few of them confessed that they were frightened, but most of them simply seemed resigned to the idea of waiting to see what would happen.

He met one man who told him that he walked the entire periphery of the bubble (though he called it *the circle,* instead) every morning before he went to work. Every day another little piece of the city went missing, he said, and every day his walk became that much shorter. The man was a dentist, and when the blind man opened his mouth to yawn, he commented, "Those molars of yours look absolutely terrible. You should come by my office sometime and let me take a better look at them." As he left, he handed the blind man a business card with a perfectly matte surface. The card was illegible to the blind man's fingers, so he threw it away.

After a while, it seemed, somebody would always begin to compare the disappearances along the border of the city to the crossing, suggesting that the city was undergoing a crossing of its own, that it was dreaming itself out of existence, or moving from one sphere of being into another. Though the metaphor was not an obvious one, it was certainly common, which made him think that there might be some truth to it.

Soon after the subject of the crossing was mentioned, the blind man would invariably start talking about the desert again. He couldn't help himself. The experience had nearly broken him in two, and it was one of the few things he was certain he would never forget.

He was passing by the open door of a restaurant one day, after a long morning in the park, when he heard two men arguing about whether the people in the city should more properly be considered bodies or spirits. "Of course we're bodies," one of the men said. "Bodies and nothing but. Have you ever heard of a *spirit* that ate hamburgers and chili dogs for lunch, a *spirit* that got leg cramps in the middle of the night?"

The other man answered, "How can you be so sure what spirits do and don't do? Have you ever been one before?"

"I know because of the world's entire history of spirit commentary. People have been writing about spirits for thousands of years, Puckett. What do you think all that writing was about? It was about constructing the spirit, that's what—building the concept from scratch. I would say I've learned as much about the idea of the spirit as the next guy over the years, and let me tell you"—he made the hollowed-out double thumping sound that meant he was striking his chest—"this isn't it."

"But surely," the second man said, "surely if there's one thing that everybody who's ever written about the spirit agrees on, it's that when you die, your spirit is released from your body. That's got to be right at the center of the concept, doesn't it?"

"But who's to say we haven't been *re*embodied?"

"I'm to say it. Me. Right here."

There was a flaw at the heart of their discussion, the blind man realized. They were mistaking the spirit for the soul. Many people tended to use the words casually, interchangeably, as though there was no difference at all between them, but the spirit and the soul were not the same thing. The body was the material component of a person. The soul was the nonmaterial component. The spirit was simply the connecting line.

This was what his father, a pastor at the First Church of God in Christ, had taught him when he was a boy, and though the blind man had long since ceased to believe in God, or at least in the teachings of the First Church of God in Christ, the distinction remained meaningful to him. When you died, the connecting line of the spirit snapped, and what remained of you was simply the body on one side—a heap of clay and minerals—and the soul on the other. The spirit was nothing more than a function of their interaction, like the ripples that formed where the wind blew over the water. If you took away the wind, and you took away the water, the ripples would vanish. And if they didn't vanish? Well, if they didn't—and this was just speculation on the blind man's part—then you got what people called a ghost. A ghost was what became of a spirit when it lingered past its time. It was the ripple without the wind and the water, the connecting line separated from the body and the soul. But the blind man was not a ghost. He knew that much.

He thought about approaching the table where the two men were discussing the issue and interrupting them with, "Gentlemen, I may be a body, and I may be a soul, but I'm certainly no spirit." Their conversation had already moved on, though, and they were arguing about something else now.

He heard a chair scraping across the floor, someone grinding pepper with a pepper mill, a woman laughing and slapping her table with an open palm.

Somewhere a bell was ringing.

Fat sizzled on a grill.

The birds sounded closer than ever.

The blind man turned his attention back to the street and walked on. That night he fell asleep sitting on a tall stool beside his kitchen counter. When he woke up the next morning and felt the cool layer of Formica under his forehead and the still air around his shoulders, it took him a moment to remember where he was. Instinctively he reached out for his leather satchel, the one in which he had carried his keys and his extra shoes and identification papers for so many years when he was alive. But of course it wasn't there. It was one of the many things he had lost in the desert, along with his eyeglasses and the better part of his wits. Most of the time he barely missed them.

The wind was not blowing, but something must have shaken the tree outside his window, because he could hear the budded end of a dogwood twig tapping delicately against the glass. It had the soft, clear, cadenced sound of a walking cane striking the ground, and he thought of the last time he himself had used such a cane, an entire lifetime of years ago. It was shortly after the day Mary Elizabeth dropped the coin into his thermos cap, when he was eight or nine years old. His school bus had just dropped him off at the corner of the block when he heard a few of the older boys in his neighborhood approaching him from across the crisped grass of someone's lawn. "Why are you blind?" they asked him. "Hey, you, why are you *blind*?"

He never knew quite what to say to this question. It seemed obvious that the boys were teasing him again, but there was always the chance that they were genuinely curious, that they honestly wanted to know for once, and he hated to imagine himself hurting their feelings. Why would they keep asking him if they didn't really care? he wondered. They wouldn't, would they? What would be the point?

He decided to try answering them. "My mama says it happened right after I was born. I was an incubator baby, and they gave me too much oxygen."

This made the boys laugh for some reason, and so he guessed that they had not been curious, after all. They repeated the word "incubator": "*Incubator*. He says he's an *incubator*. Even as a *baby*, dude was an incubator—man, that's sick."

Then they fell quiet, and one of the boys asked him, "So how often do you incubate? Once a day? What about in the shower? Do you incubate in the shower?"

He was confused. "Just that one time," he said. This set off a second round of laughter and jostling. Soon the boys were jostling him, as well, and though he wasn't sure, he thought that they might be coaxing him to join in with the fun—to laugh along with the joke, whatever it was. He gave a tiny experimental chuckle, but it didn't sound right. It was raspy and low, much deeper than his normal laugh.

All of a sudden he needed to swallow. He allowed the boys' voices to die out before he told them, "Well, I need to get home now."

One of them stepped in front of him. "Hey, that's a great cane you've got there. Can I see that cane?"

"I don't think so."

"Aw, man." A shoe scuffed at the asphalt. "Little dude burned me. That's no way to treat a buddy."

Another boy said, "Yeah. Come on, kid. Let him see the cane. He'll give it right back."

"That's right. All I want to do is take a look at it."

And the last boy said, "You don't want us to think you don't like us, do you?"

He didn't believe them at first—why would he?—but then something in his conscience gave itself over to the possibility that they might be telling the truth, as it always did, no matter how often they deceived him, and he knew that he was going to give them the cane. There was a little man who lived inside him, gripping his heart and repeating, *Believe everybody. Never hurt a soul. Believe everybody. Never hurt a soul,* and though sometimes he tried to shut his ears to the man, in the end he could never help but listen to him. "Do you promise you'll give it right back?" he asked the boys.

"Cross my heart, hope to die."

"Well, okay, then."

As soon as he held the cane out, one of them yanked it out of his grip. "I like this cane," he said, and another whistled, "Man, that cane makes you look bad*ass*," and the third said, "A cane fit for a pimp," to which the first one answered, "I know. I think I just might have to keep this cane for myself," and he listened to them praising the cane and passing it back and forth for what seemed like forever, until its absence in his hands began to itch at him.

"Okay. Give it back now," he said. "I need to go home."

"Hold your horses."

"What's your hurry?"

"Yeah, who said it was *your* cane anyway?"

"You guys—" He complained. But they rapped him once over the head with the cane, then a second time across the butt, and when he fell down, they took off running. He heard one of them say, *"Clon-n-n-ng!,"* making his voice vibrate the way the cane had as it struck his skull. Then a door slammed a few houses down the block from him and they were gone.

That was the last he saw of his cane. He had never gotten another one.

When he heard the same boys talking in the cul-de-sac a few days later, they insisted that they had never met him before, and he couldn't seem to convince them otherwise. "Cane?" they said. "I don't know anything about a cane. Maybe you mean 'stain.' Did somebody take your stain? All that incubation will give a man stains. You know what I think? I think you're just making up stories to impress the chickadees."

It didn't take long for him to give up on the idea of getting the cane back from them. Over the next few weeks he learned to walk by the sound of his footsteps, by an outstretched hand and a small measure of intuition. He stored the shape of his own neighborhood in his head, gradually unfolding it like a map at the boundaries. He avoided the older boys whenever he could until, eventually, they grew up, got jobs and got married, or just exhausted themselves and forgot what it had been like when they were children.

This was what he remembered as he sat in his kitchen listening to the dogwood tree tapping against his window.

~

But why did he remember only the things in his life that had hurt him? Why couldn't he remember the things that had given him joy or caused him to smile: the jokes he had heard, the songs that had made him lift his arms in the air, the people who had loved him, whose cheeks he had touched with his fingers?

There had been a time, and not that long ago, when he had taken pride in the fineness of his memory. He had thought of the history of his life as a perfect unfraying string, spooling out in a single line behind him; all he had to do was take it in his hands, give it a few strong hitches, and he could reexamine it at any point. But now the string had become tangled and knotted, and he was afraid that it would never be straight again.

It was late that afternoon when he heard someone say that the rest of the golf course had disappeared, along with the fire station, the arboretum, and the back half of one of the office buildings on Eréndira Street. The next morning it was the natural science museum and most of the shopping plaza. And a couple of days after that, for the first time, a woman reported that the phenomenon had extended its great blank barriers below the ground. The woman said that she had been crossing through the subway tunnel that ran beneath Christopher Street when she paused at the edge of the platform to tie her shoes. She noticed that the tracks and the track bed were no longer there. She backed away, then peered over the edge to look again. Nothing. She found the crushed red and silver disk of a Coke can on the platform and tried to drop it into the empty space. But she must have miscalculated, she said, because it landed at her feet, bounced a few times, then rolled away behind her. "It was like there was a river running between this side of the platform and the other. Except that there was nothing to it. No clay, no water—so basically no river." She gave a muffled laugh. "I guess I don't really know how to describe it."

"You don't have to describe it," someone said. "We've all seen it for ourselves."

But the blind man had not seen it. "You're talking about what's happening down below," he said. "That's one thing. But what about what's happening up above?"

He heard a half dozen collars rustling as the people around him craned their heads to look into the sky. "It's hard to tell," someone answered. "But *something's* definitely going on up there."

There was an unusual shearing pattern to the tops of the clouds, apparently, but no one could say whether it was the effect of the bubble or just some strange wind blowing high in the atmosphere. The blind man listened as they talked the matter over. Was the top corner of one of the high-rises missing? Had the sky always been that same powdery shade of blue? Finally, a gravelly voice summed things up for him: "It looks a little washed out, maybe, but everything's still up there, at least as far as I can tell."

After that, the crowd began to dissipate. As the blind man was leaving, a finger tapped his shoulder. He smelled a faint whiff of lavender. "How are you doing?" The voice belonged to a woman.

"I've seen worse times," the blind man said.

"You don't remember me, do you?"

"I don't. I'm sorry."

"I'm Minny Rings. I met you after the evacuation. We made coffee and English muffins together."

"Did we?"

"Mm-hmm. You and me and Luka Sims. And this makes six to ten."

Luka Sims? The blind man thought about the name for a moment, and then he remembered. "The newspaperman."

"That's right."

What he remembered about the newspaperman was the quality of his breathing, which had been quick and nervous, reminding him of the pulsing heart of a rabbit he had once held in his lap. Also, there was the astringent smell of ink that rose from his clothing and his irritating habit of trying to take the blind man's arm whenever it came time for them to cross the street. Nothing else came to him.

Still, he knew that he had liked the newspaperman, though he could not have explained why. "My regards to you both," he said to the woman.

How long had he been standing there rooting through the tag ends of his memories? It seemed like only a few seconds, but he wasn't sure. He waited for the woman to answer him, and when she didn't say anything, he presumed that the conversation was over. He walked home by way of Park Street and M.

When he got back to his apartment, he opened the window and turned his ears to the sound of a flock of birds that were roosting in a nearby tree. The birds whistled and cooed to each other, efficient little one- and two-note songs, until a car with a broken radiator passed beneath them and they gave a chorus of fluttery peeping sounds. A couple of kids dashed by, smacking the tree with their palms, and the birds took to the air with a sudden explosive snap of their wings. How wonderful it must have been, he thought—to run with a body meant for running, to see with eyes meant for seeing, to fly with wings meant for flying. Sometimes he thought that the most joyful sound in the world would be the sound of the birds taking over the city after everyone else was gone.

It was midway through the next day when the blind man's own building disappeared. He was standing in the colonnade when a man who had spent the last few hours circling the edge of the city stopped to give some of the people around him a report. Another few blocks were gone, he said, and when he listed them off, the blind man recognized the name of his own.

His building had still been there when he left his front door that morning. He was sure of that. How closely behind him had it been extinguished? he wondered.

A group of rollerbladers went skating by. Someone dropped a rubber ball.

There was nothing in his home that he truly needed. He could always find someplace else to sleep the night. But it was disquieting to know that for the moment, at least, he had nowhere else to go.

"Where's your cane, little man?" his mother had asked him the day the boys on his block took it away from him. And he had answered her, "I don't need it anymore."

For a long time it had seemed to him that there were more people on the streets, more people in the park, than ever before, but it was only now that he understood why. As the city became smaller, they were all being drawn toward the center. They were like pieces of bark and foam caught in a giant whirlpool.

And at last he apprehended what was happening.

When the walls came together and the bubble finally collapsed, this was where they would all end up: right here, between these benches and rustling trees. It would happen in a matter of days or weeks. There would be no way for them to avoid it. They would gather together in the clearing around the monument, however many thousand of them there were, and they would stand there shoulder to shoulder. They would listen to each other's voices, and they would breathe each other's breath. And they would wait for that power that would pull them like a chain into whatever came next, into that distant world where broken souls are wrenched out of their histories.

I owe thanks to my editors, Edward Kastenmeier and Anya Serota; to my agent, Jennifer Carlson; and to Carin Besser at *The New Yorker* for her skillful reading of this book's first chapter; as well as to the Arkansas Arts Council for its generous financial support and to Chris Columbus, Michael Barnathan, and Angela Cheng Caplan for their interest in the story I've told. In researching Antarctica for the even-numbered chapters of this book, I turned first to the anthology *Ice: Stories of Survival from Polar Exploration*, edited by Clint Willis, which led me directly to Apsley Cherry-Garrard's unparalleled memoir of Antarctic exploration, *The Worst Journey in the World*, portions of which Laura's own journey recapitulates.